Wanting Forever

T0352258

Wanting Forever

A Nelson Island Novel

DIANA GARDIN

New York Boston

Copyright © 2014 by Diana Gardin
A Preview of *Ever Always* copyright © 2014 by Diana Gardin
Cover design by Elizabeth Turner
Cover copyright © 2014 by Hachette Book Group, Inc.

Forever Yours
Hachette Book Group
1290 Avenue of the Americas
New York, NY 10104
hachettebookgroup.com
twitter.com/foreverromance

First ebook edition: October 2014

Forever Yours is an imprint of Grand Central Publishing.
The Forever Yours name and logo are trademarks of Hachette Book Group, Inc.

The Hachette Speakers Bureau provides a wide range of authors for speaking events. To find out more, go to www.hachettespeakersbureau.com or call (866) 376-6591.

The publisher is not responsible for websites (or their content) that are not owned by the publisher.

ISBN 978-1-4555-6092-9

POD ISBN is 978-1-4555-6089-9

I've wanted Forever for as long as I can remember. This story is dedicated to my very own version of that. Thank you, Tyson.

Prologue

Two Months Previously in Duck Creek

Ever sniffled once, twice, wiping her red nose on her plaid flannel shirtsleeve. Each tear she shed sliced like a dagger through his heart. He hated that he was the one doing this to her. More than once, he'd vowed never to be the one to hurt her. She'd had enough pain from that asshole father of hers. He used her like a punching bag on the nights he came home stumbling drunk. Too many times her nose looked just like this on those nights she climbed into Sam's window long after her father had fallen into a stupor.

But now, here he was, the one making her cry. Like he'd said he'd never do.

Damn it all to hell.

"Listen to me," he said fiercely as he grabbed both sides of her face in his calloused hands. "I promise you I'll be back for you. Don't spend a day missing me. Don't drop your guard. I'll come back, and

when I do, we'll go away together and we won't look back at this god-forsaken town. You hear me?"

She nodded, and he leaned down to claim her lips. He kissed her long and hard. When he pulled back, her tears were mixed with his on both their faces.

"I don't want you to go," she said. "You don't have to go, Sam. I can tell them—"

"You tell them nothing," he insisted. "Nothing. We agreed, didn't we? You let them look for me. They can search 'til the cows come home, but they won't find me. And when things die down, I am coming for you. Have I ever let you down?"

She shook her head. "No, Sam. Never."

"And I'm not about to start now." He lifted his head sharply as sirens blared in the distance. It always took the county sheriff longer than it should to get anywhere. Sam had the time he needed to get gone.

He stepped backward but stopped at the stricken look on her face. He stepped quickly in front of her again and took her chin in one hand, lifting it up so she would meet his eyes.

"Be strong, Ev. You be strong for both of us. Stick to the story. You'll be safe now. I promise."

He bent his head to hers, letting the feel of her lips envelope him for the last time. He pulled away too quickly and backed away.

One last look allowed him to memorize the familiar curves and the way her auburn hair fell in waves around her. Then he took off through the woods. Sharp branches slapped his face, leaving burning, angry marks behind. Tiny twigs snapped beneath his feet as they pounded through the brush. He'd keep running until he emerged on the other side where the state highway ran around the outskirt of Duck Creek. That's where his brother, Hunter, had hidden his Harley for him as soon as they'd realized what had to be done. Sam would take off, headed south, and wouldn't stop until he crossed state lines and then some.

Ever would be safe now. He'd made sure of it. He'd protected her most of their lives, and he wasn't going to stop now.

He didn't care that it turned him into a wanted man. Because she was worth it.

One

Keep stacking those bales, son. When you're finished, we'll head back up to the main house and I'll let you go for the day." Leon, the ranch manager, scratched his forehead as he lifted his Stetson in the steamy, late afternoon heat.

"Yes, sir." Sam stood back from the hay bale and wiped the sweat dripping from his forehead. It was unusually hot for May. On a day like this, he'd guzzled two gallon-size jugs of water, and he'd need more by the time he was done. He'd lost his shirt hours ago, and the brazen heat sizzled into the now-golden skin of his chiseled torso.

When Sam finished spreading the hay through the pasture for the horses for the day, he met Leon in front of the stables.

"I want to run something by you, Leon. Do you mind?"

"Go ahead, son." Leon's expression teetered between tense and exhausted. He was down a few workers, which was why the ranch had hired Sam on as a temp without asking a whole lot of questions.

"How's the new scheduling procedure working out?"

"Savin' my ass. Your suggestion of having some of the trainers pitch in was a great way to get around the shortage of hands. You done a lot of this scheduling stuff before, kid?"

The corner of Sam's mouth tilted upward in a smile. He grabbed his shirt, lying atop the swinging barn door, and used it as a rag to wipe the sweat dripping from his chin. "A little bit. I helped the owner of the garage where I used to work with a lot with stuff like that. Ended up managing the place when I was eighteen."

They climbed into Leon's work truck and turned up the gravel path toward the main house.

"So, Sam," Leon began. He removed his well-worn Stetson and scratched his head. Replacing the hat, he glanced at Sam. "You plannin' on stayin' around just for the summer? Or you gonna be here in Nelson Island longer than that?"

"You know, sir, I really don't know yet. I'm just trying to figure things out. Taking it one day at a time."

Leon nodded. "I can understand that. You're young. What…twenty or so?"

"I was twenty-one last month."

"Twenty-one. You got a lot of road stretched out in front of you, Sam. Nelson Island is a great place to figure it all out."

"Thank you, sir. I can see that."

"And you moved from where?"

"North of here, sir."

Sam wasn't willing to go into details about exactly where he was from. Too much information may lead someone to draw conclusions about what he'd done back home, about why he was running.

Leon pulled the truck onto the circular driveway that curved into a horseshoe in front of the main house. He turned off the ignition and climbed out of the truck.

"Got any special plans this evening?" Leon asked.

"No," Sam answered, shaking his head. "I think I'll just go back to the tack house and crash for the night."

He nodded. "It's almost dinnertime, son. Shouldn't be skipping meals while you're doing all this hard work. Go on, then. I'll see you early tomorrow. Seven o'clock."

"I'll be there," answered Sam.

Leon headed up the steps leading to the front door.

Sam watched him go, thinking back to when he'd first met Leon on his way down from Virginia. He'd stopped at a gas station to fill up, and Leon had stopped him to ask about the Harley. They'd gotten to talking, or rather Leon talked and Sam listened. The ranch manager was looking for some workers. Sam ended up leaving the gas station and following behind Leon's truck while Leon led him straight over the bridge from Charleston, South Carolina, to Mr. Hopewell at his horse ranch in Nelson Island.

Sam shoved his hands in his pockets and walked around the driveway and down the stone-paved path through wooded land that led to the tack house.

Greenery surrounded the ranch, from old magnificent magnolia trees to palmettos flapping in the breeze. Lush, green pastures rose and fell gently with the rolling hills. The property was perfectly pristine due to Leon Jackson's running the place like a well-oiled machine. He was the man who made sure every job was handled, every animal was well looked after, and every building on the property was spic-and-span. Details and organization were law to Leon.

As he made his way through the trees, Sam had a flash of the night he'd left Duck Creek. He'd left Ever standing alone in woods so similar to these. The mountains of southwest Virginia accompanied him like a friend during his childhood, and the contrast he found on the coast of South Carolina was both comforting and disconcerting.

He couldn't wait to show Ever—just as soon as it was safe.

Walking into the tack house, Sam clicked the door closed behind him and stood just inside, surveying the living room.

Mr. Hopewell had fashioned several of the buildings on his property into guesthouses. He used the larger ones for actual guests and the couple of smaller ones as houses for the hired help who needed to stay on the property. Sam qualified, as he had no other place to live on the island. Most of the staff drove to work. Leon lived in quite a nice house only a couple of miles away, with his wife.

Leaning against the door, he pulled the well-worn sheet of stationery out of his back jeans pocket. He pulled it out and began to read.

Sam,

If you only knew how it felt being in Duck Creek without you, you'd come running back to me. I know you don't want to do that. But I really am miserable here without you. The only silver lining about you being gone is that my dad is gone too. He can't hurt me anymore, thanks to you. And Hunter.

I've known you my whole life, Sam, and I've known I loved you for the same amount of time. We've never been so far apart. How are you? I know you can't e-mail without access to a computer. I was so excited to get a letter from you. Letters are more romantic than e-mail anyway. So I've written you this one. Maybe it will make you a little less lonely if you read it at night before bed.

Thank you for asking Hunter to take care of me while you're gone. He's been doing just that. Hovering a little, but I appreciate the help he's given me. I was able to use the insurance money from Daddy to pay off the house and car. Now I only have to worry about the monthly bills, and my job at the bakery is doing a pretty good job of covering that.

Without you, Sam, none of this would be possible. I'd still be terrified to sleep in my own bed every night. I'll be forever grateful.

I want this to be over soon, so we can be together again.

Love you forever, and

Ever

His daily readings gave Sam the strength he needed to stay away from her. Until the whole thing with her father's death blew over, they had to stay apart.

He carefully folded the letter on its worn creases and placed it back into his pocket. Then he wandered over to the desk in the corner and waited.

The phone on the desk jangled a few minutes later. He picked up the cordless handset.

"Hello?"

"It's me." Hunter's gravelly voice.

"I know."

"How are you, man?" Worry laced the edges of Hunter's tone. He'd always taken care of Sam. He took the big brother role way too seriously, if you asked Sam. They were only eighteen months apart.

"Couldn't be better, considering. The Hopewells have been real nice so far. Can't do much better than that. There's been a lot of fixing fences, cleaning out barns, and lifting heavy-ass feed bags, but the money's good. It's not like I haven't done hard work before. So I'm gonna be okay here, Hunter."

"Glad to hear it."

"How is she, Hunter?"

He couldn't wait any longer to hear about Ever.

"She's missing the shit out of you, Sam. Like you'd expect. I try to drive over most nights after work to check on her. But sometimes I leave the site too late. On those days I call to see if she needs anything."

"Good. Keep doing that, Hunter. You keep taking care of her, since I can't right now."

"Sam...look. You could come home if we'd just—"

"We've been through this. It's not going to happen. This is the best way for everyone."

"How's it the best way for you, Sam? You're on the run. I never thought you'd—"

"Just stop. We don't need to rehash this over the phone. What's done is done. No one will understand the truth except the three of us. Now, do your damn job and take care of Ever."

"Done, man." Hunter sighed.

A rhythmic knock sounded on the heavy wooden door of the tack house. Sam glanced at it quickly.

"I gotta go, Hunt. Stick to the plan. Love you, bro."

He hung up the phone and strode to the door.

When he opened it, the slick grin of Reed Hopewell shined up at him from the stoop. Reed leaned against the doorjamb, looking casual in a pale blue T-shirt and jeans.

"What's up, man?" he drawled. "Dad sent me down here to ask you to come on up to the main house for dinner tonight."

Sam stepped back so Reed could come inside. He closed the door behind him.

"Yeah, okay. It's always nice enjoying a meal up there."

The too-familiar panic began to set in deep in Sam's bones.

"That's what Dad does. He treats all the help like family." He smiled playfully and slapped Sam on the back.

Sam chuckled, not quite relieved. He'd been invited to the main house a couple of times for dinner since he'd been working at the ranch. Each time his heart ended up in his throat, anxiously waiting to hear that his short-term employment was terminated. Or worse…that the sheriff would be there waiting to haul him back to Duck Creek.

Mr. and Mrs. Hopewell didn't seem to suspect a thing. They

were gracious employers and seemed to want to include Sam for purely innocent reasons. They claimed they didn't like thinking of him always alone, fending for himself.

"All right, man. Let me change and I'll be right out."

Reed sank onto the soft plaid couch, propping his scuffed boots up on the coffee table. Then he straightened, staring at the couch cushions with eyes full of doubt.

"You haven't been…" He glanced pointedly at Sam, and then back at the couch.

Sam caught his gist, and cleared his throat. "Uh, no. Definitely not."

"Cool. Just had to ask. So my sister's in town for the summer. Mom and Dad have asked the kitchen staff to do it up right. It's gonna be bangin.'"

"Oh yeah?" Sam called as he walked to the bedroom, stripping off his work clothes as he entered the attached bath.

He showered quickly and changed into a fresh pair of jeans and the nicest shirt he owned, a striped button-down. He preferred T-shirts to shirts with collars. But if he was having dinner with the Hopewells, he'd play the part as best he could.

"Yeah. My sister stays gone most of the year. So when she's home for the summer, they really go all out."

Sam nodded. He was aware of the Hopewells' other child, a girl who attended college in Louisiana. She hadn't been home during his time in Nelson Island, so he'd never met her.

"I'm ready," he told Reed.

"All right, dude. Let's head on up."

Their easy conversation as they walked up the path brought

Hunter back to the forefront of Sam's mind. Reed, although younger than he and Hunter were, was friendly and good-natured, with a wild streak and a wicked sense of humor. He'd just completed his senior year of high school, so the summer stretching ahead of him was the last he'd spend as a carefree teenager.

When they arrived at the main house, all of the windows were alight. The front doors swung open, and Mrs. Hopewell stood at the top step, waiting for them.

"Sam." She greeted him with a sweet smile. "I'm glad you could join us. We know you must get lonely down there all by yourself. What were you going to eat for dinner if Reed hadn't come to drag you on up here?"

His answering smile was impossible to prevent. "Peanut butter on crackers."

She frowned. "See? Fate intervened at just the right time."

"I guess so, ma'am."

"Well, come on, boys. Appetizers are being served as we speak."

She took off down the hall. Sam marveled at the sheer size of the home's interior. His entire trailer back in Duck Creek would have fit in the foyer.

He and Reed followed Mrs. Hopewell down the hall. The ivory-paneled walls flashed by Sam as he went. His eyes traveled up to the high ceiling, where a large crystal chandelier hung over an ornate fountain in the center of the entry. He was used to seeing family photos covering the walls of houses he'd entered, but not here. Expensive-looking tapestries and paintings adorned the paneled walls.

At the end of the entry hall, they turned right and entered the massive dining room. A huge rectangular glass-top table was laden with china. The middle of the glossy surface was completely occupied by a centerpiece dripping with flowers and fruit. The flickering of candles set the entire room aglow.

"Wow," Sam murmured under his breath.

"I know." Reed nudged him hard in the ribs with an elbow. "You'll get used to how the other half lives, my friend." His voice was barely loud enough for Sam to hear. "Like fucking gluttons."

A laugh rumbled up from Sam's chest, but he smothered it just before it could escape.

Gregory Hopewell sat at the far end of the table, and he stood as they entered.

"Sam, my boy! Good to see you!"

His hearty voice filled the dining room. Sam had never once heard Mr. Hopewell's voice do anything other than boom. Mrs. Hopewell smiled at them from the other end of the gargantuan table.

"Come sit, boys. We're waiting on Aston, of course, but try some of the miniature crab cakes."

Sam was still trying to figure out why they were waiting for a car when Reed's sister swept into the room.

"Ah! There you are, sis. Sam Waters, meet Aston Hopewell. The one and only."

Reed smirked at Sam, as if he were expecting a certain reaction from him.

Sam held out his hand. "Nice to meet you, Aston."

The girl who took his hand shook out a long tumble of dark

hair, pulled off to the side to hang over one shoulder and pinned in place with a glimmering clip. Her crazy high heels and short white sundress showed off her tanned legs to perfection. Her face was exotically beautiful, her bright blue eyes a stark contrast to her raven-colored hair. The clear gloss on her lips made her mouth look deliciously kissable. For the briefest moment, Sam wondered what she'd taste like.

"Hello." Her voice was strong and clear. She rolled her eyes at her brother. "They bringing in strays again?"

"Always," Reed answered solemnly.

Sam quickly brought himself to reality…and Ever. Aston was the opposite of the girl-next-door type, completely unlike anyone Sam had ever met back in Duck Creek.

As Sam pulled out Aston's chair for her, he caught her mouthing, "Is he for real?" toward her brother.

Reed merely smirked, then motioned at a chair for Sam next to his seat.

"Now that Her Highness has arrived, can we eat?" Reed grumbled.

"Don't tease your sister," Mrs. Hopewell admonished. "Louise?"

A tiny woman carrying a tray of dishes bustled into the room.

Sam gazed around the table as he ate, trying to take mental notes so that he would be able to describe it all perfectly to Ever in his next letter.

"So, Sam," Mrs. Hopewell began. "Greg has told me how lucky Leon feels to have stumbled upon you earlier this spring. We're glad you're with us. How long do you plan on staying in Nelson Island? Do we get to keep you past August?"

Sam took a bite of a crab cake, chewing slowly to savor the delicious flavor. He thought of the best way to answer her question so as to discourage any further wonderings.

"I'm not sure, ma'am. I'd like to stay on at least until the end of summer. My plans depend on, uh, a friend back home and a special situation. So after summer ends I'll have to play things by ear. I'm grateful to y'all for having me, though. I really needed the work."

"Dude, you've gotta drop the 'ma'am' thing. I can't take it much longer." Reed leaned forward, lacing his fingers together above his plate.

Sam shook his head. "Can't help it, man. It's called manners. You ever try them?"

"Oh, low blow, Sam! Low blow. You don't need to impress them, dude. They clearly already love you."

Mr. Hopewell cleared his throat. "Stop it, Reed. Sam, don't listen to him. We really do appreciate your hard work. We want you to know that you can think of yourself as part of the family while you're here."

"Yeah right, Daddy." Aston rolled her eyes skyward again. "One of the family who works in the fields, right?"

"Actually," Mr. Hopewell began. "Leon has seen some management potential in Sam. He told me about the improvements you've made to the efficiency of the ranch. But you realize raising horses is only one arm of Hopewell Enterprises. Most of the capital comes from our energy division. And finding efficiencies is our biggest goal there. Leon mentioned that you were employed in automotive repair previously?"

Sam nodded. "I worked on a lot of cars at the garage back home. None ran on alternative fuels, but I know something about it. I rebuilt the engine on my Harley myself."

"Well, if you're interested, I thought you might help out my assistant. She's got her hands full with a brand-new baby at home, and Leon found a few more people to do day-to-day labor at the ranch. I thought this could give you the opportunity to learn more of the business end of things. You remind me of a young me. I didn't grow up with the kind of advantages my children"—he shot pointed glances at Aston and Reed—"enjoy. I had to work my way through college, and I started Hopewell Enterprises from the ground up. You're a hard worker and I think all you need is a break and the right hand guiding you."

"I don't know what to say, sir—"

"Of course, I'll increase your hourly wage as befits the new position," Mr. Hopewell added.

"Mr. Hopewell, that's beyond generous. I don't even know what to say."

Sam had been so busy worrying about how he could help Ever for as long as he could remember, he'd never thought much about what came next for him. His 3.5 GPA in high school had gone untapped because, even though he was scouted by some D III schools for football, he hadn't ever been able to think about leaving her and going to college. Her father would have never let her go.

"Just think about what you want for your future, son. That's all I'm asking. And I can help put you on the path to get there."

Sam nodded slowly. "Thank you, sir. I will."

Louise brought out the main course, Cornish hens laden with dried fruit and tiny pearl onions and potatoes. Sam inhaled every bite, dimly aware of Aston's crystal blue eyes burning into him from across the table.

Two

"Why are you doing this, Daddy? What does this guy have that makes you so eager to help him succeed? He's a complete stranger."

Long after dinner was over and Sam was gone, Aston stood arguing with her father in his office, glass French doors shut and rattling from the volume in her voice.

"Usually I'm the one who fills in for Lonna during the summers," she continued.

Aston had been working for as long as she could remember toward a place in her father's corporation. She'd attended the best private school in the area, and now she was earning a double degree in business and finance from Xavier University. She'd earned the right to work under her father as soon as she graduated, and one day she hoped to run the entire company. She'd worked for it.

So seeing her father hand this Sam guy a job out of nowhere with no regard to his lack of training and education...it burned her from the inside out. Fury shot through her veins like fire in a rain-starved wood.

"Sweetheart." Gregory's tone was placating, which made her seethe. Daddy's Little Girl had been her role for as long as she could remember, but she was made with hard edges and a tough center. She didn't need his patronizing.

"Don't do that, Daddy. Don't give me something to settle me down. I want the truth. Who is this kid?"

"First of all, he's not a kid. You can see that, surely. He's a grown man. A young man, yes, but grown. And I can see myself in him, just like I said at dinner. It's been a long time since I've run into a young man with Sam's heart and goodness, and his strength and work ethic. It's not something I see every day in the business world, my dear. And I value those qualities more than you could possibly know. I don't know much about him, it's true. I don't know exactly where he came from or why he's struggling, but he is. He's gotten himself into trouble in his past, I'm sure of that, and I want to help him move forward with his life, because the boy deserves that. I've been watching him for months now, Aston, and you'll just have to trust me."

"But he's—"

"That's enough!" His open palm slapped down on his desk, effectively silencing her.

Aston took an involuntary step backward, and his tone softened when he spoke again.

"I love you more than the entire empire, Aston, you know that. And I'm proud of how hard you've worked. I'm offering Sam my guidance and that takes nothing away from you. You'll still have a place at Hopewell. In fact, I thought you could help supervise Sam—show him the ropes a bit and introduce him to the people he needs to know. If he has the initiative I think he does, I can see him becoming quite valuable to the company."

"And you don't see me being valuable?" Aston bit out.

"Of course, sweetheart. But someday you're going to want more than Hopewell Enterprises. You'll want to get married, settle down with kids of your own."

Aston turned her face like she'd been slapped. "I don't know what kind of 1950s world you're living in, Daddy, but you'll see this is a big mistake." There was obviously nothing she could do to change his mind. She turned on her heel and strode for the French doors.

"I'll prove myself to you," she called back over her shoulder. "You'll see that I'm the future of this company. Who is this Sam Waters? You don't even know him. When you find out, he may be a big disappointment to you. And I'll be there to pick up the pieces, as usual."

Her voice trailed off on her last words until it was no louder than a whisper.

She grabbed her purse and stalked outside, pulling out her phone as her heels echoed on the brick steps outside the house.

"Prince? It's me. Yeah, I got here earlier today. Can you come and get me?"

She clicked END on the phone and stuffed it into the red leather bag hanging from her shoulder. She began walking down the long paved drive that led from the Hopewell property to the main road. Halfway down, she stopped to pull off her heels and then continued the rest of the trek holding them in one hand.

When she reached the end of the lengthy stretch of pavement she sat down on the asphalt and pulled out a cigarette, stretching her long legs out in front of her. She lit it, covering the flame of the lighter with one hand to shield it from the May breeze. She took a long drag, and tilted her head backward to stare up at the stars.

Being the backbone of her family sucked. It was a role she'd filled for years, especially for her father. She'd been there for him when he'd walked in on her mother screwing one of his business consultants, and she was there when they unbelievably reconciled. She'd been there when his favorite horse died; she was there when the company had gone international. She'd grown up before she had to, because she knew her mother was too weak to stand by her father's side the way he needed. She figured that out at an early age. So she stepped up.

And this was how he repaid her.

You're going to want more than Hopewell Enterprises one day, Aston. His words echoed in her head over and over again until the cigarette smoke that wafted in rings around her head was blurred from the tears stinging her eyes.

Pounding footsteps jerked her out of her reverie. Her head snapped up to see a runner coming down the road. As he got closer, she could make out his muscular legs, a flat, muscled stomach rippling with total abdominal beauty, and a hard, toned chest. Then her gaze locked onto the chestnut brown eyes of Sam Waters.

He took his earbuds out as he studied her, breathing hard and glistening with sweat. "Aston? Are you okay?"

She angrily brushed away the tears of frustration. The fact that he'd seen her crying infuriated her, but the beauty of his body definitely wasn't lost on her. Which made her even angrier.

"I'm fine," she snapped. "You're running in the dark? On this road? Do you have a death wish?"

She couldn't stop herself. Her eyes traveled back down his body, stopping at his stomach. He had a tattoo stretched out over his muscles; Old English letters spelling out the word RISE.

He smiled and squatted until his face was level with hers. She quickly pulled her legs underneath her as he reached out and brushed a stray tear away. The tender gesture sent a shiver through her body, and she told herself to stop acting like a hormonal teenager and get it together.

"What's wrong?" he asked.

She sighed, pressing the cigarette butt into the ground beside her. Hating him wasn't going to be easy if he was going to be this nice. But she would be damned if she was going to melt into a puddle over the man who was pulling up a front-row seat in her father's life.

"I'm really fine," she said. "Just go on with your run and forget about me."

He sat, grinning and pulling his knees to his chest, settling in. "I'm done with my run, actually. So I have nothing to do now but sit here and wait with you. What are you waiting for, anyway?"

That smile was dangerous. Infectious, boyishly rogue with one side of his mouth tilting up. Wide eyes crinkling at the corners.

Aston was sure it was a smile that made all the girls back where he was from just sink into mush at his feet and drop their panties at his bedside.

She wasn't one of those girls.

"I'm waiting for my boyfriend, actually."

"Boyfriend, huh?" he drawled. He definitely had the country boy charm turned up on high tonight. "Well he can't be the reason you're so upset, he's not even here yet. And it can't be me, I just got here."

He raised his eyebrows at her with an unspoken question.

"Oh, get over yourself. I told you I'm fine." She was quickly losing the ability to snap at him, and it was driving her mad. Her body language was softening as she attempted to keep the anger turned up in her brain. She flexed her fingers, fisting her hands in her lap. She wanted to hate this man. So why couldn't he be a jerk?

"I'm over myself. I'll just wait with you until he gets here. After all, you just told me this was a dangerous road."

They sat in silence for a moment, close enough to touch but not doing so, the heat from his body rolling off him and stretching out to meet hers.

She jumped up when she heard the engine of Princeton's Corvette tearing up the road. Relief swirled through her as she pulled on her heels.

"He's here," she announced.

"I can see that," answered Sam, solemn amusement scrawled all over his face.

Princeton pulled to a stop at the curb and left the engine

idling. He stepped out of the driver-side door and approached Sam and Aston.

"Babe, you ready to go?"

She nodded, walking up to Princeton and wrapping her arms around his neck. His eyebrows rose as he gazed down, and his mouth dropped the slightest bit at each corner.

"I missed you, baby," she crooned, loud enough for Sam's ears.

Sam watched silently for a moment before moving over and extending his hand.

"Hey," he said. "Princeton, right? I'm Sam Waters. Working out here on the Hopewell property this summer."

Princeton disentangled himself from Aston's arms and shook Sam's hand. "Nice to meet you. Thanks for, uh, waiting with Aston here."

As the two stood side by side, it was easy to see how dissimilar they were. Aston noted Sam was a few inches taller than Princeton and definitely more muscular—like the difference between a tennis player and footballer. Princeton was all perfectly pressed in his khaki shorts and white polo. Whereas Sam looked like the type who wasn't afraid to get a little down and dirty. The sweat from his run still gleamed on his chest, and his tousled hair was practically begging to have her fingers run through it. *Eep,* Aston immediately cut off the thought.

Sam nodded. "Yeah. Kind of dangerous for a woman to be sitting out here by herself at night."

Aston rolled her eyes. "Okay, Dad, thanks for the babysitting service. I'll see you around. Let's go, Prince," she said as she climbed into the low-slung Corvette.

She couldn't help turning back once after they drove off to see Sam standing in the road watching them go.

Dear Ever,

I miss you. You know that if I had any other choice, I wouldn't have left you, right? It was the only way to keep you protected. You shouldn't have to suffer any more because of that man. You've already gone through a lifetime of pain. You deserve to be happy now. The truth never needs to come out.

On a brighter note, you'll never guess what happened to me here. You know the family I've been working for? Well the man, the business owner, offered me a different position in his company so I can learn more about how the operation runs. He wants me to begin thinking more about my future, and that's something I need to start doing. How will I support you if I don't start making something of myself? And I really do think we could have a great life here together when things die down back home.

Amazing things start happening in places you never expected them to. I can't wait to see you again.

Love you For Ever,

                                Sam

He folded the letter, stuffed it into a crisp white envelope, and addressed it. He left no return address, just in case. It didn't matter. Hunter knew where he was.

He stuffed the letter in his little mailbox for the postman on his way out to work. It had been a few days since Mr. Hopewell had made the new job offer, and Sam hadn't yet had a chance to see him to accept.

"Morning," Leon greeted him when he arrived in the stable. "Heard you might not be with me much longer."

"Did Mr. Hopewell tell you that?" Sam asked. "I haven't officially accepted yet."

Sam grabbed a large, heavy bag of pony feed and hefted it over one shoulder. He hauled the bag to the back of Leon's truck, exhaling as he threw it down onto the bed. Returning for the next bag, he faced Leon once again.

"Well maybe not, but you'd be a fool not to take it." Leon's tone sounded as if he were scolding a disobedient teen. "A chance to quit workin' in these fields and learn somethin' about that fancy business out there isn't somethin' Mr. Hopewell gives too often. Actually, to my recollection he's never given it. So take it and run, boy."

Sam placed both hands on top of his head and wandered over to one of the softly whinnying horses in its stall. He stroked the mare's snout, smiling when she nuzzled the side of his head.

What Leon said made perfect sense. It just all seemed too good to be true. These weren't the kinds of things that happened to people like him. He wasn't used to being treated this way. It was unnerving. No one, apart from Ever and Hunter, had ever shown him that he had value. His father had left his mother before he was old enough to have memories. His mother never forgave Sam for his dad's departure, and she never let him forget

it. The man hadn't left after Hunter was born; it was after Sam
had arrived. She laid the fault at Sam's tiny feet. She'd never hit
him like Ever's father had done to her, but she let him know every
chance she got what a mistake he was.

His football coach in high school valued him, but only for
what he could do on the field. Sam had learned to think of himself as a means to an end. A tool to be used to win games on the
field. A route Ever could use to escape the horror that was her father.

"You're right. It's an amazing opportunity. You sure you'll have
enough help without me, though? I could still probably come
down at dawn or something if you need me, or help brush the
horses down after office hours."

"*Ach,* I'll be fine. Got two new guys starting tomorrow, thanks
to that ad you put online. You should let Mr. Hopewell know today. I happen to know he's only working a half day in the office in
Charleston, and he'll be home around lunchtime."

After eating the peanut butter sandwich and apple he'd packed
in his cooler for lunch, Sam headed up the back of the property
toward the main house. As he strolled around the slanted-brick
pathway rounding the thick green hedges that lined the entire
area, he caught a glimpse of long tan legs crossed on a lounge
chair adjacent to the path. He stopped short and peeked around
the hedge.

Aston was lying poolside, giant aviator sunglasses covering the
top half of her face. He crept closer, a grin tugging the corners of
his lips. He grabbed a pool noodle and dipped it silently into the

water as he approached. He raised it in his arms, ready to attack. The idea of surprising her with the gentle slap of a wet pool noodle was just too tempting to ignore. He knew, judging from her reaction to him the other night, that she'd be absolutely furious. And he couldn't wait to see the look on her face. The girl clearly needed to lighten up.

"Go ahead and hit me with that, Waters, as long as you've written your last will and testament." Her lazy drawl penetrated Sam's offensive as she pushed her glasses up onto her head.

He froze, stunned. "How'd you know?"

"Just count on me always knowing more than anyone else in the room," she answered wryly.

She sat up, adjusting the top of the tiny royal blue bikini she wore.

Sam wasn't blind. Aston was ridiculously gorgeous. He knew that the guys he'd grown up with would shit themselves just to stand next to her.

"Man." Sam replaced the noodle, grinning. "You're no fun, Aston."

She arched an eyebrow. "You have no idea what fun is, Sam Waters. What the hell are you doing here, anyway? Stalking me?"

"Not on my list of things to do today." He chuckled. "I was on my way around to talk to your dad."

Aston sat up a little straighter in her seat. "Oh, really? It wouldn't happen to be about the bogus offer he made you the other night, would it?"

Now it was Sam's turn to raise a brow.

"Bogus? You know something I don't?"

She smirked. "Want to hand over your résumé?"

Sam shifted uncomfortably. The subtle reminder that he wasn't good enough sank painfully into his chest. *He left because you weren't good enough.* His mother's voice echoed in his ears as if she were standing right beside him.

"Your dad seems to think actions count more than any piece of paper."

"Just remember, no one gets something for nothing in this life," Aston answered, rolling her eyes.

Sam sat down on the lounger next to Aston's and leaned forward, placing his forearms on his knees. He took off his cap and let it play in his hands while looking Aston directly in the eye. He swallowed, surprised by the fire burning in those eyes and his speech faltered. He tried to identify the emotion he noticed brewing in the azure depths and failed.

"Did I do something to offend you the other night?" he asked bluntly. "Because you don't seem to like me very much. And other than my mother, everyone likes me."

Her controlled expression faltered. "Your own mother doesn't like you? How is that possible?"

"Doesn't matter." He shook his head. "We're talking about you right now. Why don't *you* like me?"

She studied him. "I thought I had you all figured out, Waters. It's rare that I'm ever wrong about people. But maybe you'll surprise me. If you take my dad's offer, I'll be seeing a lot more of you. So then we'll know what you're really made of."

She slipped her glasses back down over her eyes.

On impulse, Sam reached out and plucked them off her face. She opened her mouth, genuine surprise registering all over her features.

He leaned in close, lining his face up with hers. "You definitely don't have me figured out, Princess. Not even a little bit."

He leaned back, dragging sparks of electricity with him. What the hell? What kind of static cling was this girl holding on to? He'd never experienced such a physical connection from just sitting so close to someone before. It freaked him out. But damn if he was going to let her see it.

"What do you do there? At your dad's company, I mean." Sam watched her expression change back to guarded.

Aston grabbed her glasses back and placed them on her nose. "I've been interning with Hopewell Enterprises since I was eighteen, every summer. I've worked mostly in the finance department. I have a weird thing for numbers. I like them."

"I don't think that's weird," said Sam. He tipped his head to the side as he studied her. "This corporate thing is going to be new for me, but I like a challenge."

She nodded, assessing him more fully. "Then we have that in common. All my father does is challenge me."

Sam's eyebrows rose. "And Reed?"

She laughed. "I think he wrote Reed off awhile ago. It's always been me asking him questions about the business. So he's been teaching me for a long time."

"It sounds like you work a lot. Between school and working with your dad in the summers. Reed said you don't get home much during the school year."

Aston was quiet a minute. Sam couldn't tell which direction she aimed her gaze, her glasses were so darkly tinted. Finally, she lifted one slim shoulder in a half shrug. "I'm used to taking care of things around here. It's what I've always done."

Sam opened his mouth to say more just as the back door swung open and Reed stepped out. He had a towel thrown over his shoulder and he sported red-and-white-striped board shorts.

"Sam!" he called. "Good to see you, buddy! Slacking off today, huh? Nice! Grab a suit and come hang out."

Sam threw a look at Aston and stood up. "No, I'm not slacking off. I'm actually getting ready to head inside to take your dad up on his job offer."

"That's amazing, man! Congrats. We should celebrate. Tonight, we party!"

"Uh…" Sam wasn't quite sure how to respond, especially since partying wasn't part of the plan in being here. He needed to save money for Ever.

Reed continued, undaunted. "I'll come down and get you around ten. We'll head over to that bar and grill down at the pier. Sunny's."

Sam nodded reluctantly, knowing Reed wouldn't take no for an answer. He glanced at Aston for a reaction. She was lying on her lounge chair again, eyes lost behind her glasses. She tilted her head in his direction, though, when he spoke.

"All right. I guess I'm riding with you, then. Unless you want to sit on the back of my bike."

Aston snorted.

"As awesome as that sounds, Sam, you can ride with A and me.

We'll see you later tonight." With that, Reed did a running cannonball into the pool, very deliberately soaking his sister in the process. Aston squealed, vowing vengeance. Sam shook his head and grinned, their banter ringing in his ears as he opened the French door to his new future.

Sam's feet pounded against the highway. Mr. Hopewell had been thrilled to have him accept the new position. Tomorrow would be his official first day. Right now, he had a lot to think about. It was way too hot to be running with the afternoon sun blazing, but it was the only way he knew to clear his mind. He owed Hunter a phone call, and he had no idea what to say.

He'd chosen the same route he'd run the night he'd met Aston at the dinner in the main house. He chugged up the state highway for three miles, then turned to jog back.

Sam was close to a mile into his return when he zeroed in on a car pulled over to the side of the road. As he approached, the little silver convertible and its driver came into clear view.

"Aston?" His voice was ragged as he drew deep breaths and slowed his run to a walk beside her motionless car. "What the hell are you doing?"

Aston stood from where she was crouched by the rear tire. Sam's breath hitched and his body went completely still. Her form-fitting black dress and strappy red sandals screamed business-sexy.

He allowed himself about five seconds to rake her appearance from head to toe, before focusing on her eyes.

She smiled. "What does it look like I'm doing?"

She squatted back down next to a small doughnut tire and a shiny tire jack.

His eyes glazed over momentarily before he reached down and grabbed both of her elbows, pulling her back up to her feet.

"It looks like you're about to change a tire."

She smirked, her elbows still held firmly in his grasp. "I see why my father has such faith in your big brains."

He laughed, letting go of her elbow to run a hand through his hair. "Don't you have Triple A?"

She glanced down the road, and then back up into Sam's eyes. "Sam, my house is two miles up the road. It would take Triple A longer to get here than it would for me to change the damn thing and drive on home. Hell, I could probably walk it."

"Yeah, but…why didn't you call your dad? Or Reed?"

She sucked on the corner of her bottom lip, and his stomach flipped. "Because I know how to change a tire. Why would I?"

Her eyes finally left his, and she took in the fact that he was shirtless and wearing running shorts. "Didn't I tell you it was suicide running on this road?"

"You're gonna lecture *me*? Step aside, I'm changing your tire."

She shook her head, staying firmly planted beside the vehicle. "Nuh-huh, Waters. I can change my own damn tire."

He let her go, reaching both hands behind his head and barking a laugh up at the clear, blue sky. The evening was approaching, and they both needed to get home if they were going to be ready to go out later with Reed.

"Wow, you're stubborn. Okay, Princess. We can change your tire together. I'm sure as hell not leaving you out here to do it by yourself."

Her eyes narrowed. "Fine."

She squatted down again, and Sam muttered a curse into the sky.

He could do this job in his sleep. In fact, he'd changed the tire on Ever's truck for her plenty of times. Taking care of people was what he did.

But he'd never come across anyone like Aston Hopewell, and he was sure he hadn't even scratched the surface yet.

He knelt down next to her, firmly moving her hands out of the way as he jacked the car up a little higher.

"Always jack the car up higher than you think you need to," he said gruffly as he worked.

Aston set her mouth in a firm line but nodded.

He glanced at her. "Can I have that wrench you're holding in a death grip?"

She handed it over. He caught her eyes on his bare biceps as he removed the lug nuts from the ruined tire. "Hold these."

She held out her hands, and he dropped the lug nuts into them. Then he exchanged the flat tire for her smaller spare.

"When do you think you'll have this replaced?"

Her face was no longer irritated, and she shrugged a shoulder as she thought. "My dad has a mechanic he uses regularly. He'll probably have him bring me a new tire in the morning."

Sam nodded. "At-home service? Nice. Lug nuts?"

She handed them over, and he replaced them. When he

was all done, he stood, reaching out to pull her to her feet beside him.

"See? We make a good team," he said.

"You did all the heavy lifting," she pointed out.

"You need to learn to let someone help you out every once in awhile. Are you going to make me run back, or can I have a ride?"

She walked around to the driver's side and climbed inside. "Get in, Waters. And thanks for helping me."

He chuckled as he got into the car. "Anytime, Aston."

Three

When he arrived back at the tack house, Sam jumped into the shower. After rinsing off the sweat from the run and helping Aston change her tire, he toweled off and put on a clean pair of jeans and a T-shirt with his night at the bar in mind.

Anxiously pacing the circular driveway, waiting for Aston and Reed, Sam recalled his conversation with Hunter. Hunter had been at Ever's house. Being able to hear her voice made the tension he was constantly holding in his stomach melt away. However, he clenched up again when he heard the catch in her tone after he told them what he was doing that night.

"You're going out?" Ever had asked tersely.

Sam could tell she didn't like the idea. He thought she might be right. He wasn't in South Carolina to make new friends and spend nights out on the town. He was here to work, save money, and lie low until he was able to reunite with his girl and his brother.

"I'll talk to her, Sam," Hunter had said when Ever was out of earshot. "This is hard on her."

So he'd hung up, showered, and dressed. He was now wearing clean jeans and a fitted white tee. He felt comfortable and laid-back on the outside, but the knots trying up his insides were pulling tighter.

Was he doing something wrong?

Then he found his mind pulling him in a completely different direction as he pictured Aston, sexily and professionally clad, bending down beside her car to *change her tire.*

"Stop it." Aston's voice rang out in the darkness as she and Reed stepped into the clear night. "You're wearing a hole in the asphalt."

"Yeah, dude, we're going out. Remember? What's got your shit twisted up?"

"Nothing," Sam muttered. "Look, I'm not sure I should be doing this tonight. I think I'm gonna just—"

Reed made a loud buzzer noise. "Don't even think about pussing out on us, Sam! You're about to get in my truck, and we're going out. Period. You clearly need a shot more than anyone on the island right now."

Sam tugged his ear thoughtfully, and then hung his head in defeat. He heard the doors to Reed's Silverado unlock, and he pulled himself into the crew cab seat.

Aston climbed into the front and turned around to peer back at him. "Country boy gentleman like you, and you just let me climb my ass up into this truck by myself?"

He stared at her, stricken. "Dammit. Aston, I'm sorry. I'm kinda distracted. I usually would never—"

"Easy, Waters. I was kidding. I'm perfectly capable of climbing up into a vehicle on my own."

She grinned at him, and then turned back to face the front of the truck.

"Seems like you're capable of a lot. Doesn't mean you have to do it all on your own, though." The words came from somewhere inside of him, the part of him that had really been listening while she had spoken to him beside the pool. The part of him that had watched how doggedly determined she'd been to change her own tire by the side of the road.

She turned again and stared at him with those deep baby blues, her eyes piercing right through the dark. He held her gaze, feeling the electricity begin to shoot through him again. He didn't want to think about the strange feelings she brought out of him, especially not tonight when he was so torn up about Ever's feelings.

When Reed climbed behind the wheel and started the ignition, he glanced back at Sam in the rearview. "Ten minutes, man. Then we're drinking your sorrows away."

He eased the truck out of the driveway and down the long entry drive. Once at the end, he turned onto the state route and headed east, toward the ocean.

Sam settled back into his seat, staring out the window as Nelson Island's nighttime scenery flew by. When he heard Aston address Reed, he turned his attention back to the front of the cab.

"It would make Daddy really happy if you came to work this summer, you know." The soft glow of the dashboard lights reflected against her profile, and Sam had trouble taking his eyes off of her.

"Yeah, I'm sure he would." Reed's answer was clipped.

"You don't have to keep hating him," she said softly. "It's not his fault he is the way he is."

"It's not?" asked Reed, his voice rising slightly. "He has a son not interested in the family business, so what does he do? Does he take an interest in that son's activities? Nope. He decides that son isn't worth his time, instead."

Aston watched him for nearly a full minute, then she turned her head back to the front windshield with a sigh.

"I heard you playing today," she said. "It was good."

The obvious subject change was welcome to her brother. "Thanks."

Sam wondered about the rapport between the siblings. Aston was clearly so business-focused, but Reed was as far on the other side of the spectrum as was possible. How could they have been raised by the same father, with such vastly different values?

When they arrived at Sunny's, the gravel parking lot was teeming. Cars were parked haphazardly in crooked rows outside the building. The bar itself was settled precariously on an old wooden pier looking out over the twinkling lights of Charleston just across Charleston Harbor.

Sam jumped down from his seat and immediately opened Aston's door.

"When I mess up, I only do it once." He smirked at her, nodding his head once.

She took his outstretched hand and stepped down, squeezing his hand just before she pulled it away.

"It looks dangerous." Sam appraised the way the bar leaned toward the water, his head tilted to one side.

Aston laughed. "You'll live. Just don't lean too far over the rails."

Sam nodded seriously and Reed snorted.

"She's teasing you, Sam. No one has ever fallen over the side. Not sober, anyway."

When they walked inside, they headed straight back to the outdoor deck and to a large table in the far back corner. The tables were all round and wooden, with a worn-in appearance. The entire place was comfortable and laid-back. Neon beer signs adorned the walls around them, and servers were walking around in tight black polos and jeans or cutoffs. The relaxed atmosphere struck the right chord with Sam, and he sighed with relief.

He was able to take a deep breath for the first time since speaking with Hunter and Ever.

"Sam, meet the crew. Crew, this is Sam." Reed gestured grandly around the table and back at Sam as they approached.

Sam scanned the table. Six seats were occupied. He picked out Aston's boyfriend, Princeton, immediately. He sat with his chair facing backward and his elbows leaning on the table.

"Hey, Sam." A lanky guy with brown hair curling around his ears held out a hand and shook Sam's enthusiastically.

"I'm Finn. This is my girlfriend, Ashley." He gestured toward the petite blonde sitting next to him. She smiled and waved at Sam.

"Yeah, and that's Blaze, Tate, and Tamara. Tate and Tamara are twins." Reed gestured toward the other half of the table while taking his seat.

The twins glanced over at Sam, Tamara's eyes lingering longer than necessary. Sam thought it was obvious they were siblings: They both had red hair and their faces shared the same bone structure. Tate's hair, of course, fell shorter than his sister's, curling around his ears in a rare shade of coppery gold.

"Blaze?" Sam asked, looking at the burly guy with dark brown skin. He was huge. He could have played on the O-line on Sam's high school football team, and probably one of the colleges around too.

"You play ball?"

Blaze grinned. His dark skin, tattooed arms, and giant's build made him intimidating until he aimed that smile at anyone nearby. Then it was clear he was as dangerous as a teddy bear. Sam guessed that in spite of that, he still wasn't someone to be crossed.

"Got that nickname back in school. They started calling me Blaze after they saw how I lit guys up on the field." Sam returned Blaze's wide grin.

Blaze was his kind of guy.

Sam aimed his gaze at Princeton. "We meet again."

Princeton nodded in his direction. "Since when do y'all invite field hands to come and hang out with the crew?"

Aston shot him a glare, which piqued Sam's curiosity. "Shut up, Prince. Sam will be working in our father's offices soon."

So maybe she wasn't a fan of Sam joining the ranks of her father's company. But she was quick to defend him.

Even against her boyfriend.

Princeton's eyebrows shot toward the sky. "Oh, really? How'd you pull that off, Sam?"

Sam shrugged. "I didn't. It was Mr. Hopewell's idea."

Princeton's eyes narrowed.

Tamara got up from her seat and nudged Reed out of the way so she could have his spot. "Where you from, Sam? We're all from boring old Nelson Island. We meet a lot of newbies over the summer, though. They're always fun. You...you look like you're gonna be a *lot* of fun."

She pinched his cheek good-naturedly and tilted her mouth in a crooked smile.

"Down, girl," admonished her brother, rolling his eyes. "The guy just sat down, Tam. Give him a second."

Sam glanced around the table. "Nice to meet all of you. Let me buy the first round."

A cheer went up, and everyone put in their beer orders.

As Tamara scooted her chair a little closer to Sam's, he eyed her a little warily. Where he was from, girls weren't so forward. Not to mention they all knew he belonged to Ever. So he'd never had to fight off a female, and he wasn't looking forward to the task.

Reed must have seen Sam's apprehensive expression, because he spoke up.

"Better back off, Tam," he warned. "Sam's girlfriend wouldn't like you so close."

Aston's head snapped up. Her eyes burned into Sam's. "Girl-friend?"

"Yeah, sis, you didn't know? Our Sam here is spoken for."

Sam met Aston's eyes and instantly averted his gaze. The emotions swirling in her eyes, and in his own gut, were more than he wanted to consider.

"Where's your girl?" Finn asked curiously.

He put his arm casually around Ashley, pushing a strand of her hair back behind one ear.

"She's back home," Sam explained. "She had to stay behind to take care of some, uh, business."

"Business, huh?" Princeton smirked from across the table. "Know what it sounds like to me, country boy? Sounds like you're hiding something. What town did you say you were from?"

"I didn't." Sam kept his tone cool and hard, but his stomach was sinking fast. "I might be country, but it doesn't mean I can't still knock the shit out of someone if I have to. Especially someone getting into my personal business."

He stood and walked away from the table, headed for the bar.

"I know it's hard for you, Prince, but try not to be such an ass tonight, would you?" Reed glared at Princeton as Sam walked away.

Sam leaned against the bar with both palms flat against the smooth wood, breathing deeply. He wasn't trying to make any enemies here. He was trying to lie low. Why was that so hard?

"Another Michelob, please," he told the pretty female bartender.

She nodded and slid the brown bottle over the wooden surface until it reached him. He wrapped his fist around the chilled glass and took a long swig, swishing the lager around in his mouth before swallowing. He turned around and looked out over the bar. He wasn't sure if he was going to be able to sit at a table with Princeton tonight. Maybe he'd hang out here until it was time to go home.

Home.

He was nine hours away from his real home. His gut twisted as he thought of Ever and Hunter. But he didn't miss Duck Creek. The town had served as a prison for him his entire childhood, and he finally felt free of it for the first time in his life.

Thinking about Duck Creek forced Sam's thoughts to wander back to his girlfriend. He only hoped the police weren't giving Ever too hard of a time, hounding her about where he had run off to. Everyone in Duck Creek knew they were a package deal. Since childhood, they'd never been separated. If Sam was buying candy and soda at the convenience store on Route 8, Ever would be waiting on a bench outside. And Hunter was never far away either. That was the way things had always been. So the sheriff's department had to be questioning them pretty hard.

Nelson Island was comfortable for him with its rolling green pastures and long, winding back roads that reminded him of home. But the fresh sea air with a hint of salt and the ability to squish sand between his toes if he had the inclination was new and kind of wonderful.

Maybe this could be his home.

If he weren't hiding the blackest secret he'd ever known from everyone he met here.

"Princeton's always been a jackass." Tamara's tone was dry as she sidled up to him at the bar. "We only tolerate him 'cause he's always been one of us. Ignore him and come on back to the table. I won't bite."

He looked down at her and sighed. It was time to set the record straight with Tamara and avoid an uncomfortable situation. "I will come back, on one condition."

"Name it, sweetness."

"You have to stop flirting with me, Tamara. I really am taken."

She frowned. Her dark red lips, so close to her hair color, made an exaggerated pout.

"Look, Sam, I'm a flirty girl. I can't stop being who I am, can I? But I understand you're off-limits. We can be friends, though, can't we?" She looked up at him through long lashes and tossed her long, straight hair over her shoulder.

She really was cute with a flirty, sultry flair. She reminded Sam of home, too.

He chuckled and put an arm around her neck, already feeling brotherly love for the girl. "Nope, guess you can't. I sure as hell keep trying. It's not working out so well for me, either. We're friends, sure."

She smiled and led him back to their seats at the table. He was able to continue drinking his beer, staying away from conversation with Princeton while joining in with the others.

But he found his gaze wandering back to Princeton and Aston often. He waited for them to get all close and cuddly like the other couple at the table, Finn and Ashley. They never did.

Sam watched Aston's hands as if they called to him. He couldn't shake the vision of those slender fingers twisting the lug nuts to loosen her flat tire.

And he watched, her hands balled into fists on top of the table.

He quickly glanced to her face, and she was gazing at Finn and Ashley with an unreadable expression. Then her glance slid to Princeton, who still sat backward on his chair with both hands cupped around his frosty mug of imported beer. Awareness dawned on Sam, a blazing sunrise in an area of his consciousness that had previously been dark with night.

She wanted him to touch her. It was as clear as day to Sam, but apparently Princeton didn't have a clue.

The men in Aston's life clearly treated her like the strong, capable woman she was. She wanted that, she demanded that.

But there was so much more to her than that. How long had she gone without any of them realizing it?

Aston bit down on her tongue as Princeton pounded his sixth tequila shot of the night with Blaze and Tate. She rolled her eyes and glanced over at Ashley, who gave Aston a sympathetic shake of her head. She extracted herself from Finn's arm and came to sit next to her friend.

"He's hitting it pretty hard, huh?" she asked in a low voice.

"Is that new?" Aston asked, her voice dripping with sarcasm.

Ashley clearly had a better leash on her man, but then it had always been that way. Ashley and Finn had been together about as long as Aston and Princeton, since junior year of high school. They'd been through all the ups and downs together. Aston knew Finn and Ashley had the ability to make it for the long haul. They were *it* for each other. It was obvious every time Finn looked at Ashley and that dumb, dopey expression appeared in his eyes. Every time Ashley absently placed her hand in Finn's, Aston felt reality jab her in the gut.

She had no illusions about her relationship with Princeton. She'd been enamored with him in high school, but since graduation when she'd gone to Xavier and he'd stayed behind at the

University of Charleston, she'd known they weren't going to make it to marriage. She didn't think Princeton knew that, though. She stayed with him because they'd been together so long, the relationship was like an old, comfortable quilt she could pull on to shield her from chilly nights. But now, at this point in her life, it felt like the quilt was heavy on her limbs in the middle of a hot, steamy summer. They didn't have the connection that Finn and Ashley had.

Maybe they'd never had it.

It was glaringly obvious on nights like this when the whole gang was together, and Finn and Ashley were right there, acting like they were already married.

"And Reed is still Reed," Ashley said with a giggle. She was staring in fascination as Reed wound his fingers through the bra strap of the giggling blonde sitting in his lap. He let it snap back down on her exposed shoulder and she gasped, batting her lashes at him.

Reed found a new girl to occupy his lap every time they went out. He didn't do commitments.

"You barely came home this year, Aston." Ashley's expression was sad. "I miss you."

"I miss you too, Ash." Aston sighed. "I just didn't feel like coming home and watching my dad fawn all over my mom like she never cheated on him. It makes me sick. They healed, but Reed and I didn't. I love being at school, away from all the N.I. drama."

What she didn't say was that now that she was home again, every time she looked at Sam she felt like she was doing the same thing to Princeton her mother had done to her dad.

"I have no idea what that would be like." Ashley nodded sympathetically. Ashley and Finn both attended Charleston like Princeton. "Going to U of C is just like being in N.I. Only a bigger version of it." She presented Aston with a wry expression.

Aston smiled at her friend. She and Ashley had known each other since they walked into kindergarten and found they had matching Barbie backpacks. She considered her a best friend, and she was sad she'd seen a lot less of her over the past three years.

She reached over and squeezed Ashley's hand. "We'll just have to spend a lot of time together this summer to make up for it."

"Done." Ashley grinned and smoothed a hand over her short blond bob. "Tamara's laying it on thick with Sam tonight, huh? I think she really likes him. I can see why. He's sweet as pie."

Aston glanced over at Tamara and frowned. "We told her he had a girlfriend. Why is she still after him? She looks like an idiot."

Ashley turned surprised eyes on Aston. "Easy. She's just being Tamara. She's always like that around new guys. Especially new guys who look like Sam. I mean, damn. The boy is gorgeous."

And he was. Aston couldn't deny it. She actually had a chance to look at him tonight, really look at him without being obvious. His dark wash jeans fit him just right. She could see how tight his ass was beneath them, and she couldn't help wondering what it would feel like to reach out and pinch it. The fact that Sam was such a sweet guy made her want to do not-so-sweet things to him.

Ugh! The temptation to think about him in ways she shouldn't was overwhelming. Sam was working for her father.

He wasn't from around here, which meant he'd eventually leave like all the summer people did. He was also, as she'd found out tonight, taken. And so was she.

And she couldn't stand the guy! There were times when he acted like he could see straight through her, to parts of herself she kept locked away deep inside. And that drove her crazy in ways she'd never been driven.

So why did she melt a little inside when those tawny-colored eyes locked onto hers? And why did her stomach clench when he spoke her name with that adorable drawl of his? And why the *hell* did she have to cross her legs and clench her muscles on the rare occasions when he touched her?

She barely knew Sam Waters. But she knew that something sizzled between them in a way she'd never felt. And it was so good, so *tempting,* that she almost wanted to throw everything else she knew out the window and straddle his lap.

But she couldn't afford to think that way. She had to be on her guard with Sam, or he would end up taking advantage of her father. She knew the look her father got in his eyes when he was talking with Sam. He saw potential in him, and he would pull Sam up by his bootstraps until he became everything Gregory Hopewell wanted him to be.

"Come here, baby," Princeton slurred as he pulled her roughly against him. Aston had to rise part of the way out of her chair in order to keep her arm in its socket.

"Hey, Prince," Ashley warned. "Be easy. You're hurting Aston's arm."

Sam's head snapped around at Ashley's declaration. His gaze

locked on Aston's arm where Princeton's hand squeezed. Sam's eyes narrowed and he glanced at her face. She deciphered the look in his eye almost as if she'd known him all her life and could read his mind. He was asking her if she was okay.

No one ever checked with her to see if she was okay. Everyone just always assumed that she was. A strange heat saturated her chest cavity, squeezing her heart so hard in its cage that she winced against the ache.

She nodded, just a slight tilt, hoping he understood it meant to stay where he was. He scrutinized her and Princeton, his body tense. But he didn't come toward them.

"Get off me, Prince," she said. She grabbed Princeton's hand and pried his fingers off her arm. He only replaced it with his entire right arm draped across her shoulders. He pulled her face toward his with his left hand.

"You're so fucking gorgeous," he said. "Kiss me."

"No!" Aston exclaimed. "You're trashed, Prince. Get off. I think you're done for the night."

Sam stood up quickly, causing panic to course through Aston. Part of her, the part way deep down inside that she tried to keep hidden, glowed at the prospect of Sam inserting himself in the middle of her and Princeton. But the rational part of her won.

It always did.

She shook her head firmly at Sam.

"No," she mouthed. He hesitated, standing in front of his seat but still glaring at Princeton.

Reed finally noticed the silent standoff between Sam and his sister and stepped in. He shoved Sam back into his seat, and stepped around Aston to grab Princeton by the shoulders. "Come on, Prince. I'll buy your drunk ass another."

"Reed!" Aston's tone was sharp.

"Hey," he tossed over his shoulder as he walked toward the bar with a weaving Princeton. "I'm getting him away from you, aren't I?"

Sam watched them go, his mouth hanging open. Then he looked at Aston.

"Is he always like that?" His tone was accusing.

Blaze let out a booming guffaw. "That's our Princeton. Charming, ain't he? We cut him off at a certain point, and then we take his keys and someone always gets his drunk ass home."

Sam didn't look amused. "He's an ass. And you guys shouldn't keep putting up with it." His eyes never left Aston's. His disappointment echoed a hard line deep in her soul. She didn't like it.

Tamara looked first at Aston, and then at Sam. She slid up to Sam's side.

"Oh, don't worry about her, Sam. She's a hell of a lot tougher than she looks. If anybody can handle a drunk Princeton, Aston can."

"Yeah? Well I'm no stranger to men acting badly when they drink. And no one can handle that. No matter how strong they are."

Aston's body tensed as Sam pushed back from the table and stormed away toward the parking lot. Everyone's heads followed his exit.

"I think I love that guy." Blaze chuckled.

"It's about time someone stuck up for you, Aston," Finn agreed. "You'd never catch me treating Ash that way, or getting trashed like that in front of her."

"Yeah, we all know how perfect you and Ashley are, Finn," Aston snapped.

She rose from the table and followed Sam outside the bar.

She caught up with him at the far end of the dock. He was peering out at the dark water silently lapping against the wet wood. She stood beside him, watching him watch the water.

"Look," he said without glancing at her. "I'm sorry. I have a hard time watching drunk assholes treating women badly. Brings up a lot of stuff for me. I'm not going back in there."

"No one said you had to," Aston spoke softly. "But I'm not some helpless little girl. I can take care of myself. I don't need a caveman."

His eyes shot to hers, flashing with anger. "You're calling me a caveman? Maybe you should go back in there and take another look at your man. All I'm saying is that I won't watch him treat you like that."

Anger flared up inside of Aston, a shocking fiery blast of red heat. "Why the hell do you give a shit, Sam? You don't even know me. Or Princeton. Why do you care what he says to me or how he touches me?"

She took a step closer until she was able to jab a finger in his chest.

"Why aren't you back home, Sam? Looking out for *her*?"

He stepped back, as if she'd shoved him. He stared at her for a minute, then at the finger she jabbed in his chest.

"Maybe I should be." His voice sounded soft and broken. "Maybe I should be at home. But I can't be there right now. I shouldn't be here, either."

He walked away from her. A tumult of emotions battered her chest as she watched him. Something in his voice squeezed her heart almost painfully for the second time that night. Hearing him sound so torn was wrong, somehow. She took a step to go after him, and then stopped.

Sam wasn't her responsibility, and she wasn't his. She watched him through the bar windows as he walked over and said something to Reed. Reed nodded and stood up, waving to their friends. She watched Reed and Sam trudge back out of the bar.

"Hey, sis," Reed called to her. "I'm gonna head home with Sam. You gonna drive Princeton?"

She nodded. She'd drive Princeton home, like she always ended up doing, and then Finn and Ashley would bring her back to the ranch, like they always did.

As Sam and her brother drove away, her chest still ached from the expression she glimpsed on Sam's face.

He never glanced back at her.

Early the next morning, Sam's sneakers pounded along the trail winding around the pastures on the Hopewell ranch. He ran with the cover of the trees on his left, with a clear view of rolling grass on his right. Music blasting in his ears, he was met with his idea of a perfect morning.

He slowed as he neared the training ring where the polo ponies received their daily workouts. A large black quarter horse stood bucking in the center of the ring, a long rope attached to its bridle.

Sam paused. He knew they'd recently acquired the horse, and that it had yet to be tamed and broken. Aston stood across the ring, her small hands firmly gripping the rope.

Her worn jeans were a far cry from the polished outfit he'd seen her in the previous night, and his jaw fell open as he followed her movement around the ring.

She circled with the horse as he bucked wildly, pulling on the rope with the force she needed to keep him from knocking her to the ground.

Sam stood frozen to the spot, inspecting Aston as she expertly weaved a path around the ring with the wild horse. His body was taut, ready to run to her aid if she needed it.

She didn't.

After several long moments, the horse slowly lay down on the ground, breathing heavily, his large nostrils flaring. Aston approached, moving as slowly as a toddler learning to walk.

She murmured calming words of appreciation as she grew closer to the horse, who tracked her approach with wary eyes. Crouching low, she reached out to him.

"Easy, boy. Easy. That's it, you big, sweet thing. That's it."

When she was finally close enough to touch the giant, she stroked a gentle hand along its flank, continued words of encouragement and love reaching not only the horse's ears, but also Sam's.

Incredulity washed over him as he watched her with the now quiet horse. Large, grown men had been working with the horse all week and had yet to manage to get close enough to touch it.

Aston, with the power of a sweetness and gentleness he'd never before seen in her, had literally stroked a wild beast and nearly turned him into a harmless pet.

He swallowed hard.

When she finally led the horse back to his stable, Sam followed, approaching the large double doors as she was exiting them. She started at the sight of him, placing her hand on her chest.

"That was impressive." He leaned against the barn door, taking in her flushed skin. Her long, dark hair was pulled into a ponytail high on her head, with tendrils of loose strands hovering around her face. Her turquoise V-neck tank hugged her curves, and her battered leather boots had seen better days.

A small smile pulled at her lips. "You think so, Waters? Just a little breaking-in."

Sam chuckled. "A little breaking-in? I saw that horse make grown men cry this week. It could've turned on you."

She laughed and reached for a water bottle sitting on a barrel. She brought the plastic to her lips and sipped, keeping her clear blue eyes trained on Sam.

"You think that's the first horse I've worked with? I've been breaking horses for years, Sam. I didn't need any help with this one. The guys did all the hard stuff earlier in the week, anyway."

"So." Sam ticked a list on his fingers. "She...is a genius at school. She manhandles her drunk boyfriend. She changes her own tires. She breaks wild horses. Is there anything else I need to know about you before I say or do something that might have you kicking my ass?"

Aston sized him up, allowing her gaze to travel from his legs, up his bare stomach and chest, and finally looking way up to meet his stare. The corners of her mouth twitched upward as she tried to fight a smile. She lost the battle, and a huge grin broke out on her face.

A grin that nearly stole his breath. Seeing her smile like this was rare, and he wanted to pluck it from her lips and place it into his pocket for safekeeping.

She should smile like that more often. She should smile like that every damn day.

"You have absolutely nothing to worry about, Waters."

He tried not to stare as she walked away.

Tried, but failed.

Four

Dear Sam,

This long-distance thing sucks. I've never been away from you for a day, much less months at a time. It's killing me, Sam. Thank God I have Hunter here. Without him I think I'd go crazy.

I'm going to be honest. Life with Daddy gone is...eye-opening. Every night when I lie down without wincing in pain from what he'd done to me, I breathe another sigh of relief. Thank you for giving me the strength I needed to live this life.

I finally went back to work at the bakery. You know it's the only thing I know how to do, and getting back to work is helping me adjust to everything. I have a new friend. Her name is Rilla and she opened a florist next door to Sugar Coated. We even went out to a bar!

It feels weird knowing you are there, living this new life

by the beach. Sun and sand compared to fishing by the creek?
Sounds like a vacation. I haven't heard from the sheriff's office
in weeks. Don't you think it's time we figured out what to do
next? Maybe we can even find a way for you to come home. I
have to go, Sam. Hunter is walking in the front door.

I love you.

Ever

He placed Ever's most recent letter in the desk drawer. His feelings about the letter were jumbled. He still got the aching in his heart whenever he read a letter from her. But the daily living without her was getting easier. He was getting used to not waking up panicked if she wasn't in his room with him. On those mornings, he'd ride his bike as fast as he could over to the house she shared with her father and check to make sure she was still breathing. Her father would be passed out on the couch, and Sam would creep back to her room, having to encounter whatever new horror would present itself to him that morning in the form of a bruise, cut, or broken bone.

Their childhood together was horrible. And apart from Hunter, they were all the other had.

Sam had stumbled onto this life of hard work, yes, but also comfort and relaxation. When he stepped into the little tack house he occupied, he would breathe deep and sigh, because he was alone and he was safe. It was strange and exhilarating.

Guilt enveloped him. Guilt, for liking life without Ever here to enjoy it with him. But she'd be here eventually. He'd promised her that.

He stepped out of the tack house front door and locked it behind him, whistling as he strode toward the main house.

Today marked a week and four days after the night out at Sunny's. Despite the drama with Princeton that night, he'd felt at home among the group. He and Blaze had talked football, and he'd taken a shot with him and Tate. He never took shots, so it was a new experience. In Duck Creek, on the brief occasion he'd been at a bar, he'd refused to lose control in case he had to face Ever's dad when they arrived back home. So the freedom to drink with friends had been nice. Tamara was adorable and so easy to talk to, and he'd admired the easy and carefree love Ashley and Finn shared. He and Ever had the love part down, but easy and carefree? Never.

And then there was Aston. He had known love. True, deep, devotional love. He'd been devoted to Ever since before he knew what *devoted* meant. So the farce of a relationship she was sharing with that tool, Princeton, was baffling to Sam. And it drove hot, angry fire through his veins, too, because even though he had only known Aston for a little over a week, he felt he already saw her much more clearly than Princeton did. The way she and Princeton had greeted each other when he'd found her crying by the state highway the night of her welcome-home dinner had been a joke. They hadn't kissed or even hugged. Hell, he'd expect a girl who'd been separated from the man she loved to go running straight into his arms the moment she saw him. And he'd expect a man who'd been apart from the girl he loved to scoop her up in his arms and never let go. That was what a girl like Aston deserved, and she clearly wasn't getting it from Princeton.

Sure, he knew she was tough. He saw straight through her hard exterior to the little girl underneath who had never found the kind of love she wanted to believe existed in the world. And he bristled, acknowledging that Princeton didn't see that in her.

She deserved better.

Sam was mulling all of this over in his brain as he approached the main house for his first day working as Mr. Hopewell's business assistant at home. Mr. Hopewell had asked him to meet him in his home office first thing this morning so he could further explain the tasks Sam would be expected to complete.

Sam stopped short as he cleared the tree line beside the driveway. He noted a sheriff's cruiser parked directly in front of the steps leading to the front door. His heart banged inside his chest as he stared at the vehicle.

What the hell? Why was the sheriff here? Could they have put it together? Had he been careless going out last week, meeting all of those people? Princeton had indicated he suspected Sam had something to hide. What if he'd done some digging and discovered what the Duck Creek sheriff thought he'd done?

The front door creaked open and Sam ducked back behind the line of trees for cover. He peered out as the sheriff himself came walking out of the house with Mr. Hopewell. Sam couldn't hear what they were saying, but he watched as they shook hands and the sheriff climbed into his car. He drove slowly around the driveway and down the road leading off the Hopewell estate.

Mr. Hopewell looked in Sam's direction. "You can come on out now, Sam. He's gone."

Sam's pulse stuttered before it began beating more quickly

than ever. He stepped out from the cover of the tree line and headed toward Gregory Hopewell. He felt his face redden as he approached, and Mr. Hopewell's grim expression did nothing to slow the rapid pattering of his heart.

"I think we have some things to discuss, don't we?" Mr. Hopewell turned and strode up the front steps. Sam stood frozen down below, watching his mentor walk away.

Gregory turned around at the top and indicated that Sam follow. "Aren't you coming? It is the day I asked you to meet me here, is it not?"

Sam took a deep breath, let it out, and followed.

As the office doors closed behind them, Mr. Hopewell took a seat at his impressive mahogany desk and gestured toward the chair situated in front of him. Sam sat.

"Sam, that sheriff wasn't here for you. I spotted you out of the corner of my eye the second we emerged from the house, and the fact that you hid confirmed some of the suspicions I already had."

Sam set his jaw in preparation for fight-or-flight. If Mr. Hopewell had suspicions about him, then why had he invited Sam here? Why was he allowing him to work on his property? And now in his office?

"Get comfortable, Sam. Let me tell you a little story."

"I've got to ask you, Aston. Point blank, okay? What's going on with you and Sam?"

Aston curved her slender hand to shade her eyes from the sun. She craned her neck forward so that she could zero in on

Ashley's face. Then, deciding the angle she received wasn't good enough, she sat all the way up in her lounge chair and stared at her friend.

"What the hell are you talking about, Ash?"

Ashley lifted her sunglasses so Aston could see her face. She wore a solemn expression, but the corners of her mouth twitched as she evaluated Aston's hostile posture.

"I mean exactly what I asked. What's going on? You two most definitely had some fireworks sparking the other night."

"Sam has a girlfriend back home. And I'm with Princeton. So there's zero action going on between us."

"I'm not saying you two have done anything. And hell, Aston, maybe you don't even realize it. But there's something about you and Sam. I've never seen it with you and Princeton. When we were sitting around the table at Sunny's, you kept turning toward him when he talked, even if he wasn't talking to you. And every time you got up to go to the bar, his eyes followed you across the room. I swear I could feel the electricity coming off the two of you in currents. It was weird, Aston. And kind of amazing."

Ashley sat back in her chair and replaced her sunglasses, as if that was all that needed to be said on the subject. She knew Aston well enough to know that she'd have to have this conversation a few more times before Aston was ready to admit anything.

Aston's back was ramrod straight in the luxe chair, her legs stretched out straight in front of her, her apple-red painted toes curled into the soft fabric of the seat. She crossed her arms rigidly against her chest as she stared at Ashley.

"I really wish you'd stop watching us so closely, Ash. It's creepy.

And Sam is just a guy here for the summer, working for my father. That's all. Don't read more into it. You can be so dramatic sometimes."

Ashley let out a bark of a laugh without bothering to look at her friend. "Okay, A. I'll humor you. But can you just admit one thing?"

"Admit what?" Aston sighed, her body slowly releasing its tension as she relaxed back into the lounger.

"Admit you think he's hot."

Aston closed her eyes briefly, glad they were hidden behind her aviators. "He's hot, I guess. I mean if you like the whole big-muscled, six-foot-four thing. And the deep brown eyes that see right through you. And he does have all of that country-boy charm that he uses like a weapon when he wants to."

"Right." Ashley laughed. "All of that's true. But you haven't been looking at him or anything, right A?"

"Right," Aston agreed, turning onto her stomach so the sun's rays could warm her back.

"I love Princeton like a brother, Aston. We all grew up together; I don't even have a choice at this point. But I don't know how long you're going to pretend he's forever for you. You don't feel the same way about him that I do about Finn."

Aston rolled her eyes. "Not everyone is going to find what you two have, Ash. If I didn't know the two of you, I wouldn't even think it existed. But I sure as hell haven't seen it anywhere else. So I have no illusions about the fact that Princeton is probably as good as it's going to get for me."

Ashley made a mental note right there to talk to Finn, ask him to get Sam alone. She wasn't willing to watch her best friend set-tle. Aston deserved better than that.

"Well, Ashley White! I didn't know you were here! Come on over here and give me a hug!"

Lillian Hopewell glided onto the patio smocked in a turquoise cover-up and donning her own pair of aviators. She held her arms open, and Ashley rose from her chair to greet her.

"Mrs. Hopewell, hey. It's good to see you!" Ashley hugged the woman warmly.

She and Aston had spent so much time together here over the years; she knew all of the drama that had happened between As-ton and her mother. In spite of all of it, she still loved the woman like a second mother.

"Oh, please, call me Lillian now. We're all adults here these days, aren't we?"

Aston remained frozen on her lounger, never bothering to ac-knowledge her mother's arrival.

"What are we doing today, girls?" Lillian asked, settling com-fortably onto her own lounger with a fruity drink in one hand.

"Oh, we're just discussing Aston's crazy attraction to Sam Waters." She glanced sideways at Aston.

"Ashley!" Aston gasped, finally sitting up.

"Oh, Aston, don't get shy. I am your mother, for God's sakes. I hadn't noticed an attraction, Ashley. Is it true, Aston?"

"You wouldn't have noticed, would you?" Aston grumbled. "You were probably thinking of him as eye candy for yourself."

The silence hung heavy in the sweet summer air. Ashley cleared her throat.

Lillian forced a smile. "Actually, no. I'm starting to think of Sam like a son. He's absolutely darling, and there would be nothing wrong with you feeling an attraction toward him. Why not?"

"Um, because I don't cheat, Mom. I have a boyfriend."

Lillian chose to ignore Aston's rudeness and waved her hand dismissively. "Aston, you and Princeton are the only ones who think you and Princeton are going to make it much longer. You two are about as hot for each other as your grandparents. When you finally realize it, it'll be the best decision you'll ever make."

Aston rose, adjusting her halter-top bikini as she did so. Without another word, she strode into the house, slamming the door behind her. The windowpanes rattled in her absence.

"Well, that went well," murmured Lillian.

"It's going to take time," Ashley said sympathetically, patting Lillian's hand.

"It's been years, Ashley. She knows it was the biggest mistake of my life. Is she going to hold it against me forever?"

Ashley blew out a breath. "Aston's one of the most pigheaded people I know. But she also loves harder than anyone else. You're her mother. She was hurt when it all came out. But she'll come around eventually."

Lillian nodded tightly. She pursed her lips until they were white. "Thank you, Ashley. At least one of my children still loves me."

"They both do," Ashley responded as she stood. She raised both arms above her head and arched luxuriously in the sunlight. She threw one last smile at Lillian as she went inside in search of her friend.

Five

Ten years Previously in Nelson Island

*C*ome on, honey," Gregory said as he watched his only daughter shut the car door. "You're moving like a turtle."

She grinned her happy smile at him, the one that always tugged his heartstrings and made him do whatever she wanted. Whenever she smiled, it made him want to give her the entire world. Because most of the time, she was oh-so-serious, much too melancholy and focused for a little girl. She was a people-pleaser. She always wanted to be the best, and not just for herself but also for the other people in her life. Especially her father.

And as she entered her adolescent years, he was worried that she may never get the happy, carefree childhood he'd always wanted for her. She was always worried about the future, and about what was going to happen next in life.

"I'm going as fast as I can, Daddy." She giggled. "You could help me carry this stuff, you know."

"Oh, I guess I could," he answered, walking back to grab the sack of groceries from her skinny arms.

He hefted the sack in one arm, and placed his other around his daughter as they walked inside the house.

They walked straight back to the kitchen and set the sack on the counter. Aston climbed up onto a barstool at the counter while Gregory began putting the things away in the pantry.

"So, you've got a big science fair coming up this weekend," Gregory commented. "Is your project ready?"

"Yep," Aston murmured. "It's all ready to go. Will you be there, Daddy?"

"Of course, I will, sweetheart," he answered. "When have I ever missed one of your big events?"

She considered that, and then shook her head. "Never."

Ballet recitals, school plays, science fairs. He'd always shown up. Her mother was a little on the flighty side, but she always knew she could count on her father to remember where to be and get himself and her mother there on time, seated in the front row.

"And I don't plan to start now," he answered.

THUMP. The sound from upstairs sent both of their gazes up toward the ceiling. No one was supposed to be home; Lillian was out shopping with friends, and Reed was at a sleepover. Gregory and Aston were supposed to be out still, but they'd gotten done with their errands early.

Gregory's face went hard, his expression cold and determined.

"Go outside, Aston," he ordered. "Right now."

"But, Daddy—" she protested.

"No," he cut her off. "Outside. Don't argue!"

She did as she was told, looking back once before she scurried out the door.

Gregory walked to his office and over to the tall, locked cabinet in the corner. He bypassed his shotgun and retrieved the 9 mm Glock in the back. He grabbed the ammunition from its separate case and deftly loaded the weapon.

He left his office and crept slowly up the stairs, listening hard for more sounds of the intruder.

When he reached the door to the master suite, the voices coming from inside were too soft for him to make out. But then, faintly, he heard the muffled sound of his wife's giggle.

And he knew. He just knew that she was in there, with another man.

His world crashed down around him, one jagged piece at a time as he slowly opened the door to the bedroom he shared with his wife.

He didn't stop at the threshold, just continued walking until he was right beside the bed. His bed. Their bed.

"Gregory!" she gasped, sitting up quickly and pulling the sheet up over her bare body.

At least she had the courtesy to look ashamed. The man she was with, however, had a lazy grin spread over his cocky face.

Gregory raised the gun.

"Gregory!" Lillian screamed. "No!"

He stared at them both, the gun pointed directly at the man's head. A business associate. He'd laugh if it weren't so screwed up.

"Get out," he said flatly.

The man, no longer grinning, quickly got up from the bed and grabbed an armful of clothes from the floor. He ran out of the room.

Lillian and Gregory stared at each other for a long moment. He couldn't read the expression in her eyes, and likewise, she couldn't read his. In that moment, something between them had shattered, even though Gregory realized it had already been broken.

"I can't be here," he finally said. "Your daughter's outside. Go and get her, and try not to fuck anyone else while she's in the house."

He turned, and walked out of his bedroom. He stumbled numbly down the stairs and out the front door, where Aston was sitting on the porch steps.

"Daddy!" she screamed.

Tears were streaming down her face.

"Who was that man who ran out of here?"

The panic in her voice was evident, and as he looked down at her he realized her clever brain had already figured things out. But he couldn't stay to console her. He had to get himself together first, before he would ever be able to comfort his daughter.

"I have to go, honey," he said, kneeling down beside her. "I'll be back in a few days."

"Daddy," she sobbed. "I don't want you to go. And you promised you'd never miss the science fair."

He gazed into her shockingly blue eyes, the ones that had always managed to wrap him around her little finger, and his heart broke all over again. This time, he was going to have to say no to her. And it was going to kill a small piece of them both.

Six

"Did you know that I didn't grow up here in Nelson Island, Sam? Or Charleston, either. I'm actually from Tennessee. My parents owned a farm outside of Nashville."

"No, Mr. Hopewell. I didn't know that." Sam pulled his earlobe. He couldn't see far enough ahead in this story to tell yet whether it was going to end with Gregory turning him in.

Gregory Hopewell nodded. "It's true. I ended up here in a roundabout way in my early twenties. A lot like you."

Sam brushed a hand over his hair. He cocked his head, staring openmouthed at the older man, still puzzling over the fact that Gregory obviously knew he was hiding something vital. It was likely that he knew that Sam was on the run.

"I had a girlfriend back then. High school sweetheart. We did everything together. Now, I had an okay family life growing up. My parents were loving, but they had to work hard for everything we got. And what we got wasn't much. So I wanted out. I wanted to break out of that small town and find more for myself. I told my girl I was leaving and that I wanted her to come with me."

Sam shivered. Gregory Hopewell's story so closely mirrored his own. What kind of bomb was Gregory about to drop?

"She didn't want me to go, Sam. She begged and pleaded. I told her I wanted her with me, but she loved our town. She loved the slow, familiar life it provided. She said she was okay with inheriting my parents' farm one day and living out the rest of our days the exact same way they had.

"It wasn't me. I couldn't do it. So that last day, we argued. A kerosene lamp fell over in the barn on my parents' property. I knew it was only a matter of time until the whole place was engulfed in flames. So I got her out. But instead of staying to fight the fire, I ran. I was too scared to stay and face up to my mistake. I took off out of town that day and I never looked back. My parents' farm burned to the ground.

"They lost everything. But they never knew I was the one responsible. I came here, found a job, and worked my way through college. Then I started my company and built it up to what it is today. But the fact that I ran when I should have stayed will never, ever, be too far from my mind. It haunts me every single day of my life."

When his story ended, he studied Sam. Sam stared back, unblinking. His heart squeezed as sadness overtook him, and his eyes burned. His story wasn't like Mr. Hopewell's. He hadn't done the cowardly thing. It was just the opposite. But he'd still left his girl behind. And the possibility that he'd made a mistake haunted him.

"Sam, look at me."

He glanced back up at Gregory.

"I don't know what your story is, son. And maybe you aren't willing to share it with me. But I can see the same haunted look in your eyes I see when I look in the mirror every day."

Every muscle in Sam's body tensed. The gears in his brain were moving too slowly to keep up with his emotions. Suddenly, he felt close enough to Gregory to disclose everything. The father figure he'd missed growing up was sitting right in front of him with open arms. All he had to do was walk into them, and everything would be okay.

"I can't," he whispered, his voice thick and full of pain. "I can't tell you."

Mr. Hopewell sighed. "That's okay, son. I understand you still don't trust me yet."

"No, it's not that...you've been a saving grace for me, sir. You don't even know how much your taking me in means to me. I just...it's not my secret to tell. I promised her...I promised someone back home I'd keep her safe no matter what the cost. I did that, and now I can't tell anyone what happened or her security would be threatened. I just can't."

Gregory Hopewell's eyes softened. He looked at Sam across the desk, and felt the bond of a son forming that he'd never expected from a kid who just happened to be working on his ranch.

"Okay, Sam. When you're ready, just know that I'm here. You clearly need someone to talk to, and I hope I can be that for you. Or if it's not me, I sure as hell hope it's someone soon. Because the secret and the pressure of keeping it, is clearly killing you."

Sam's chest constricted and he let his head fall into his hands. Gregory came around the side of the desk and put his hand on Sam's shoulder. "It'll be okay, son. Whatever it is. It will be okay because you're a good man. Remember that."

Sam only nodded.

"Listen, now. We're going to take it slow. I have to have your ID and forms for HR, but I can't do that if you're hiding from the law. So there's some things you obviously need to work out. In the meantime, though, you'll need to look the part of an administrative intern in a corporate environment."

Sam bristled. "All I have are jeans and work shirts."

"That's why I'm going to give you this." Gregory walked back around his desk and opened a drawer, pulling out a credit card. It was black.

"Take it and go shopping. You need to get a few suits, but also just some slacks and shirts to wear around here. New shoes wouldn't hurt, either."

He laughed again at Sam's vacant expression. "I know that look. You need help, don't you? I'll send Aston with you. That girl knows style and fashion about as well as she knows business. And that's a hell of a lot."

Sam nodded blankly. "I don't even know what to say, Mr. Hopewell. This is…a lot. Thank you."

"First of all, you may call me Gregory when we're not at the office. You're welcome, Sam. Now go and find my daughter."

Aston stumbled away from the door where she'd been eavesdropping on the conversation between Sam and her father. She'd been about to storm upstairs when she'd heard her father usher Sam into the office.

With every word she'd heard, a tiny jolt of shock frayed her nerves. The story her father had told Sam...she'd never known any of it. Her lungs contracted, and she struggled to draw deep breaths. She retreated from the office door and turned the corner into the kitchen, where she ran smack into Ashley.

"Hey!" Ashley exclaimed. "I was just coming to look—Aston? What's the matter?"

Ashley's arms went around her. "What is it, A? What happened?"

Aston stared at Ashley without really seeing her. Her dad had never told her that story...but he'd told Sam. She was halfway between jealousy toward Sam, and sympathy for his pain. She'd heard what he had to say, too. What he'd said about having a secret he couldn't divulge, and the fact that he was protecting someone else. She knew it had to be the girlfriend he'd left back home. She wondered angrily if that girl was worthy of Sam's love. He'd given up so much for her. Was she doing the same for him?

Aston's legs wobbled dangerously and she quickly pulled out a chair to sit down. She'd never felt such a tumult of clashing emotions pulling her in all directions at once. She thought she'd been emotional when she'd found out about her mother's affair.

At that time in her life, she'd just down her emotions before they could bury her. Her father had needed her. She had refused to crumble to pieces because of her own heartbreak and disappointment in the woman who'd birthed her. The way she was feeling about Sam was different. She could try to turn it off, but she had a feeling she wouldn't be able to if she tried. The ocean of feelings crashing over her in regards to Sam Waters and his mysterious secret was devastatingly big.

"Aston?" Sam's voice wafted through the kitchen from his place just outside the door.

She looked up and saw him filling the entrance.

"Yeah?"

Ashley's curious stare flickered between the two of them. "Are you okay, A?" she asked again. "You look…"

"Are you sick?" Sam moved briskly into the kitchen to stand next to Aston's chair. "Can I get you something?"

He stared at her with concern, his head tilted to one side as he gripped the back of her chair.

"No, I'm fine," she told them both. "I just…I'm fine. Do you need something, Sam?"

She steeled herself and rose from her chair, looking up into his eyes.

"Well, actually…I was going to ask you to come shopping with me."

She must have missed that part. She'd been reeling about the revelations they'd made in the office; she hadn't even heard the end of their conversation.

"Shopping?" she asked faintly.

"Yeah," Sam answered, shifting his feet uncomfortably. "Your dad wants me to start interning for him, you know…and he thinks maybe I should, uh, restock my wardrobe a bit. Buy some more formal clothes for work. He gave me the expense card. Can you help me?"

The plaintive tone in his voice and those lost little boy eyes...she couldn't say no. Just thinking about helping him out of the clothes he was wearing...a bead of sweat trickled slowly down her back. She wasn't going to be doing that. She was only taking him shopping.

"Of course," she answered. "Let me go upstairs and change. Give me fifteen minutes."

She wasted no time practically flying from the room.

Closing her bedroom door behind her, she closed her eyes and leaned against it. She could do this. She could spend time with Sam Waters. It was shopping. Granted, it was shopping for an internship she didn't necessarily want him to have, but she loved shopping. And the more time she spent around Sam, the more she realized he didn't have designs on moving up in her father's company. Maybe he had just been in the right place at the right time and he deserved a shot at something good.

Maybe.

Actually, she'd been itching to get her hands on his wardrobe since she met him. Not that the clothes he wore weren't sexy, in a country boy kind of way. He had simple tastes. But holy hell...how delectable he could be if she could sink her stylish teeth into him?

Okay. Thinking like that wasn't helping. The heat that had been building in her center since he'd approached her in the kitchen was only getting hotter. He'd been so genuinely concerned about her, and the nurturing reaction from him made her want to curl up into his body and just let him hold her.

This line of thought wasn't helping her calm down at all. Not a bit.

She took a cool shower, dressed quickly in short white shorts and a low-cut red tank top, and topped the outfit off with wedge-heeled sandals. Sam wasn't blind. If he was elevating her blood pressure like this, then she sure as hell was going to set him aflame as well. Two could play at this game.

She descended the staircase to find him waiting for her by the front door. Ashley was standing next to him, smirking as she watched Aston walk down the stairs. One look at Ashley told Aston her friend knew exactly what she was doing with her outfit…and liked it. Aston narrowed her eyes, and Ashley laughed.

"Well, y'all have fun, okay? I can't wait to see your new look, Sam. You're in good hands with my girl Aston here. But I think you know that, now don't you?"

She opened the front door and left before Aston could throw her another dirty look.

"Well," Aston asked Sam. "You ready?"

"You recover fast," Sam commented.

She didn't miss his eyes roving up her legs as he took in her appearance. She smiled. The boy was taken, but he wasn't dead.

"Recover? From what?"

"You seemed kinda ill in the kitchen awhile ago. You feeling better?"

"Oh, that," she said cheerfully. "All better. You mentioned the word *shopping,* and I perked right up."

Sam's head fell back as he laughed. "I'm so glad I could help you out, Princess. Now, I have a feeling that going shopping with you on my Harley isn't a good idea. We're coming back with a bunch of stuff, aren't we?"

She recovered quickly from the thought of sitting on the back of his bike, and then chuckled at the worried tone in his voice. "Oh, tons and tons. We'll take my car."

He nodded and held the door open and ushered her through it. She couldn't remember the last time Princeton had held a door for her. As she brushed past him, she received a delicious whiff of his scent: outdoorsy, fresh, and all-man.

Driving down the state highway with Sam in her silver BMW M3 convertible, the top down, the wind blowing through their hair, Aston's heart lifted and all of the worries she had about her father and Sam floated away. Her gaze drifted over to him, and she saw that his soulful eyes were burning into hers.

"What?" she asked curiously.

"You weren't sick earlier, were you?"

Startled, she looked back at the road. "No."

"That was more like shock I saw on your face. Right?"

Aston saw him reach for her hand, which was resting on the gearshift. Her breath caught in her throat as she felt the heat from his skin when his hand neared hers, and then he pulled it away. He fisted it on his lap.

When she glanced over at him again, his jaw was clenching. The little muscle there was pulsing gently. His eyes focused on the road ahead of them.

"Sam, I heard what my father said to you in the office. I was shocked because I'd never heard that story before. He never told me."

She felt him staring at her. "But you two seem so close."

"That's what I thought."

Sam was silent for a moment. "Sometimes stories like that, the ones that make you feel uncertain about the person you are inside…sometimes it's easier to share them with a stranger than with the people you care about."

"Maybe," she agreed. "Or maybe you just bring something out in people, Sam. Something that makes them want to unveil themselves in front of you."

She almost couldn't hear his voice over the wind roaring in her ears. "That's funny. That's how I feel about you."

She glanced over at him again to see him staring at his fisted hands. "Does that make you feel guilty, Sam? Talking to another girl isn't cheating on your girlfriend. She's not here. If you need someone to talk to…well, you can talk to me."

His eyebrows lifted. "Really, Princess? I thought you didn't like me."

She bristled. "It's not that I don't like you. You're just somehow working your way into my father's heart and his company. I don't like it. But I feel sorry for you. My father was right. You're holding something in, and it's not healthy."

"Oh, you're concerned about my health now?" He laughed.

She pursed her lips and continued to drive.

Seven

Sam attempted to avert his eyes from Aston's exposed collarbone as she reached out to turn down the collar on the shirt he was trying on. The dressing room in the upscale department store she'd brought him to was roomy, with mirrors on every surface and comfortable lounge chairs scattered about the space. He'd never tried on clothes at a place this nice in his life.

And *dammit,* he was distracted. Aston was a distraction. She made him forget about the fact that he was only in N.I. because he was running from the cops. How would she feel about it if she knew? How would she feel about him?

She also made him forget about the ache he felt deep in his bones when he thought about Ever. Aston kept him, just for a little while, from thinking about how he was letting Ever down every time his face broke into a smile or every time he let himself think he might have a future here.

It wasn't fair. Because he knew she was miserable back in Duck Creek.

So when Aston leaned into him, he used every ounce of strength he had not to inhale. Inhaling would allow the scent of wildflower and vanilla musk, the perfect mixture of spicy and sweet, to envelop him. He couldn't allow that to happen.

He was a man. He and Ever had sex, of course they did. They were a couple, and that's what couples did. He'd known her for as long as he could remember. So they had sex. With Ever, it was comforting. Like coming home to a warm fire after a long day out in the cold. But the attraction he was fighting with everything in him for Aston…that was something new. Something that had nothing to do with duty and protection, and everything to do with chemistry and heat.

He turned away from Aston's nimble fingers and looked at himself in the mirror. His jaw dropped.

In the dark gray slacks and light blue pinstriped button-down shirt, he looked…professional. Like a man with goals and drive.

"Amazing," Aston said, breathing.

He read her expression behind him in the mirror. His mouth watered a bit when her blue eyes darkened with a mixture of emotions. She pretended to dislike him, but what he saw in those eyes of hers? That sure as hell wasn't hate.

"You think?" He put his arms out to the side and turned. "I honestly didn't think this store was going to have clothes that fit me."

"Well, it was a feat," she admitted. "You're a giant, Sam."

She reached up and grazed her fingers against the scruff on his chin.

"This doesn't…exactly go with your suit," she murmured.

He remained very still while she touched him. She'd never touched him before, and for him, a nonreaction was the safest bet. Her fingers were soft and delicate, a complete juxtaposition to the strength he knew they were capable of. He struggled to keep his eyes from closing with the pleasure of her touch.

"I should shave?" he asked softly.

"No," she admitted. "Because I kind of like it."

He chuckled quietly and stepped back. "Okay, Princess. Now that your work here is done, I'd like to thank you by buying you lunch."

She wrinkled her nose. "You can't afford me."

His laughter rumbled around them. "That's true. But I can feed you. Let me get changed out of this and we can get the hell out of here."

When he emerged, back in his comfortable jeans and T-shirt, she grinned at him.

"I hate to say it, Waters, but I like you this way, too."

He stopped short. "I'm sorry, Princess, but can you say that again? Because I could be wrong, but I'm sure that's twice in ten minutes."

"No."

His laughter followed them as they left the store and headed out into the sunny Charleston afternoon.

"This city's pretty cool," he admitted.

"I wouldn't want to live anywhere else. Charleston feels alive to me. Like the history here just envelops you and breathes life into everyone here."

He studied the architecture as they passed. The buildings impressed him in a way he didn't think they would in a larger, more notorious city. He appreciated the muted colors and the long, wraparound porches that adorned houses and businesses alike. He loved how the houses all had wide square posts holding up their illustrious balconies.

When they reached the meter where Aston had parked her car, he placed the mound of bags they had acquired in the trunk. He was surprised they all fit.

"So," he said. "Is this what life has always been like for you? You just grab Daddy's credit card and take off to get whatever you want? I'm going to pay him back for this, you know. There's no way I'm letting him pay for my clothes."

He wasn't trying to insult her; he genuinely wanted to know what it would be like to live that way. Always knowing you had the money to pay for the things you need. And also being so carefree that you didn't have to wonder where your next meal or pair of shoes was going to come from.

Her brows furrowed. "Financially, yeah. I know it's weird to you. But I've worked my ass off for everything else I've gotten. I was always at the top of my class in school. I know what hard work looks like, Sam. You don't always need to get paid for it with money, either."

He raised an eyebrow at her. "How else would you get paid?"

"Well…never mind."

He shook his head. "Nope. Not gonna happen. Tell me, Princess."

She kept her eyes aimed down at the sidewalk. "In Louisiana, I work with underprivileged kids. You know, the ones whose parents don't give a shit about them. There's this place they can come to after school, and I work there three nights a week helping them get homework done and just hanging out. So, that's hard work, too, but it pays me in a different way than a corporate job will one day."

He stared, marveled, and melted just a little inside. This girl, with her rock-hard exterior and ice-cold beauty, worked with *kids* who had so much less than her in her spare time. His heart pounded in his ears as he watched her. "Impressive."

"I didn't tell you to impress you."

"I know." He nodded. "All this money stuff is new to me, though. If you knew what life was like for me and Ever growing up, you'd be horrified. I *was* one of those kids you work with."

Aston looked at him sharply. "Ever?"

He sighed. "Ever's my girlfriend."

"Oh? We're going to talk about the girlfriend? Finally."

She opened her car door and climbed inside, and Sam did the same. She looked at him expectantly once he was buckled in.

He tugged on his earlobe and avoided her stare. "What do you want to know?"

"Let's start with how you met."

"I don't know the answer to that."

Aston kept her eyes on the road. "Huh?"

"What I mean is, I've known her pretty much my whole life. The town where I grew up isn't very big. It's probably even smaller than N.I. And a hell of a lot poorer. So everyone knows everyone, and Ever, Hunter, and I have just always been together. There was a field separating her house from our trailer."

"Who's Hunter?"

"My brother. He's eighteen months older than I am."

"I see," Aston replied. "And…if you and Ever are so close, why are you here and she's not?"

"Uh, next question."

This time she took her eyes off the road to glance at him. "Why?"

"I can't tell you that. Honestly, Aston, there's more I can't tell you than stuff I can. That's just the way it has to be."

"I see. Sam…I really hope she deserves your loyalty. And your love."

"What do you mean? Of course she deserves it." Sam leaned his head back on the headrest behind him. "I'm not so sure I deserve hers."

"Why would you say that?"

"Look around, Princess. The town I'm from isn't like this. She's miserable right now, trust me. And I'm here doing all of this…stuff I'm doing. I'm starting to think it's wrong, and I should go back and do what's right."

"I wish you'd stop feeling so guilty all the time. Whatever happened, whatever secret you and Ever are keeping, it doesn't mean you don't get to live your life. You're not on pause."

"I know I'm not. God, I know."

She watched him smooth his hands through his hair, watched the frustration and pain chase each other across his face.

He couldn't believe that Aston was wondering whether or not Ever deserved him. The thought was insane. Ever was his reason. Without her, he wouldn't have made it through the verbal assaults he'd internalized from his mother. She'd torn him down, made him feel like less than nothing. Then he'd be able to help Ever through another beating, and he'd know he wasn't worthless after all. Without Ever, he wouldn't be strong enough to protect anyone.

She deserved nothing less than loyalty from him. And nothing but his undying love.

So far, Sam had only worn his brand-new clothes to Gregory's home office.

"So, here's the program we use when we're setting up travel and reimbursement procedures for the researchers." Aston's mane of hair surrounded her face as she leaned over Sam's shoulder.

She pointed to the computer screen. "See? There's a group of them heading to South America in a few weeks. They're going to meet with a small business that has been harnessing geothermal energy off the coast of Peru."

Sam studied her actions, taking mental notes of what she showed him. Her scent was a bit distracting. He inhaled, and the spicy-sweet aroma of her hair kicked him in his gut. He held his breath as she leaned back.

"You see?" Her brusque tone reminded him that she had no idea what just went through his head, and he was snapped back to his senses.

"Got it."

She'd been training him every single day for two weeks. They worked together at the home office while she showed him what Gregory's assistant usually did at the corporate office in Charleston. Gregory popped in on occasion, when he was home.

He was pleased at how quickly Sam was learning the ropes.

Sam leaned back in the plush office chair, eyeing the computer screen, and then slid his gaze to Aston.

"So, you usually spend your summers working for your dad?"

She nodded. "Built-in internship. The only company I want to work for after college is this one, but it's nice to earn internship credits, anyway."

He nodded. "And you're a finance major?"

She nodded.

"Okay, so I've seen you working here for the past couple of weeks. I've seen you training horses. What else do you like to do?"

Aston's icy blue eyes settled on his. "I don't know. That's pretty much it, Sam. Isn't that enough? What'd you do to relax back home?"

His mouth tugged up in a crooked smile. "I like to fish."

She clicked her tongue against her teeth and wrinkled her nose. He watched as she used her index finger to stroke the pulse point on her neck, a habit that was quickly becoming his new fascination. "As in, disgusting worms on a hook and sitting and waiting for a tug on a line…for *hours*?"

Now his face broke into a full-fledged grin. "Yeah. That's my favorite kinda day. Ever, Hunter, and I did it a lot in the creek where we grew up. It calms me down, brings me back to earth when I'm feeling like I need to hit something. Now that I'm here, and I can't fish, I just run."

"Why would you feel like you need to hit something? Not that I don't understand the feeling." She sat down in the chair across from Sam, giving him her full attention.

In a sexy white pencil skirt and sleeveless turquoise blouse, complete with plunging neckline, he found it hard to keep his full attention on their conversation.

"Lots of reasons. Back there, anyway. Here, I haven't found any reasons to want to hit something yet. Just need to clear my head with a run sometimes."

"Oh, good. Wouldn't want any of our friends to be in your line of fire, would we?" Her quiet chuckle reminded Sam of the water rushing over smooth stones in the creek, and he smiled.

"Nope. We wouldn't."

Sam walked in the front door of the tack house after a long day of working with Aston. She'd continued to show him different company routines and procedures, and their easy conversation had flourished. When he'd first met her, the last thing he'd thought was that she'd be easy to talk to.

She kept surprising him, proving his first impressions incorrect. Every time he thought he needed to step in and pull her out of a tough situation, her own capability pushed him back. It was as if she were always wearing a shirt that said I GOT THIS.

The first thing he noticed was the cell phone sitting on the desk.

The bill comes to me. You can give me the money for it each month if you want, but I want you to use it. Everyone needs a cell phone.

Gregory

The second thing he noticed was the ringing landline right next to his brand-new cell phone.

His cautious voice spoke into the receiver. "Hello?"

"Bro. Good to hear your voice, man."

"Hunter. Hey. Good to hear yours, too. How's Ever?"

"She's good. Everything seems to be dying down, Sam. Sheriff hasn't been to see her in weeks. People around town have stopped asking about you. She's just…living life."

Sam didn't miss the catch in Hunter's voice. "So…what's wrong, then?"

Hunter sighed. "She's got a lot of emotions she needs to figure out."

The panic rose like hot lava in Sam's chest. "What do you think she needs, Hunter?"

"She, uh, we…she and I both want to see you. I think I can get her out of town unnoticed, now that some of the pressure is off. Can we come for a visit?"

Sam sank down onto the desk chair. "Damn, Hunt. I want that more than anything. I'm just terrified to say yes."

"Say yes, Sam. We really need to see you. Give us a couple of days. Then we'll come back to Duck Creek."

Sam couldn't hold back his desire to see his girl and his brother. Caution flew out the window as he melted into the chair. "Yes. Bring her. When can you come?"

"Dude, we can be there this weekend."

"Okay. Listen, Hunter. I know this hasn't been easy for you. Thanks for looking out for her. I owe you everything."

"You…you don't, man. You don't owe me anything."

"I love you, Hunt."

"Love you, man. See you in a few days."

After they hung up, Sam sat staring at the phone. After almost three months apart, he was going to be reunited with Ever. Even if it was just for a little while.

Did it only have to be a little while? Why couldn't it be for good? A prospective future in Nelson Island bloomed beautifully before him. He had a job; he was making money. He could get a place for the two of them. If Hunter wanted, he could find a job and move down, too.

They could do this. It had been enough time. The cops were still looking, but they hadn't figured out that Ever was still speaking to him. They thought he was long gone. And he was.

They could do it. They could start a life together.

The comfort that thought provided surrounded him, soothing him from the inside out. Made him feel like he had his old purpose back again.

Then his thoughts drifted to Aston, and he came crashing back down to earth.

He would have to be around Aston all the time. He worked for her father. At least until the end of summer, they'd be together. They'd gotten to a place where they could work together, completely ignoring the electricity that sizzled between them when their hands accidentally touched. They managed to avoid eye contact altogether, because meeting one another's eyes led to an unconscious movement toward one another.

But he couldn't ignore the conversations they shared. The little tidbits of knowledge he was gathering about the girl he called

Princess were worming their way into his heart. Inevitably, they were growing closer with every hour they spent together.

Maybe having Ever around would fix it. Whatever was wrong with him when Aston was around, Ever could change it.

The front door opened and Reed strolled in.

"What the hell, dude?" he asked indignantly.

"I'm sorry, Reed. You just walked into my place, and you're the one saying 'what the hell'?"

"Well, yeah. I haven't seen you in weeks, man. We're supposed to be friends, remember? And what the fuck are you wearing?"

Reed stared at him, aghast.

Sam looked down at his black slacks. He'd rolled up the sleeves on his plain white dress shirt, but he still looked more formal than Reed had ever seen him.

He spread his arms and grinned. "I had to grow up sometime, Reed. Don't worry, it'll happen to you, too."

"Shut your dirty fucking mouth. Get that shit off, Sam. We're going to Sunny's tonight."

Sam groaned and fell back onto the couch. "Come on, man, I've worked all day. I have visitors to get ready for. I don't have the time or energy to go out tonight."

"Sam, if you don't get off that *motherfucking couch* right now, I'm going to call Blaze," Reed warned. "And what fucking visitors?"

"Fine," Sam answered. "But I'm taking my bike. I need to be able to come home on my own when I'm done."

Reed nodded. "Agreed. What visitors?"

Sam grinned. "My girl's coming to visit."

"No fucking kidding?"

"Yeah. And my brother."

Reed's eyes narrowed. "This will be interesting. We'll take them out this weekend. I'm out. I'll see you at Sunny's in less than an hour, right?"

"Right."

"Don't make me send Blaze, Sam."

Sam placed his hands in the air, surrendering. "Never."

Thirty minutes later, Sam rode into the parking lot of Sunny's and killed his engine. He removed his helmet and got off the bike. His boots crunched in the gravel as he carried the helmet with him up to the door.

"Well, that was a whole 'nother kind of hot." Aston's remark blasted him from the shadows beside the door.

"Oh, man." He paused in his path to the door, searching for her in the darkness. "In about a month, I've gone from shit under your feet to hot. This is definitely progress."

She stepped out into the light washing down from the door, and Sam's breath got lost somewhere between his mouth and his lungs.

She wore a lacy black bustier-style shirt that screamed at him every naughty thing he'd ever thought. As hard as he tried, he couldn't keep his eyes from traveling down to the cleavage spilling out of the front. The lush skin at her neckline played peekaboo as the creaminess contrasted sharply with the tight, black fabric. Her cutoff jean shorts had him aching for home, and she was wearing a pair of black cowboy boots.

Cowboy boots.

It was the boots that almost pushed him over the edge and stopped his feet from continuing their forward progress. Years of containing his natural urges and attractions nearly came crumbling down around him. He couldn't handle Aston Hopewell in boots. She could walk around in her spiky stilettos and expensive sundresses. But cutoffs and boots? Now she was speaking a language that led straight to the place that he tried so hard to fight; his groin twitched just enough to remind him that he was still a living, breathing *man*.

"Aston." He spoke slowly, working against the inappropriate images that flooded his mind. He couldn't disguise the tight strain in his voice no matter how hard he tried.

She stepped up beside him, dropping her cigarette on the ground beside her and stamping it out. Surprise registered on her face as she peered up at him.

"You mad at me, Waters?"

Her scent, always so spicy and sweet, wafted over him as she stood there with hands glued on her hips. He braced himself with one hand against the wooden doorjamb. "No…no, I'm not mad. It's just…you're wearing, uh…"

Shit. Now he couldn't even form a full sentence without stuttering all over himself. Aston and her damn outfit were turning him into a drunken idiot, and he hadn't even set foot inside the bar yet.

She leaned against the other side of the doorway. A teasing smirk played over her lips, and he knew…he *knew* she could read his thoughts like she was reciting them from a book.

"I'm wearing what, Sam?"

He closed his eyes briefly. When he opened them again, she was still standing there, eyes burning into his. Hers were an ocean of azure, and they were smoldering. The heat in her gaze sent a shock of caffeine straight to his lower extremities, causing an immediate erection and he cursed himself for losing his shit over a girl who was so far from being his.

He struggled for control of himself. Fought the urge to reach out for her hips so he could drag her up against him. Reminded himself that he wasn't allowed to do any of it. Her boyfriend was probably waiting for her inside. His girlfriend was his whole reason for breathing.

"Boots."

She stared down in open shock. "You like my boots? I'm a Carolina girl, Sam. Of course I own a pair of boots."

Sam stared at her, standing under a halo of yellow light from the fixture above the door. Looking for all the world like the darkest, sexiest kind of angel and causing him to forget where he came from. With just a look, she was doing things to his body he'd never felt before, never allowed himself to think about.

"Aston," he said, his voice barely a whisper.

She trembled, finally recognizing the precarious situation they were tiptoeing around. "Yes, Sam?"

"I need you to step away from me. Now. Go inside, grab me a beer, and get your ass and those *boots* under a table. Okay?"

He stood motionless, one arm still pressing firmly against the doorjamb. He towered over her, his eyes never breaking their stare.

She hesitated. "Sam..."

"*Now*, Aston. Please. Go."

She took one last, longing look at him. Then she turned and fled into the bar.

Sam let out a shaky breath he hadn't even known he was holding. He put his other hand up against the doorjamb and dropped his head forward until it was touching rough wood. He took a deep, rattling breath and wondered what the hell was happening to him. He wasn't this horny guy who walked around chasing skirts all the time. That had never been him.

And, he realized, it still wasn't. He hadn't even looked at another girl since he'd been in South Carolina. He'd only seen Aston.

He sighed heavily, scrubbing his palms over his face. Then he opened the door to the crowded bar.

The noise of voices and laughs, drinks clinking and lively music enveloped him as he entered, making what happened in the parking lot seem surreal.

He approached the table in the back where he could hear Reed's raucous laughter and Blaze's jovial voice.

"Sam!" Tamara squealed his name just before she threw herself in his arms.

"Someone's happy to see you," Ashley drawled with an eye roll.

Sam found an empty seat waiting for him next to Reed, and saw an opened Michelob sitting on the table at his place. He smiled slightly and glanced at Aston. She was sitting in her chair next to Princeton, a small smile on her lips.

And he couldn't see her boots, thank God.

He sank into his seat and took a long swallow of beer.

"What's up, man?" Reed asked in a quiet tone. "You cool?"

Sam tore his eyes away from Aston and glanced at Reed. "Uh, yeah. I'm good. Just happens to be a good night for a beer after all."

Reed nodded, and then directed his attention at Finn. "Finn, you're taking a shot tonight."

"I've got Ash in my car," Finn argued.

"I'm not listening to that shit tonight, Finn. Ash can drive. She's not an invalid."

"Go ahead, baby." Ashley shot Reed a glare, then smiled sweetly at Finn. "Have some fun."

Reed bought a round of shots for the guys, and Sam took his gladly.

With the tequila running hot through his system and the beer cooling him down again, he finally began to feel more like himself and less like a horny, emotional wreck.

Aston admitted to herself that watching Sam almost lose his stellar control was exhilarating. She'd arrived moments before he had, and when she saw him pull up on his bike she hadn't been able to resist waiting for him. His reaction to her outfit was expected; his reaction to her boots was not.

Most of the guys were slurring their words. Except for Sam and Blaze. Sam had stopped after a single shot of tequila; Blaze never seemed out of control, no matter how much he drank. Now Aston, Ashley, and Tamara were rolling their eyes watching Reed, Tate, and Princeton act like idiots.

A pretty brunette was taking up residence in Reed's lap, and he whispered into her ear. He'd found her the last time he'd been up to the bar to get a round of drinks. He'd included hers in the round as well.

Aston watched in disgust as the girl laughed at something Reed said while he nuzzled her neck. Her tank top dipped low as he brought his arms around to cup one of her breasts. She tilted her head back and closed her eyes. Somehow, Aston kept herself from gagging.

"Sam!" Reed called, looking up from the brunette. "You need another shot."

"I'm driving tonight, Reed. No more drinks. I'm all done."

"But you gotta prepare, man. Your girl is coming this weekend." He glanced at Aston. "And I'm sure you need to let off some steam before that happens."

Princeton caught the glance and rose from the table on unsteady feet. "What the fuck are you looking at Aston for, Reed?"

Reed scoffed. "She's my sister. I'll look at her however I want, Prince."

Aston's head jerked toward Sam. "What's he talking about, Sam?"

Sam sighed. "Nothing."

Princeton looked from Aston to Sam and back again. He threw his hands in the air and headed for the bar.

"Stupid slut," he muttered over his shoulder as he went.

Sam was on his feet so fast Aston barely had time to take in the insult.

"What did you just call her?" His voice was low, and laced with deadly calm.

"The way you two are always looking at each other. I'm not an idiot, man." The alcohol in Princeton made him stupid enough to take a step back toward the table.

"I don't care what the fuck you think is going on. It's not. You don't deserve her, but since you got her, you're one lucky asshole. But don't ever let me hear you call her a name like that again."

"Or what, Waters?"

Aston stood. "Stop it, Prince. That was shitty. I haven't done anything to deserve it. You're cut off for the night."

Princeton turned and jerked Aston toward him. "Then let's go. I want to leave with you. Now." He began pulling her toward the door.

Blaze quickly stepped in front of Sam as he started to follow.

"You're going to let him treat her that way?" Sam leveled an angry glare at Blaze, his voice lifting to be heard over the din of the bar.

"Chill, Sam," Blaze warned. "Those two go at it like this all the time. You don't need to stand in their way. Aston's got this. She always does."

Sam pushed Blaze's arm off of him. "I won't watch it, man. I don't care how strong she is. No woman should have to put up with that shit."

He walked toward the door that Princeton and Aston had just exited.

"Aston!" His voice echoed in the still, warm air.

She turned, still grasped in Princeton's hands.

"Back off, Sam," she called.

Princeton wrapped his arm around Aston's neck, dragging her lithe body halfway toward the ground.

Sam reached them in two strides. "Oh, *now* you want to touch her? Get the fuck off her. Now."

He wrenched Princeton's arm free of Aston, shoved Princeton backward, and pushed her behind him.

"You're trashed. You need to go home. I'll go get Blaze. Aston's not driving you tonight."

Princeton looked furious. "Really, A? You're going to let this slow-talking motherfucker tell me what to do?"

She leaned around Sam. "Yeah, Prince. Tonight I am. I'm sick of dealing with you when you're like this. Go home. We'll talk tomorrow."

Blaze was already behind them, pulling out his keys. "Come on, Prince. We can pick this up again tomorrow. You're done tonight."

Prince tossed one last angry glare back at Aston and Sam, and climbed into Blaze's F-250. The gravel crunched under the large tires as they rolled out of the parking lot.

Aston whirled on Sam. "What the *hell*, Sam?"

He gazed at her, bewildered. "What did I do?"

She shoved him in the chest, not fazed when he barely moved. "What did you mean… '*now*' he wants to touch me?"

"He never touches you! And you want him to…I know you do. The men in your life treat you like you're wearing a fucking suit of armor. Princeton, your dad…even Reed. You're tough, but you're not unbreakable. He doesn't *touch* you."

She stared at him, the scope of emotions in her eyes going from shock, to anger, to sadness, until she finally shuttered them off. Her gaze hardened, as if she'd put on that coat of armor Sam had spoken of.

"You care enough to rescue me from a drunk asshole, but you can't tell me Ever is coming to visit this weekend? Were you just going to bring her to the house and introduce her?"

She began walking away toward her car. Sam caught up to her and matched her strides.

"Aston, stop. I only just found out. Why does it piss you off so bad? You were getting ready to leave the bar and go home with that drunk asshole. What happens between you two when you're alone with him like that? When I'm not there to step in?"

She glared at him. "I'm not a weak little girl, Sam. I've told you that before. I would never be with a guy that would hurt me. He's a little rough around the edges when he's drunk, but honestly, Sam, you're bringing that out in him worse than usual."

"Me?"

"Oh, please don't widen those little-boy eyes at me, Waters. You have fun with Ever this weekend. And when you figure out what the rest of this crew already knows, let me know."

She climbed into her little car and gunned the engine. She looked at Sam again as she moved the gearshift into reverse.

"I realize that Princeton isn't the right guy for me. I plan on correcting that. So you can stop worrying about me, and start worrying about your upcoming weekend with the girl you love."

She drove away, and he caught sight of one glistening tear before the wind ripped it away. His heart lurched, and he rubbed at his chest as he watched her speed off.

The weight of the night's events nearly sent him to his knees, but he stayed standing long enough to grab his helmet from inside the bar. When he had the familiar weight of the Harley between his legs, he let himself fly along the back roads, his thoughts flipping furiously between the girl he loved and the girl he couldn't stop thinking about.

Eight

Ten years previously in Duck Creek

Y*ou're eating* again?" *Sam's mother asked as she entered the dirty kitchen.*

"*It's dinnertime,*" *he answered through a mouthful of peanut butter and jelly.*

"*If you're gonna keep eating me out of house and home, you need to get a job,*" *she snapped.*

"*A job?*" *Sam was bewildered.* "*I'm eleven.*"

"*And you're a completely worthless piece of shit!*" *Her voice rose to a scream.* "*All of this stuff I have to pay for? Football equipment, food, clothes. How do you think I'm supposed to handle it all by myself?*"

Sam sighed. She was in a mood. It was rare she wasn't, but Hunter wasn't here to take the negative attention away or deflect her sharp blows. He took another bite of his sandwich and stood.

"*I'll start looking for one, Momma. But it's dark out now.*"

"I don't care." Her answer was weary, and sad. "I don't care where you go. Just get out."

So he obliged her. He always tried to do what she wanted; it was just never enough. The difference between the way she treated Hunter and Sam was almost criminal. Sam thought mommas weren't supposed to play favorites. She doted on Hunter, giving him all of the praise and attention a child deserved. With Sam, he was an extra piece of baggage in her life she wished she could drop.

Hunter tried his best to offset his mother's abuse and neglect, being the best big brother possible. He played with Sam. They were best friends. He watched his football games and helped him with his homework when he needed it.

But it wasn't enough.

Sam walked out of the trailer and trudged through the field separating the trailer park from Ever's small brick home.

He could hear the yelling before he reached the yard, and he began to run. He crept up the steps and peeked into the beveled window next to the front door.

He saw her father towering over her small frame, screaming at the top of his lungs about how worthless she was. It was a familiar spiel, but it would end up so much worse for Ever than it did for him.

He cringed as he saw the big man's hand come down, and Ever was knocked, sobbing, to the floor.

Sam's hands fisted beside him, but the door was locked. Even if he busted in, what could he do? He was an eleven-year-old boy fighting a giant. And Ever would get it so much worse if he interfered. It had happened once before when they were nine. Sam came up behind her father and hit him with a stick.

Sam had to take Ever to the Urgent Care that night, pulling her in the wagon attached to the back of his bike. The nurse on call was the sheriff's wife, a good family friend of Ever's father. She simply nodded at Ever's story of falling off her bike and sent them on home.

So he waited. He sat on the porch steps and covered his ears, waiting for the fighting to stop. When it did, he peeked in the window again to see Ever's father sprawled out on the couch, snoring.

He walked around the house to her bedroom window. He raised it quietly and climbed over the sill.

Ever was curled into a small ball on her bed, tears flowing down her face. A welt was beginning to form just above her cheekbone, and the sight of it fueled the fire that had been burning inside of Sam since he'd met her. This man was evil, and Ever had to live in a house with the Devil every single day.

He lay down behind her, wrapping his arms around her as best he could, and just held her while she cried.

When her tears were dried up, she sat up and nodded. He helped her up and walked her to the window, where he assisted her over the sill.

They walked together, his arms cradled carefully around her, back to Sam's trailer. Sam thought there should be a trail worn into the grass, as often as they walked this route together. He poked his head in the front door, looking for his mother. When he noted that she was nowhere to be found, he brought Ever inside and towed her to his room.

He closed the door and locked it. Then they curled up on the bed and held each other, like two broken birds, tightly for the rest of the night.

Nine

W e need to talk, Prince. Can you come over?"

Aston listened as Princeton agreed, and she hung up her phone. She sighed and closed her eyes, soaking up the morning sun as it burned into her skin.

"What made you finally see the light about Princeton?" Reed asked from the chair next to hers.

"I don't know, Reed." Aston imagined taking the sun's rays and absorbing them into every portion of her body, using them for strength. "It's just time to move on, you know? Prince and I have been together for five years, and we're still in the same place we were when we were fifteen. I want to be crazy in love. I want that for him, too."

Reed nodded. He sent a sideways glance over to his sister. "I never understood what you were doing with him, A. It's not that Princeton's this horrible guy. He's just not *your* guy. Everyone knew it but you two."

"Really? Why didn't anyone say anything?"

"Say something to Aston Hopewell, queen of the Stubborn Fairies? We wouldn't have *dared*. You've always had to see a situation in your own time for it to be real for you. This wasn't any different."

"You're sounding very wise there, little brother. Are you finally growing up?"

"Hell, no. I just graduated from high school. My wild days are just beginning."

Aston sighed. She sat up and retrieved the sunblock from her bag. "I hate seeing you act like a man-whore, Reed. You're better than all of these trashy girls you keep hooking up with. I wish you'd see that." She began slathering sunblock over her bare stomach.

Reed looked out over the pool. "What? You think I should be in a relationship? So I can end up like you and Princeton? Or...Mom and Dad?"

"Mom and Dad are still together."

Reed snorted, so she tried again.

"You could end up like Finn and Ash."

"That's one in a million. At least I thought it was."

"What? You don't think that anymore?" Aston stopped rubbing and glanced over at her brother.

"I think there might be a chance for lightning to strike twice in N.I.," he answered casually.

"What do you mean?"

Reed took a deep breath. "Aston...after it's all said and done with Princeton, are you going to admit you have feelings for Sam?"

She laughed and sat back in her chair. "Sam's taken. He's not for me."

"You don't know what the future holds, Aston. Sam's honestly the best guy I've ever met. And the spark I see between the two of you…well I've never seen anything like it."

"Shut up, Reed."

"Shutting the hell up."

"Why does Reed need to shut up?" Princeton asked, walking through the gate on the side of the house.

"Does she need a reason?" Reed rose from his chair and walked toward the kitchen door.

"Don't let me ruin your tanning, Reed." Princeton smoothed his hair back from his face and grinned.

"Now it's your turn to shut up," Reed tossed back as he opened the back door and went inside.

Princeton laughed and claimed Reed's vacated chair. He looked over at Aston and took her hand in his.

"What's up, gorgeous?" he asked her.

Aston looked at their hands and her stomach flipped over. She'd spent years with Princeton. She knew his family. They'd spent countless hours together, watching movies, playing games. Hanging out, drinking at Sunny's. Every major event in her life, from the time she was fifteen, had been weathered with Princeton.

Now it would only take a few minutes to bring everything they had to an expeditious end.

"I just thought we should talk after last night." For this moment, she kept her voice quiet, but resolute.

"I'm sorry, Aston. I kind of lost it, I know. I never want to hurt you. I never mean to. It's just…I only have this time before everything starts to get so serious. I start medical school in a year. I just try to loosen up every time we go out, and I always take it too far."

"Yeah," Aston said. "You do. And I know you're anxious about what the next steps look like. But it's time to grow up. For both of us."

"I know. I plan on it. But last night…I don't know, A. I saw how he was looking at you…"

"Who?"

"Waters. He looks at you like you're the only one in the room sometimes. And it drives me crazy. I can't hurt a guy for looking, but damn. You're with me. And he's got someone back home, right? I just want him gone."

"Prince…"

He squeezed her hand tighter. "What?"

"Let's not make this about Sam, okay? This is about us. We're…we're not working, Princeton."

He sighed. "Aston—"

"No, let me say this. We've been together a long time. And I've loved you since I was fifteen. I know you love me, too. But is this what being in love is supposed to be like? We don't have that insane, passionate heat between us that Finn and Ashley do. I want more for a relationship than just a best friend. Don't you?"

His expression morphed as he drew in her words like a breath. "You think I don't feel heat for you, Aston? Look at you. You're the most beautiful girl I've ever met. I'm hot for you every time

I see you. There's a time and a place. Someone should tell that to fucking Finn and Ashley. I don't need to have my hands constantly all over you to know that I want you."

Aston agreed with that sentiment. But...she *wanted* the man she loved to have that burning need to touch her. "No, you don't. But you have to feel it, Princeton. And I think if you're honest with yourself, you don't. And I have to be honest with you, too. I just want something different from what we have."

Princeton's face darkened. "And what you want...does it look like Sam Waters?"

"I told you this isn't about Sam. I promise you it's not. I don't know where I'll end up after we go our separate ways, Princeton. I'm ending this because it's time."

Prince stood and paced along the side of the pool. "I had a plan, Aston. These were the fun years. This was our time to live a little. Maybe you just need a little more space to do that. Then, medical school and you working at your father's company. Then we were going to get married and have a family. Don't ruin the plan, A."

He stopped pacing and ran both hands through his blond hair. The desperation in his voice hammered her ears and her heart, and her face crumpled. "Princeton. You can't set a plan for your whole life like that. Especially without letting the other person in the relationship in on the plan. We're not going to make it that far. We're just not."

She stood up and grabbed his hand, halting his pacing. "When you wake up tomorrow, you're going to realize that I'm right. And you're going to be glad you have the freedom to go out and find what you really want in a partner. It's not me, Princeton. It never was."

She reached up to rest her hand on his cheek.

"I'm glad I got to be with you, Princeton. You've taught me a lot about life and about love. You were there for me during the hardest time in my life, and I'll always love you for it. But now it's time for me to let you go. And you have to let me go."

He picked up her hand and tossed it down by her side. "What if I say I don't want to?"

She took a step back. "You don't have a choice. I've made my decision. It's over, Princeton."

Sam paced in front of Gregory Hopewell's desk as the older man reviewed the agenda for an upcoming board meeting, e-mailed to him from his executive assistant.

"Sam, why are you burning a hole in my floor?"

"Oh, uh, sorry, sir. I wanted to let you know that I'm having guests come into town tomorrow. I was going to let them stay with me in the tack house, but if that's not okay with you I'll pay for them to stay in a hotel."

"Oh, really? I don't mind if you have guests in the tack house. Do you mind if I ask who's coming?"

"Of course not, sir. My brother and my girlfriend."

Gregory studied Sam. "Are you excited?"

Sam had been counting the minutes. Excited was an understatement, but there was also an undercurrent of anxiety flowing through him whenever he thought of what his reunion with Ever would be like. The best-case scenario? She'd melt into his arms like they'd never been apart. He never allowed himself to consider the worst-case scenario.

"Yes. It's been too long since I've seen them."

"All right, then. Let me know if you need anything."

"Will you be introducing your friends to Reed and Aston this weekend?" Gregory's tone was casual.

"Probably. I think Reed's expecting us to all show up at Sunny's tomorrow night."

Gregory nodded thoughtfully, still scrolling through the document on his laptop screen.

"Why do you ask?"

"I've just noticed how close you and Reed…and Aston…have become."

"Yeah," Sam said slowly. "I never expected to feel like I belonged anywhere when I left home. So what I've found here…it's going to be hard to give it up."

"Why would you need to give it up, Sam?"

"Because I'm going to have to move on eventually, and everyone here is going to forget all about me."

"Sometimes plans change, Sam. And I'm pretty sure that no one here is going to forget about you anytime soon. Keep your mind, and your eyes, open. You might be surprised at what you see."

Gregory finally looked up from his computer.

"Have a great weekend, Sam. I hope it turns out to be everything you're expecting."

Ten

W elcome to the corporate offices!" Aston couldn't keep the excitement out of her voice on Friday.

This was her world, her livelihood, her future. And although she should have been reluctant, she simply couldn't wait to share it with Sam.

When she glanced at him, he was staring up at the building ahead of them with focused eyes. He stood silently, just taking it in. She grabbed his wrist and pulled him forward.

"This isn't what I expected," he admitted as they entered the double red doors at the front. The Hopewell Enterprises logo stretched across the front, a windmill fan with the letters H and E emblazoned beneath.

The building, rather than being made of steel and glass, was of the Charleston historic style. Two mansions connected by a shared vestibule housed the corporate offices. The interior was light walls and dark, rich wooden floors. Antique bronze finishes adorned light fixtures and doorways.

"Shit." Sam breathed. "This is kind of awesome."

Aston grinned; her face hurt she was smiling so madly. She was home, and she wanted Sam to feel at home here, too.

She led him to the elevators located past the lobby, waving to the lady sitting at a generous front desk as she did so.

Once inside the elevator, Sam leaned his head back against the wall and eyed her. "Where to, Princess?"

"Daddy's office. He told me to bring you up when we arrived."

The elevator doors opened upon a traditionally decorated hallway much like the lobby downstairs, and they ended up standing in front of a large wooden door. A small atrium opened up before the office door, and an empty desk sat in the middle.

"Daddy's executive assistant usually sits here," explained Aston. "She should be back in a few weeks, when her maternity leave is over."

She knocked lightly on the door before pushing it open and escorting Sam inside.

"Sam!" boomed Gregory. "Glad you're here. How do you like the offices?"

"They're amazing, sir."

"Glad to hear it." Gregory stood from his desk, resting his palms on the top. "I've been building this business for a long time, Sam. It's my home."

The phone sitting on top of Gregory's desk buzzed. He pointed to the door. "I want you two to pull up the latest projections sent to me by the geothermal researchers. I have to sign off on the final drilling project today for their trip."

He turned to his phone, Aston and Sam's cue to exit the office.

As soon as the doors closed behind them, and they were back in the atrium outside the bustling hall, Sam grabbed Aston's forearm.

"I get it," he said softly, chocolate brown eyes holding hers.

"Get what?"

"I get why you love this…working here, being a part of it. I think I just fell in love with this place."

Shuddering slightly at his words, she sent him a small smile. "I knew you would."

She settled down in the chair behind the executive assistant's desk, and Sam stood just behind her, leaning over slightly in order to read the computer screen.

His warm breath tickled her neck, and the hairs there stood at attention. She was suddenly hyperaware of his cool, masculine aroma and his hulking manliness in such proximity. She was sure he had no idea what he was doing to her.

And what was he doing to her? He was working, and he was learning, and he was succeeding. It was sexy as hell to watch the progression and forward motion that was Sam Waters. It was as if when given the right tools and opportunities, he was unstoppable. And she just wanted to be a part of it.

They worked side by side until Sam thought he needed to go home and prepare for Ever and Hunter. Aston reluctantly shut down their desk, silently wishing she could somehow extend the workday.

Sam paced in front of the main house. Hunter had called from the gas station just before the bridge to Nelson Island, and he'd given him careful instructions on how to get to the ranch. They would pull up at the main house any minute, and he planned to walk them to the tack house from there.

Anxious didn't begin to describe Sam's current state. A thin sheen of sweat had broken out over his palms, and his skin was cold despite the summer heat.

Headlights turned onto the drive from the state highway. The early evening air was alight with fireflies, and crickets chirped noisily in the brush all around him. But as the vehicle approached, the evening noise fell silent within his bubble of existence. The lights crawled forward, and he stopped pacing as Hunter coaxed Ever's old red Chevy pickup around the curve and slowly stopped close to the opposite end of the driveway.

"I'm guessing I can't park this old thing here." Hunter opened the driver's side door and climbed out, stretching his long legs.

"Leave the keys in the console," Sam instructed. "I'll have Reed move it for you."

"Reed?" Hunter's eyebrow's rose. "Is he the butler?"

Sam grinned and grabbed Hunter in a bear hug. They slapped each other's backs, and then he turned to the passenger-side door and flung it open.

Ever stepped out, her long red hair blowing in the mid-June breeze. She looked exactly like he remembered, only without the bruises. She was a little plumper, healthier-looking, too.

"Ever." Her name was barely a breath on his lips, and he grabbed her around the waist to lift her off her feet.

As soon as he touched Ever, he rocketed back to life with her in Duck Creek. How they were always desperate; desperate for love, desperate for safety, desperate for *more*. Hugging her made it all achingly real again, and he immediately released her at the jolt of pain that staked through his chest.

"Sam." She looked up into his face and gently squeezed his solid biceps.

He held her at arm's length.

"You look good," said Sam tentatively.

"You, too," she answered, glancing around her.

Sam bent down to kiss her but missed her face as she slowly whirled, taking in her surroundings.

"This is where you've been living?" Incredulity filled her voice.

"I told you it was big." Sam offered a wry smile. "But I don't live in there. I can take you guys down to the tack house where I've been staying."

"Oh, that sounds more like it." Hunter reached into the bed of the truck to grab two duffels. "They put the help in the outhouse."

Sam laughed. "Wait until you see it. It's far from an outhouse."

Ever and Hunter exchanged a look that he couldn't decipher. That was new. Usually he and Ever were sharing looks Hunter didn't understand. Now that he'd been away, he was out of the loop and his stomach rolled uncomfortably in response. What was he missing here?

He led them through the wooded grounds until he reached the front door of the tack house. He opened it wide and grabbed Ever's bag to carry inside with him.

Shutting the door behind them after they entered, Sam gestured around him grandly.

"My accommodations," he intoned in a grand, formal voice.

"Wow." Ever stared around her with wide eyes. "Sam, this is…this isn't what I expected. I mean, from your letters and what Hunter told me, I knew you were living well here. But this crazy-ass estate and this cozy little house…I just don't know. It's wild."

"But you like it, right?" Sam pinned her with imploring eyes. "You can stay, Ever. You can stay with me if you want to. I have a job here and everything."

"Sam…" she began and then stopped.

She glanced over at Hunter, as if at a loss for the right words. She perched on the end of the couch.

The feeling that he was missing a large piece of a puzzle crept along Sam's spine. His gaze swept to his brother as he raised his brows. Hunter met his eyes, and Sam fought to comprehend the warring emotions battling in his eyes.

"What are we doing tonight?" Hunter cleared his throat, and Sam embraced the shift in subject.

"We're going to just order some dinner and relax. You guys have had a long drive and I know you're probably tired. Then tomorrow I thought we'd go on over to the beach and hang out during the day, just the three of us. Tomorrow night we're going to a bar with some people I've met here. They're the real deal. You're going to love them."

Ever stood, and Sam took a second to reabsorb every detail of her into his brain. "Okay, then. I'm, um, going to take a shower. Can you show me where it is, Sam?"

He nodded, grasping her hand and leading her into his bedroom. Something was off, something he couldn't fathom. She wasn't reacting the way he'd expected her to after their long separation.

"This is your room," she said, biting her bottom lip.

"Yeah." He pulled her around to look at him. As he stared into her jade green eyes, he was reminded of another pair of eyes he'd stared into recently. In those blue pools he was frozen solid, barely able to take in air. He shook his head, drawing a deep breath.

"Ever," he began. "Something's wrong here. I've been thinking about you all the time. I think N.I. would be a good place for us to start over together. I like it here."

He tamped down the fact that although he missed her, she was bringing up emotions he had been able to bury deep inside him while he'd been living in Nelson Island. Seeing her was doing things to his soul. Things he hadn't realized he had enclosed tightly in a glass jar. Ever was opening the lid and letting it all out again.

"I can see that," she answered. "But now that my daddy's gone, Sam, I like Duck Creek."

He stared at her, horrified. "You *like* Duck Creek? Ever, no. We hate Duck Creek."

She shrugged. "It's my home. My daddy dragged me through hell and back again, but he's gone now. Everything has changed. It's like I've woken up after a long nightmare, and the sun has broken through the clouds for the first time."

All of that had happened while Sam was gone. He didn't miss the fact that she was healing, and it was without him.

And, he realized, he was healing as well.

"But you know I can't ever go back to Duck Creek."

She sighed. "I know."

He stared at her, utter confusion controlling his features.

"Let me take a shower," she said. "We'll have some dinner and have a good time tomorrow. We don't need to worry over details right now."

She entered the bathroom and closed the door gently behind her.

"Hell," he muttered. "It's going to be a long night."

He went back out to the living room and sat on the couch beside Hunter, sprawling back against the cushions with his legs splayed. Hunter, a slightly smaller version of Sam with dark blond hair and hazel eyes, reached over and patted his back roughly.

"I missed you, dude. Ever did, too."

"Then why does everything feel so wrong between us? Shit. Ever is all I've known my whole damn life. If she and I can't figure things out now, I don't know what I'll do. I don't know how to live without her."

"Yes, you do," Hunter said softly. "You're doing it."

They had a quiet dinner of pizza and sweet tea, and Sam began pulling out blankets for the couch.

"Hunt, I'll make up the couch for you to sleep. This place isn't big enough for a guestroom."

Hunter nodded, his expression cloudy. "What about Ever?"

Sam glanced at Ever. "We've slept together a lot of nights. I'm sure we'll make it."

Ever nodded. She pushed off the couch and slipped into Sam's room. Sam could see her through the door held ajar, rifling through her suitcase.

"Hey," Hunter said, reaching out and grabbing hold of Sam's arm. "Take it slow with her, man."

Sam stared at him with unblinking eyes. "I'd never do anything different, Hunter."

He followed Ever into his bedroom and closed the door behind him.

When he turned to face the room, Ever was in the bathroom bent over the sink, brushing her teeth. Sam leaned against the doorjamb, watching her complete the normal, mundane task with a growing sense that everything was not normal and mundane.

"Feeling the effects of the long trip?" he asked her when she was done.

She nodded, squeezing past him to the bedroom and climbing up onto the big, four-poster bed. Her sleep shorts and tank top were different from what she used to sleep in, Sam noticed.

She used to sleep in his football jersey, or a T-shirt that belonged to him.

He reached up and absently tugged on his earlobe, and Ever's face broke out into the first true smile she'd demonstrated since arriving.

"Still got your nervous tic, I see," she said with a grin.

He smiled wryly. "I don't know what you're talking about. I'm never nervous."

She scooted over on the bed and patted the place next to her.

He stripped off his shirt and climbed into bed with his sweatpants still on. He stared at the ceiling, hands folded over his chest.

"Ever," he said softly. The pleading in his voice couldn't be hidden. "Are we going to be okay?"

"One way or another, yeah." Her voice was equally soft, but firm. "We'll both be okay, Sam."

When he glanced in her direction, she was staring straight up at the ceiling, her body tense. He could sense the distance between them, even though she lay right beside him. He reached out to caress her hand, rolling her palm over and clasping her fingers in his. Rolling over on his side, he brought it to his lips.

She squeezed his hand in return, and then sat up. "We've been together for as long as I can remember. It's always just been me, you, and Hunter…against the world."

He nodded, turning his head to face her. "That's never going to change."

"Isn't it, though? I feel like the minute you left, everything changed. Taking you out of Duck Creek was like flipping a switch. You seem happy here."

"I am happy…and you could be, too. You just need to give it a chance. Maybe you'll fall in love with it."

She sighed, a soft breath in the darkness. "I fell in love with *you*, Sam. Before I even knew what love was. We had to fight for every breath, and we made it through to the other side. Now…I don't know where we go from here."

The sadness in her voice was slicing a crack through his heart. Everything shouldn't be this difficult now. They should now have a clear path to happiness. Why didn't they?

"I'm going to the bathroom," she said.

He refrained from pointing out that she'd just been in the bathroom. His tongue should be bloody, due to the number of times he'd bitten it since his brother and his girlfriend had arrived.

"Okay." He yawned instead.

While she was gone, his eyes drifted closed as he tried to picture the countless nights they'd spent together sleeping on his bed after she'd crawled through his window. As he wondered how they'd gotten so far away from that easy comfort, he fell asleep. And didn't open his eyes again until the next morning, when all that was next to him in his bed was the dent where Ever had slept.

"Ouch!" Ever screamed, hopping from one foot to the other. "This sand is freaking hot as fire!"

Sam laughed, watching her hoppy little dance as they stepped onto the sand.

"It's supposed to be hot," he explained, attempting to smother his laughter. "It's the beach."

She glared at him. "I think I hate it!"

They trudged closer to the waves rolling in and set up a little camp with chairs and towels. Sam settled into a lounge chair and sighed.

"No one hates the beach."

Ever, continuing to dart irritated looks in his direction, sat on a beach towel and pulled her knees into her chest.

"So now what?" she asked.

"Now I think we're supposed to relax," Hunter offered.

Ever heaved a sigh and stared out at the water.

"You can't deny that's beautiful, right?" Sam asked, tugging her long red hair gently between his fingers.

"I guess." She never took her eyes off the waves. "I'm not going in that water though. There's probably sharks in there."

This time Hunter was the one who burst into laughter. "Sharks? Only in the movies, Ev."

They sat on the beach for an hour, just talking and watching the waves and the people. Then, Sam stood.

"Do you want to take a walk with me?" he asked Ever.

She eyed his outstretched hand. "Walk? On the sand?"

A smile tugged the corner of his lips, but he managed to keep an otherwise straight face. "Yeah."

"All right." She stood carefully and tested her feet on the sand.

"It's not as hot the closer we get to the water." Sam beckoned with his outstretched hand. "Come on."

He pulled her off of her towel and they began to move away from their spot on the sand and toward some of the small hotels farther down the beach.

"Don't you love it here?" Sam asked her quietly. He didn't understand how she could deny the beauty of the place, even if she was attached to their hometown.

"I can see that *you* love it here." Her answer was careful and pointed.

Sam heaved a sigh.

"Look, Sam," she began. "I just don't know where I'd fit in. You seem to have started this whole great new life here, and it's without me. It's kind of surreal. And I've started a great new life back in Duck Creek. I even have a new friend. Besides you and Hunt, I don't think I've ever had a friend. My eyes are open to things now they weren't before because of...you know."

"Yeah, I know." Sam sighed. He wrapped an arm around her and pulled her in close to his side. "We'll figure it out. I promise."

After a few hours on the beach, they headed home to shower and have dinner so they'd be ready for the night ahead of them at Sunny's. Sam couldn't wait to introduce them to his friends. It was Reed introducing him to the crew at Sunny's and the laid-back atmosphere he'd found inside the quirky little beachside bar that had put him on the path to comfort in this new place. He knew Hunter and Ever would really fall in love with the whole group.

How could they not?

Eleven

*S*am carried his lunch tray to a table brimming with his friends. His usual seat next to Ever was empty and waiting for him. He sat, and she smiled over at him as she tore open her carton of milk and took a sip.

Sam inspected her. He had walked her to school this morning in their usual routine, but he wanted to make sure her bruises were fading.

He silently questioned her with his eyes, and she shrugged in return.

"Hey," Chris said from across the table. "You guys coming to homecoming tonight or what?"

"I never go to dances, you know that," answered Sam.

"We know." Chris's girlfriend, Julie, rolled her eyes. "But what about Ever? Maybe she's sick of sitting them all out."

He glanced at Ever, whose face was blushing a furious crimson.

Sam chewed his bite of mac and cheese slowly. "I don't get it. Why do you think I would be holding Ever back from attending a dance?"

Ever suddenly pushed back from the table and ran from the cafeteria. Sam stared after her, a bite of food halfway to his mouth.

"What am I missing?" he asked.

Julie shot him a death glare from across the table.

"You're so clueless, Sam. You and Eve…you two are such a couple. No one takes care of her like you do. Why haven't you taken it to the next level?"

Disbelief and shock imploded Sam's world as he stared at Julie. A couple? He and Ever? That wasn't…oh, shit.

Did Ever want more than what he was giving her?

Without another word to the group, he pushed himself back from the table and left the cafeteria. He walked out of the school's big double doors and spotted Ever a few feet away, sitting alone on a bench.

He paused, just taking a breath as he watched her. Slowly, he walked over to her. "What's up, Ev?"

She didn't glance up at him as she sniffled. She rubbed her nose with a tissue, and stayed silent.

Her tears prickled his heart. She cried enough. He never wanted to be the cause of her tears. Never. He sat next to her on the bench and leaned into her until his shoulder bumped hers. Then he placed an arm around her and stared out into the parking lot.

"I messed up, didn't I?" he asked softly. "You want more, don't you?"

She turned to look at him. And he looked back at her, really looked at her, for the first time.

He noted how long and silky her thick auburn hair had gotten; he found that her cheeks weren't as chubby and freckly as they used to be. Her face had hollowed out into the slim, sculpted face of an angel.

She was thin, but not waiflike, with curves in all the right places. She had an ethereal quality about her, a beauty he hadn't quite noticed until this moment. He suddenly understood Hunter's comments about how Ever was changing, and how somebody ought to do something about it.

But it was the perfectly broken girl underneath all of that exterior beauty that he could no longer resist. Of course they should be a couple. Everyone else had realized that they already were.

He just needed to make it official. That's what should naturally happen next.

"Ever," he whispered, pulling her head down to rest on his shoulder "If we do this…if we take this friendship to the next level, there won't be any going back. That scares me, because apart from Hunter, you're all I have."

She nodded. "I know. I never would have said anything. You're all I have, too, Sam. Without you I don't know where I'd be. Dead, maybe. But I do want more. I…I love you."

He caught his breath sharply at that. His mind raced, trying to catch up with his quickly beating heart. He loved her, too. He had for a long time now, he just hadn't realized what it was.

He knew now. And maybe it wasn't the kind of love that's felt with a burning passion and an uncontrollable need to be with the other person. But it was love all the same: warm, comfortable, safe.

He lifted her chin with his finger and bent his face toward hers. The very first meeting of their lips was sweet, and warm, and friendly. She had always offered him a home where he'd never had one before. This was no different.

Twelve

Deep into the evening found Sam, Hunter, and Ever in Reed's Silverado, with Sam riding shotgun on the way to Sunny's.

"So, Hunter," Reed was asking. "Did you play football, too?"

"Naw," Hunter answered. "Sports are Sam's thing. I was more of a watch-from-the-stands kind of a guy."

"Me, too," Reed answered. "With football, anyway. But I lettered on the swim team."

"I'm sure you did," Hunter answered wryly.

Sam glanced back sharply at him. Hunter just grinned, and shrugged.

When they arrived, Ever glanced out at the lapping waters of the ocean and stopped.

"This rickety old place is sitting *right on the water*!"

"Yeah." Sam chuckled. "It threw me for a loop the first time, too."

"I'm not going in there," she announced.

Reed stared at her, incredulity filling his handsome features. "But in there is where the bar is."

"So?" she shot back. "That place is about to fall into the water!"

Reed shook his head and breezed past. "I'm going to leave you out here to deal with this, Sam. I have a shot of Cuervo and twins waiting on me inside."

Ever folded her arms and squared off against Sam. A new stubborn set to her jaw was forming that Sam didn't recognize. "I'm not going in, Sam."

Sam groaned, the vein in his neck throbbing visibly as he looked at Ever. "Ever, our ride just went inside. We have to go in."

"I'll stay out here all damn night—"

"Ever," Hunter interrupted. Sam's and Ever's heads both snapped around to stare at him. "Let's go in and get a drink. I'll order you a nice bottle of Bud. Then once we're inside, if you feel unsafe, I swear I'll wait outside with you the rest of the night."

"You don't have to wait with her," Sam said.

His annoyance with his brother and Ever was growing, and he still couldn't understand what was causing it. Why did it seem like they were the two who had bonded for years while he watched from the sidelines? "I'm here."

Ever conceded. "Fine. One drink." She took off toward the door to Sunny's, her boots crunching in the gravel as she stomped.

They entered and Sam led them toward the table on the deck where his friends waited. Ever groaned when she noticed the location of the table, but Hunter squeezed her shoulder and she didn't complain aloud.

"Guys," Sam announced. "This is my girl, Ever. And my brother, Hunter."

Greetings went up around the table, and Sam grinned as he saw Tamara's watchful eyes scoping out Ever.

When everyone was settled, Ever on one side of Sam and Hunter on the other side of Ever, Sam went up to the bar to get their drinks. He held up one finger to the now-familiar bartender to indicate his Michelob and asked for two Bud Lights for Hunter and Ever.

"She's gorgeous," said Aston from beside him as she leaned her back against the bar and crossed her arms.

Sam glanced over at her and ran a hand over his short dark hair. "Yeah, she is."

"You doing okay? You seem tense."

He watched her study him, and the familiar pang hammered in his chest. Then he looked closer. There was something different about her. Her face was less stressed somehow, and she had a genuine smile on her face as she spoke to him. He glanced back at the table, and his eyebrows rose with the curiosity now burning a trail through his mind.

"I'm doing okay," he replied. "Things are just kind of weird right now. Just the long-distance thing, I guess. We'll be okay. I just need to spend some time alone with her. It'll be fine."

"Yeah, you said that twice," Aston pointed out.

"Did I? Well, that's because it will."

"I'm sure it will," she agreed.

She stuck her hand out toward the bartender and pointed at the glass bottles behind her on the wall.

"Give me a gin and tonic with a lime, Kelly," she said.

Sam looked at her in surprise. "You're drinking tonight?"

"Seems like a night that I might need one."

"Where's the boyfriend, Princess?"

"We broke up. It was tough…but we were never going to make it, Sam. I knew it, and if Prince thinks really hard about it, so did he."

The words he wanted to say lost their way somewhere between his heart and his mouth.

Kelly brought Aston's gin and tonic over along with Sam's three longnecks. He paid for all the drinks, including Aston's highball.

"Thank you," she said. "You didn't have to do that."

"Us country boys are gentlemen," he pointed out. Then he smiled. "I had fun working with you yesterday. Glad you didn't stay mad about the other night."

She waved a dismissive hand. "Water under the bridge. Plus, you were right."

She walked back to the deck, and Sam followed, with a worry-line creasing his forehead. When he arrived back at the table, Tate was regaling Hunter and Ever with tales of the group's adventures in Sunny's over the years.

"So don't worry about this place falling in," he finished as Ever furrowed her brow doubtfully. "If it's still standing after a rumble between Blaze and that Vin Diesel look-alike last summer, it'll be standing forever."

Sam and Hunter clinked the tops of their beers together before they took a sip.

"So what took you guys so long to visit?" Ashley asked, leaning forward to rest her elbows on the table.

"We had a lot going on back home," answered Hunter. His tone was careful and succinct, and he kept his gaze coolly focused on Ashley.

Ever looked down at her beer, not meeting anyone's eyes.

"Yeah, but Sam's here," Aston pointed out. "You must have missed him. Now that we have him, we don't know what we'd do without him."

Sam stared over at her. Since when was Aston part of his fan club? Most of the time he couldn't decide if she wanted him, or if she hated him. Tonight, she *was* different. He tried not to think about it.

Not to like it.

"We did miss him," Ever said, looking up and meeting Aston's eyes. "More than he knows."

Sam put his arm around her and pulled her closer. She looked up at him and smiled tentatively.

Reed was already settled comfortably in his chair with the twins, Kelsee and Kaylee, sitting on each of his legs. Tonight he'd dialed down his usual look, opting for a plain black T-shirt and worn jeans. A single black leather cuff adorned his wrist, and the sun had turned his skin golden brown. He looked older, and somehow like he was settling into himself. He spoke up.

"We think Sam's great. My dad saw the potential in him right away. Moved him from tearin' it up out there with the horses to working in the office. Dad thinks Sam is going to make it big in the company one day. Thank God, because I sure as hell don't want to!"

Hunter studied Sam. "So you think you can make it work, Sam? Staying here and moving up the corporate ladder? What about school? What about Ever?"

"Why can't Ever come with you?" Aston asked, watching Hunter closely.

"Because they'll notice if I'm suddenly gone, too," Ever snapped.

Aston's eyes widened. "Who will notice?"

Sam cut in. "We haven't worked it all out yet, guys. We'll just see what happens at the end of summer. I enjoy working at the company. I...like it here. But I never meant to make this permanent."

He met Aston's glare head-on, his eyes searching hers for understanding, hers narrow and unwavering.

Finally, he blew out an exasperated sigh. "We'll see what happens, okay?"

The tone of his voice told her to drop it.

"I need some air," Ever said suddenly, moving to stand. Sam opened his mouth and she threw up a hand, walking toward the front of the bar.

Sam stood up to go after her. Hunter stopped him.

"Let me, bro," he instructed gently. "You two have been apart for awhile. She's having a rough time seeing how well adjusted you are here on top of...just let me go talk to her. She'll be okay."

Sam stared at him with more confusion. "*You* want to go talk to her?"

"Yeah." Hunter nodded. "I've been with her over the last few months, Sam. I know how she's been feeling. I'll bring her back in here in a minute, okay? You stay here."

He got up and followed Ever, and Sam stood there, watching his brother's exit.

"Sam," Finn said in a low voice. Sam turned to meet his gaze. "We're your friends. What the hell is going on? Did you guys get into some kind of trouble back in your old town?"

Finn's voice was full of concern, and when Sam looked over at his friends he saw it etched on everyone's faces at the table. Even Reed moved Kaylee and Kelsee off his legs, ignoring their squeals of protest, and leaned forward.

"Go get another drink," he told them, thrusting some bills into their hands.

As the twins left, Aston spoke up. "Sam. You can tell us anything."

Sam leaned back in his chair and pulled at his earlobe. He closed his eyes briefly, and when he opened them again Aston's were burning into his, looking straight through him the way she always did. It was too much for Sam, and now he was the one who wanted to bolt outside for fresh air.

"Guys…I promise I'll fill you in. Just not tonight, okay? I'm going after them."

He got up and moved quickly through the crowd now gathering on the deck as the live band set up in the corner. He brushed past the bodies squished together inside the bar and opened the door. He stepped out into the night and breathed deeply. The still air and the sound of lapping water against wood was a relief.

He looked around the parking lot for Hunter and Ever. When he didn't see them, he walked around the side of the building to head farther down the pier. He understood Ever's feelings. It was overwhelming, being together again and meeting new people and thinking about possibly making this her new home. She'd been given a lot to absorb. He wanted to give her the time she needed to take it all in, but he wanted to spend that time with her. Getting comfortable with each other again was what they desperately needed.

In the back of his mind, a voice told him that as long as he and Ever had been together, they shouldn't need any time at all to get used to each other again. They'd been the main portion of each other's lives for years; not merely as lovers but also as friends and saviors.

He pushed that voice down deep.

He saw Hunter's and Ever's shadowy forms down near the end of the dock. As he drew closer, his footsteps quiet as the wood of the pier met the rubber soles of his boots, he stopped short.

Hunter had come outside to talk to Ever. Sam could have accepted that, even though he should have been the one consoling her. But the image of their arms wrapped around each other, their *lips locked together* in a passionate kiss would haunt Sam for the rest of his life.

Thirteen

Sam stumbled backward, one of his boots catching against a loose piece of wood on the pier. He caught himself on the railing and then he was up and running. His heart was pounding wildly in his chest, and he could hear a keening in his ears that wouldn't go away.

"Sam!" Ever screamed behind him, but he didn't even pause.

He was going to confront them. He just had to be able to breathe first, and that wasn't going to happen on this dark night, on this silent pier.

He burst through the door of Sunny's and stopped next to the bar. He braced himself with one hand flat on the wood, eyes aimed down at the floor as he grabbed deep lungfuls of air. His stomach churned, making him want to bend over farther and hurl its contents onto the bar floor.

He looked up, seeing nothing but the picture of his brother and his girl lip-locked. He picked up someone's bottle sitting on the bar and threw it as hard as he could across the room, watching with a smatter of satisfaction as it shattered against the wall and splashed lager in all directions.

"Hey!" Kelly shouted. "Sam!"

Blaze was upon him then, grabbing his arms and pulling them behind him.

He didn't see Aston's features as she stood in front of him, didn't hear her voice as she spoke urgently into his face. She wrapped both hands behind his neck, begging him to listen, to stop and talk to her.

Hunter and Ever entered the bar. Sam turned to them and quickly averted his eyes. The muscles beneath Blaze's grip tensed, and he flexed his hands in agitation.

"No," he mumbled. "Get the fuck out."

Blaze tightened his grip on Sam's arms. "Easy, man."

Sam was a big guy, but Blaze was bigger. He held Sam tightly.

Aston turned to look at Ever and Hunter. "What the hell happened?" she asked.

"Sam!" Ever pleaded. Her voice was nearly hysterical. "Come outside and talk to us."

Sam looked up. He shook himself, and threw Blaze a warning glance. Blaze let go, but stayed right next to Sam.

"Us? You two are an 'us'? You really want me to talk to you two right now? Do you *really* want that, Ever?"

"Yes," Ever said, tears streaming down her face. "*Yes,* Sam. Come outside."

Hunter's eyes never left Sam's. "Ever. Give him a few minutes. We'll be outside, Sam. When you're ready."

They walked out, and Aston turned to Sam. Her long dark tresses brushed her bare shoulders as she studied him. "Sam. Talk to me. What happened?"

"I walked outside…" he whispered roughly. He cleared his throat, searching for his voice. When he spoke again, it was a little clearer.

"I walked outside and saw my brother and Ever making out."

He looked down at Aston's shocked face, and heard Blaze mutter, "Shit."

"I'll be right back." Sam headed for the door.

"Sam," Blaze said. "You think that's a good idea? You don't look good, man."

"How would you look, Blaze, if you walked in on the love of your life kissing your brother?" Sam's voice was deadly calm, but he wobbled slightly on his feet.

"What'd you just say?" Reed asked, walking up behind Blaze.

"You heard me," Sam answered. "I have to go outside and talk to them, now. I'll be back…I guess."

"You want me to come with you, bro? You shouldn't have to deal with this shit alone." Reed's concern was plastered all over his face.

"No," Sam answered shortly. "Alone is what I am now."

He felt that loneliness settling in, deep within his bones. The two most important people in his life had just betrayed him. Hell, up until three months ago, they were the only two people in his life that mattered.

He walked out the door.

Hunter and Ever were standing huddled by the door, Hunter's

arm curled around her protectively. He pushed her behind him slightly when Sam stepped outside next to them.

Sam laughed, but there was no humor in it. "Are you protecting her from *me*?"

Hunter stayed silent, but his arm tightened around Ever as she tensed.

"Do you know how fucking funny that is, Hunt?"

"Sam..." Hunter began.

"I've been protecting her my entire life, Hunter. But you know that, don't you? You are my mother*fucking* brother!" Sam put both of his hands on his head and shook it in disbelief.

"Are you two about to try to explain this? Because I really can't wait. I really can't fucking wait to hear what you have to say."

He folded his arms and stood a few steps away from them, staring at them as if he wished lasers could shoot from his eyes.

"Sam," Ever began. "I'm so sorry. I didn't want you to find out this way."

"Wait a minute," Sam said, holding up both hands. "*Find out* this way? This wasn't the first time you two..."

"Stop, Sam," Hunter warned.

"Have you two *slept* together?" Sam asked, the incredulity in his voice making it rise louder than he'd like.

"It just happened, Sam!" Ever exploded. "Hunter was with me this entire time, getting me through my father's funeral, then that horrible investigation, the missing you..." She trailed off.

"Yeah," Sam scoffed. "You missed me so much you just fell onto my brother's dick because of the despair? That's what you're going with? You're really not the girl I thought you were, are you, Ever?"

"Shut the fuck up, Sam," Hunter said. He stepped forward, blocking Ever from Sam's view. "You don't get to talk to her like that. You gave her the gun for protection. You were the one who told her to tell the cops you did it. And then you just *left*. You made all the decisions, and then you left her."

"I did that for her!" Sam shouted. "I took the blame to protect her. After everything he did to her for all those years, her father deserved what he got! And I might have given her the gun, but she *had* to use it! He would have killed her if she didn't!"

Ever's sobs rang in his ears. He shoved Hunter aside so he could look into her face, the freckles lightly dusting her nose now slick with tears.

"I did all of this for *you*, Ever. And now you're telling me you want my brother instead? Huh? Is that what you're telling me?"

She sobbed harder, shaking her head wildly. "We never meant for it to happen. We just…we're…" She lost the ability to speak.

"Sam, you were so busy protecting her all the time you forgot to love her. You know it deep down, if you stop being an ass long enough to think about it. You have this whole new life here. Don't kid yourself. Ever doesn't fit into it. She and I belong in Duck Creek. We'll get you off the hook with the cops. We'll tell them the truth; it was self-defense. She never needed you to step in and be her hero."

Sam took a step back. She never needed him? They were acting like everything he'd done, he'd done for nothing.

Ever was still sobbing, her body heaving as she leaned against Hunter. He took one last look at her, and then turned his back.

"Where are you going?" Hunter called.

"I'm going to call you two a cab. Get your shit out of my place and go home. I'm done."

"Done with what?" Hunter yelled. "I'm your brother, Sam."

Sam looked back at him. He shook his head.

"No, you're not."

Aston perched on a barstool, nervously twisting her hands as she watched the door. When Sam walked back through it, she breathed a sigh of relief, and then pain shot through her chest as she took in the expression on his face.

"Is your brother still standing?" Reed asked suspiciously.

"Yeah," Sam answered, his voice dull and void of emotion. "But he's not my brother anymore."

He gestured to Kelly, and she came over reluctantly. "I'm sorry, Kelly. I'll pay for any damage. Give me a shot. Of anything. And please call my brother and my...call them a cab."

Kelly nodded and brought him a tiny glass filled with amber liquid. He picked it up and slammed it back, and then indicated for her to bring him another one.

"Sam..." Aston began slowly.

He held up a hand. "I just can't right now, Princess. Give me a day to digest it. You can tell me how sorry you feel for me tomorrow."

Aston stared at him as he pounded his second shot, and then she nodded.

"I'm not leaving you, though. I'm going to just sit here next to you. I won't say a word."

He turned and held her gaze. Something in his eyes was duller, broken somehow.

"I don't want you to sit next to me while I drink myself into oblivion. Go home, Aston."

Reed grabbed her shoulder and turned her around.

"A," he said. "Give him tonight. He doesn't want you to see him this way." He walked with her toward the door.

"You good to drive?" he asked her.

She nodded numbly. "Take care of him, Reed. Don't leave him alone."

"I promise." He nodded.

She drove home without the music playing, something she never did. All she could think about was Sam's face when he'd been bent over the bar.

She'd known. Somehow, she'd known that Ever didn't deserve him. He'd been holding back from Aston, holding back the same feelings she harbored, because of his duty and his love for his girl-friend. And it was all for nothing. Because she'd been sleeping with his brother.

She'd laugh if it weren't so screwed up.

She wasn't sure where she and Sam could go from here. Sam didn't want her with him tonight. She didn't expect him to jump into her arms, but above all else they were friends. They'd finally gotten to a place where she could call him that. She wanted to help him through this pain.

When she arrived home she dressed for bed and was turning

back the covers when a knock sounded on her bedroom door.

"Yeah?" she called.

"Aston? Can I come in?" Her mother's tentative voice drifted through the door.

Aston sighed. Her mother was the last person she wanted to see right now.

She wiped the tearstains from her face and opened her bedroom door. She turned and walked back to her bed, sitting down.

The bedsprings squeaked when her mother sat down beside her.

"I heard you come in," Lillian said. "Is everything okay?"

She studied Aston's face, and Aston turned away.

"Everything's fine," Aston answered. "I'm just tired."

"Reed told me you broke things off with Princeton. Is that true?"

Aston sighed and leaned back onto her mound of pillows. "Yeah, Mom. Princeton and I are done."

Lillian studied her daughter carefully. They hadn't been close for years, and they'd never been as close as Aston and Gregory. But she could still read her daughter like a book.

"That's not what has you so upset tonight, though."

"No."

"Sometimes talking about things gives you perspective. You don't always have to be so tough all the time."

"Really, Mom? Because if I wasn't the one being tough all the time, who else would be? You?"

Her mother stiffened. "I can see that you don't want to talk right now. But I'm your mother, Aston. No matter what's happened, I'm still your mom. Try to remember that as you're hating me for the mistakes I've made. I've made my bed, I know that. But I'm trying. Your dad and Reed forgave me. You're the only one holding a grudge."

She left the room, closing the door softly behind her.

Aston stared at her bedroom door for a moment. Then she rolled over, pulled a pillow over her head, and sobbed. She wept for Sam and the pain she knew he was in; she cried for her mother and the relationship they'd never have again.

When she woke the next morning with puffy eyes and a tangled mess of wavy hair, she went in search of Reed. She found him in the kitchen.

"How is he?" she asked her brother, getting straight to the point.

Reed glanced at her, chewing his toast thoughtfully. "He's pissed. And hurt, too, but right now it's mostly the pissed that's coming out."

"You got him home last night, right?" she asked.

"Yeah, A, of course I did. He's probably still sleeping off the tequila."

She took off for the front door.

"Whoa, Aston! What the hell do you think you're doing?" Reed stepped in front of her, holding his hands out in front of him to block her passing.

"I'm going to talk to him. He needs a friend."

"And you really think you're the best person to be that friend?" Reed assessed his sister, taking in her appearance. "You look like a hot mess yourself."

"He needs me right now."

"Now isn't a good time to talk to him, A. Give him some space. Let him find you when he's ready. He will be ready eventually. Just give him some time."

She heaved a deep sigh. "You don't think he'll do anything stupid, do you?"

Reed was watching her closely. "Like what?"

"Like leave."

"No. I think we're all the guy's got. He's not going anywhere."

Fourteen

Sam wished like hell he'd let his boss give him Monday off.

He sat at Gregory's glossy mahogany desk in the office, limply typing the travel itinerary he'd been asked to complete while Gregory was off working in corporate headquarters this morning.

Sam felt like he'd been hit by a Mack truck, then run over twice by a train. He'd gotten drunker than he'd ever been on Saturday night, and then he'd spent Sunday sitting on the beach with Reed, Blaze, Tate, and Tamara. Aston was noticeably absent, and he knew it was because he'd asked her to leave him at the bar the previous night. He had mixed feelings about her empty spot, but he eventually decided it was for the best. He'd become closer to her than he'd ever expected to in his time on the island. He considered her a friend, and the way she made him feel physically was dangerous. After what had happened with Ever and Hunter, the intimacy he felt growing with Aston was something he couldn't allow to take over. Anything that emotional had the power to hurt, and giving that power away again just wasn't an option he could live with.

Sunday evening, Hunter had called the landline in the tack house several times. He knew it was Hunter because everyone here had his new cell phone number. He also knew that Ever was forcing Hunter to keep calling. Hunter would have known that Sam wasn't ready to talk to them.

Sam didn't know if he'd ever be ready to talk to them again. He'd never felt so turned upside down by emotions. His whole life, he'd had one purpose. Protect Ever. From her father, and then from the consequences of killing him.

When that purpose had been taken away, Sam wasn't sure what he was supposed to do now. So he was just living hour by hour.

He looked up when he heard the soft knock on the office doors and they creaked open.

"Tamara," he said in surprise. "Hey. What are you doing here?"

"I'm here to see you," she answered, her dry smile strangely comforting. "I wanted to check on you. You hit it pretty hard this weekend. Not that anyone can blame you. Feeling okay today?"

Sam leaned back in the large leather chair and ran a hand over the recent scruff on his chin. "Do you mean physically or mentally?"

"Both."

"I feel like shit," he admitted.

Tamara shook her head sympathetically. "Then why are you working?"

"It's a workday." Sam shrugged. "The days of the week don't stop because I got my heart broken." He squinted, rubbing his forehead. "Or because I still have a hangover."

Tamara knit her eyebrows together and frowned. Sam assumed she didn't understand anything about coming to work when you didn't exactly feel your best, because Tamara and Tate had never worked a day in their lives. They had gone straight from high school to college, and their parents never required them to work for spending money. They came from a wealthy family, just like everyone else Sam had met in Nelson Island.

"Well, what are you doing tonight?" Tamara asked. "Want to get together? You should probably keep busy, right? Get your mind off of…things?"

"Um, sure. We can hang out. Do you know where my place is?"

As Tamara nodded, Aston opened the French doors, and Sam was almost pushed backward in his chair by the sheer energy she carried with her whenever she entered a room.

As her eyes locked on his, he was finally able to see Aston Hopewell for the first time with a free heart. Now he knew exactly what he'd been missing, despite how much he wanted to ignore it. His heart clenched tightly in his chest, forcing the breath he was holding to come whooshing out of his lungs.

He closed his eyes briefly, steeling himself against the rush of emotion washing through his entire body. He couldn't let himself feel this way about…anyone. Not after what had happened. He'd given everything he had to Ever, and look what had happened. After Ever, he didn't have anything left to give.

He glanced at Aston again, and her bottom lip disappeared into her mouth as she studied his expression. He found himself wondering if that lip felt as plump as it looked, and his body reacted. Immediately. And strongly.

"Yeah, Tamara," he said in a clear voice. "We should definitely get together tonight. Come over to my place around eight."

Aston stood just inside the door, her eyes roving between Sam and Tamara.

"Hi, Aston." Tamara greeted her with a grin. "I'm guessing you and Sam have some work to do, so I'm gonna get out of y'all's hair. I'm looking forward to tonight, Sam. It'll be a good...distraction for you."

She gave him a flirty little wave to go with her sexy little smirk, and brushed past Aston on her way out.

Sam shuffled papers on the desk vigorously as Aston entered and closed the doors behind her.

"Sam," she said, quiet disbelief ringing through her voice. "Did I just hear you arrange a *date* with Tamara?"

He glanced up at her after he'd had a chance to slow his rapidly beating heartbeat.

"Nah," he answered flippantly. "We're just hanging out at my place."

"Just the two of you?" Aston's eyes flashed an angry ocean blue. "That's what constitutes a date, Sam."

"What can I do for you, Aston?" He made his voice bored, hoping she'd rush through whatever business he was sure she had to share with him. Her face, her voice, the way she rubbed her finger along her neck when she was thinking...these were all things he wanted desperately to avoid. He held his breath so her soft scent wouldn't overwhelm him.

Her eyes narrowed. "Sam. I know you're hurting. But we're friends, right?"

"Yeah," Sam answered. "We're friends. So why are you grilling me about who I'm spending time with?"

Aston's mouth dropped open. "I'm not grilling you, Sam. I'm just concerned. Do you really think you should be throwing yourself into dating someone like Tamara after what happened?"

His eyes hardened against her questioning. "What do you mean 'someone like Tamara'? I can do what I damn well please, Aston. Did you have a reason to be in here right now? Do you have some accounting stuff to go over?"

"Nothing that can't wait," she shot back over her shoulder as she whirled around.

He flinched as she slammed the door behind her so hard the panes shook.

Then he sank back into the soft cushion of the chair and let out a shaking breath.

He sucked it right back into his lungs when Aston came sweeping back into the room.

"Work's over for the day." She stalked over to the desk and leaned forward, placing her palms against the shiny top.

The spicy sweetness overpowered him before he could protect himself, and his body swelled in response. "What?"

"Get your ass to the tack house and change, Waters. We're getting out of here."

His heartbeat took off again, pulling him out of his seat. She held up a hand.

"No questions. Just meet me out by my car in twenty. Think you can handle that?"

He nodded. Her demeanor when she was bossy was…appealing. He couldn't say no to her.

"You going to tell me where we're headed?" Sam glanced at Aston.

He'd been with Ever since they were teenagers, and he'd loved her. He'd thought she was beautiful and fragile and innocent, but he'd never thought of her as sexy. Aston, with her confidence and her take-charge attitude, the way she handled the BMW on the highway as she drove him to an unknown destination?

Sexy.

He fought against the thought. He was aware of how much he didn't need the feelings forcing their way to the forefront of his mind.

"We're almost there." Her smile was reassuring, and he allowed himself to sit back in the seat and enjoy the ride.

They were on a part of the island he hadn't yet visited. The homes were spread farther out, and the upscale feel of the rest of the island became more rural, more remote as they pulled over.

Aston hopped out, smoothing her hands over her cutoff jean shorts.

He wondered if she knew how much he liked it when she wore those shorts.

"Okay, Princess. What's going on?"

"Check the trunk, Waters." She took off toward the water. They were parked next to the entrance to a private beach, and beyond the sea grass and thin stretch of sand lay a long pier. There were boats dotting the shoreline in the distance, but the area was deserted otherwise.

He eyed her receding figure before he went around to the trunk and pulled it open.

Fishing poles.

Two fishing poles and a tackle box were sitting in Aston's otherwise pristine trunk, looking so out of place and foreign that a laugh rumbled deep in his chest.

He glanced to where she'd retreated and found her standing on the pier, just staring out at the water.

His heart clenched. He reached for the spot, rubbing it beneath the tank he wore under his button-down. A warmth, starting in his chest, radiated outward until he was filled with it. The conversation they'd had while working together flashed into his mind.

"Hell," he muttered. "She brought me fishing."

The tackle box was stocked with bait and lures, and he busied himself readying both the rods while she dangled her bare feet in the water, staring out at the rippling sea.

When they were settled, his pant legs rolled up and a fishing pole in his hands, a tiny piece of his soul was restored.

Silence blanketed them as they sat side by side, dangling their feet and their lines into the ocean.

Finally, he bumped her shoulder with his own. Looking down at her, her long hair flowing loose in the breeze, the warmth he'd experienced earlier burst into flame inside of him. "Thank you."

She used her small bare foot to nudge his much bigger one. Tingles permeated the area at her slight touch. "Welcome."

"How'd you pull this off?"

She smiled. "Borrowed the gear from Leon."

He didn't need any more words, and he was thankful for that. Because there weren't any that would express how she'd made him feel. Nothing about Aston Hopewell was predictable, and he was finding out more and more every day that her feisty spontaneity was exactly what he craved.

When he arrived back at the tack house that evening, he sank onto the couch. He flipped on the TV and stared at the screen without watching it. She'd taken him fishing. He'd mentioned it once, in passing, and she'd committed it to memory. Awe filled him when he considered how much it had affected him. He contemplated picking up the phone to thank her again until he heard a knock at the front door.

Shit, he thought, remembering Tamara. He liked her; he appreciated her sweetness and her desire to help him through a difficult time. He also knew that she wanted more from him than he'd ever be able to give.

He got up and opened the door.

"Hey, there." Tamara breezed past him, carrying a brown paper grocery bag.

"Hey, yourself," he answered. "What's in the bag?" He warily watched her unload the bag on the island in his kitchen.

"Some snacks to go with our movie. And some beer, of course.

I got you your Michelob, because I wasn't sure you were keeping your fridge stocked. A single guy like you, living all by your lonesome over here."

Sam let out a rumble of laughter. "Well, you come prepared, don't you?" He sat on a barstool and watched her fill a bowl with Chex Mix. "Actually, I don't do the stocking at all. The Hopewell's housekeeper comes once a week, and I'm not picky. She doesn't know I like Michelob, though. So thank you."

The unexpected warmth he felt in his chest at having a female presence in his house wasn't lost on him. He liked the feeling. He just found himself wishing it were a different presence.

"What movie?" he asked, expecting her to name a RomCom.

"Man of Steel," she announced.

Sam's eyes widened. "The Superman movie? You brought an action flick to my house? Girl, you should come with a warning! You're dangerous."

She smirked. "Why? Because there's a superhero nerd under all this hotness?"

This time he threw back his head and roared with laughter. Maybe tonight was going to help him forget, after all.

Aston watched the path leading from the tack house to the main house driveway sporadically all night. Her afternoon with Sam had been like taking a deep breath of fresh air after being underwater for a long time. She'd never been fishing. She'd never had the desire to do something so simple and mundane. She liked fast cars, the rush of a bucking horse. She loved corporate dealings, and luxury shopping trips in a big city.

But spending a day sitting on a pier beside a man who made her *feel* something in her stomach and her chest and her core she'd never felt before…it was a whole different kind of rush.

She knew when Tamara had arrived, because her little red Porsche Cayenne was parked in the curve of the driveway. She kept checking to see if she'd left yet.

But every time she looked, her heart sank when she saw that the car was still parked in the same spot, taunting her. She secretly hoped that Sam couldn't forget his afternoon with her while he sat in his house alone with Tamara.

"You're making yourself crazy, you know," Reed said.

They were sitting on the couch in the great room, watching a movie. She didn't even know what movie it was. She kept getting up to go check the window.

"What are you talking about?" she asked.

"I haven't talked to Sam today, but I'm guessing he let Tamara come keep him company tonight, since her car is parked in the driveway. Am I right?"

Her brother's lazy drawl irritated her. "So?"

"So, if you're so curious, why don't you just go down there and crash their party?"

She glared at him. "Weren't you the one who told me to stay away? Tamara wasn't that stupid. *She* didn't stay away! Now she's cuddled up in the tack house with Sam. She's the last thing he needs right now." She left out the tiny detail that she'd also spent time with Sam alone today.

Reed reached out and squeezed her hand. "So go tell him. I said give him a few days. It's been a few days, A."

"I'm not going over there, Reed. I know Tamara. Who knows what I'd be walking in on?"

"Come on, Aston. You know Sam, too. You think he'd sleep with anyone so soon after his breakup?"

"He's a guy." Aston sighed. "I don't know what he'd do." She sat back against the pillows of the couch and crossed her arms over her chest.

She watched the rest of the movie in silence, wondering what Sam and Tamara were doing but refusing to go back and check the window.

On her way upstairs later that night, however, she did glance outside and noticed that the little red Porsche was gone. She went to bed with a smile on her face.

Two weeks passed of Aston having to work with Sam in her father's office. He almost never met her eyes, and when he did she felt a sharp jolt of magnetism before he inevitably glanced away. She noticed how quickly he was picking up on the nuances of the company. The last time she'd worked with him, Sam had troubleshot an accounting program issue with IT personnel completely on his own. She'd merely watched him handle it, feeling proud and completely turned on.

Her attraction to Sam Waters was growing, while their closeness was dwindling away.

He hadn't once mentioned their fishing trip, and she was damned if she'd be the one to bring it up, or suggest they hang out again.

She missed the days when they would discuss life's little surprises and the companionable silences they endured while working together. Everything was different now.

It was as if when Sam had lost Ever, Aston had lost Sam.

On the weekends, she watched, tortured, while Sam sat with Tamara in his lap, or when Tamara brought him another beer from the bar. She couldn't comprehend their relationship. She knew Tamara wanted Sam, she could see it in every move the other girl made. But she didn't think they'd slept together. Sam kept a smidgeon of distance between his body and Tamara's whenever the girl attempted to snuggle up to him. He kept his hands firmly on the table or on his beer when she settled into his lap at Sunny's. So even though her heart thumped painfully when she looked at them, she felt vindicated when they weren't acting like a physical couple.

It was on one of these nights that she caught him, outside on the pier, while everyone else was inside listening to the band perform Maroon 5 covers.

"Hey, Sam," she said, sidling up behind him.

"Princess," he answered cautiously, watching her approach. "What's up?"

She let out a painful breath, wincing.

"What?" he asked in alarm. "What'd I say?"

"You called me Princess," she said, her voice barely audible above the lapping waves. "You haven't done that in awhile."

He nodded, studying her in silence.

She stopped in front of him. "What's up is that I finally got you alone for a minute without Tamara winding herself around you in one way or another, like a slutty snake."

He shot her a cocky smirk that was so un-Sam-like she wanted to smack it off his face.

"Oh yeah? You wanted to get me alone? Well, Princess, all you had to do was ask."

Her blood boiled inside her veins. She knew he was acting like this because he was still raw and hurt over losing Ever. She got it. But she wasn't going to tolerate it when it was just her and Sam. She was going to demand that he talk to her.

"Stop that," she said as the anger rolled off her. "I'm not having that attitude, Sam. It's not you."

"What the hell do you know?" he asked, his voice cold and hard. "This is me. Me without Ever. What, you don't like it? You seemed to like me a whole lot before. Single Sam isn't as appealing to you?"

"That's not what I'm talking about and you know it, Sam. I liked you before for the sweet, caring, down-to-earth guy you were. The guy I haven't seen since I took him fishing on the pier. This new Sam I've seen over the last few weeks annoys the hell out of me in a way you never did before. I want you to snap out of it!"

His eyes flashed angrily. "Oh, so Aston Hopewell snaps her fingers and *poof!* Everything is the way you want it to be? I'm not one of your minions, Princess. Your magic doesn't work on me."

They stared each other down.

"Sam," she relented in a softer tone. "I want to be here for you. I want you to open up to me. Please."

His eyes melted at the corners, and he looked at her in a way that softened her heart. Her hope rose. And then he shook his head and his eyes hardened again. The cocky swagger was back.

"You want me to open up to you?" He grabbed her tightly around the waist with one big hand, pulled her against his chest, and crushed his lips to hers.

The zing that went straight from her lips to her core weakened her knees. Her arms automatically went up and around his neck, tugging the soft hair at his nape. She felt so small and vulnerable wrapped in his arms; he was enormous. He surrounded her, swallowed her whole in the best way possible. She couldn't fight the desire that welled up inside her; she moved her lips against his hungrily for an instant before her brain caught up with her body.

She braced both hands against his chest and shoved with all her strength. He stepped back immediately, rubbing his lips with his fingers, his eyes blazing into hers.

As he stood there staring at her, panting with ragged breaths, she slapped him as hard as she could across the face.

"I'm not Tamara, Sam. You can't just use me to soothe your pain. I won't let you treat me like a goddamn substitute."

"Aston," he began, his voice rough. "I—"

"That was worse than anything Princeton ever did to me, Sam. Congratulations. You got what you wanted. Don't ever touch me again."

She whirled around and ran for the safety of Sunny's. Her heart was cracking inside her chest and her heels sent a *thwack, thwack, thwack* into the too-still night.

Fifteen

Five Years Previously in Nelson Island

*A*ston stumbled down the hardwood staircase, her heels flying across the wood as she ran blindly away from the sight she'd just seen. When she reached the bottom, she didn't have the energy to run anymore. She just sank onto the last step and buried her head in her arms. Sobs shook her body.

She didn't look up as the familiar young man brushed by her, only shuddered and cringed into the wall so he wouldn't graze her skin again.

"Aston." Her mother's whisper earned a look from Aston so poisonous Lillian could have dropped dead right on the steps.

"I'm so sorry," Lillian said.

Her voice was so quiet Aston barely heard her.

"You're what?" asked Aston, aghast. "You're sorry? For what, Mother? Cheating on Daddy? Or sorry you got caught *again*? *God, you are the most pathetic excuse for a woman on the planet!"*

"Don't do that, honey," Lillian snapped, straightening from where she'd crouched next to her daughter. She tightened the belt on her satin robe and frowned.

"Don't presume to understand me, Aston. Where is your father right now? Do you see him? Do you ever see him? No, it's always just me, always alone."

The last words were spoken on the cusp of tears, and they now flowed freely down her cheeks as she stared at her daughter. Her expression was pleading, begging her to understand.

But Aston didn't understand. She never would.

"Alone? You're not alone! You have two kids you're supposed to be taking care of. And Reed's only fourteen! He needs his mom! Daddy's working. He's working for you, and for this family!" She shook, disgust overwhelming her. "I hate you," she spat. "You're disgusting. The pool boy? Really? How much more cliché could you get? He's barely legal!"

"Are you going to tell your father?" Lillian asked what she'd been wondering since Aston walked in on her and Toby. She knew that Gregory wouldn't be able to forgive her a second time.

Aston just stared at her, her bottom lip curling with the contempt she felt for her mother.

"Tell him he's not enough for you? Tell him you slept with another man yet again, so that I can pick up the pieces of his dignity one more time? Like I did last time?"

Lillian only stared, waiting to hear the answer. She sniffled and wiped more tears from her cheeks.

The truth was, Lillian had a problem. She was lonely. She never felt the kind of love from her husband that she'd felt when they first got married. She'd married young, and they'd had Aston right away. And then Gregory had begun to build Hopewell Enterprises, and all attempts at romance and wooing were left by the wayside. She loved her husband. She just didn't feel loved by him. And she had always been starving for love, since the only father she'd ever known had walked out on her and her mother as a child. Gregory had rescued her from a life of looking for love in all the wrong places. But he'd forgotten how much she needed his strong arms around her.

He'd forgotten how much she needed him.

"No," Aston said finally. "I'm not going to tell Daddy. You've hurt him enough. God, get some help or something. And if you ever do this to him again…"

"I won't," Lillian answered quickly. She stepped toward Aston, who backed up onto the step above her.

Lillian dropped her arms and bit her lip.

"I hate you," Aston said softly. "I hate you so damn much. And that's never going to change."

She flew down the steps and ran outside, where Princeton was just pulling up with Reed in the front seat.

"Prince," she said, surprised to see him. "What are you two doing?"

"Just picked Reed up from practice," Princeton explained. "He's gotten pretty fast in the pool. Didn't think he had it in him."

Reed rolled his eyes and closed the car door. He walked over to Aston in his swim team sweats, staring closely at her face.

"What's wrong, A?" he asked.

She shook her head at her brother. "Nothing."

She'd always tried to protect him from her parents and their issues. She'd never stop trying.

"Okay," answered Reed. He knew she was lying, but he also knew her well enough not to push the issue. "I'm going to go shower."

Princeton leaned against the car, staring at Aston.

"So," he began.

"So," she said, leaning next to him.

"So there's a field party tomorrow night," he continued. "And I was wondering if you'd like to go with me. Like, as my date."

She stared at him. She'd known Princeton since grade school; they'd all grown up together. But he'd never made a move on her. Why now?

"Uh, sure," she said. "What's the catch?"

"No catch," he answered, smiling. "I just like you, Aston. I always have. We'll have fun together, okay?"

"Okay," she agreed, with a smile.

Aston decided right there that she'd stick with Princeton, if he wanted her. He was safe. He wouldn't hurt her. He wouldn't be able to even if he tried, because he'd never have the power to.

She would never go through the same issues her parents did. With Princeton, she'd never be in danger of that happening. She'd never be in danger of giving him her entire heart.

Sixteen

Sam stared after Aston, his lips still burning from the kiss that had set his whole body on fire.

He had no idea what he was thinking. One minute, he was trying so hard to keep his guard up because he knew that letting it down in front of her would be his undoing. The next minute an angry pyre burned inside him, consuming him, and he reacted to it by pulling her to him and plating his lips on hers.

He'd thought that she was livid with him for violating her space and her body, and rightfully so. But *damn*, he'd thought that kiss would finally get her out of his system, but it had only made him more ravenous for her. Especially when he remembered her initial response.

She wanted the kiss. She'd reacted to him, moving her lips against his and pressing her body tightly against him. If she hadn't pushed him away a second later, he never would have stopped kissing her. Never. The next step would have been picking her up and carrying her to her car. He wouldn't have been able to help himself.

Thank God she'd stopped him.

He was now stumped as to where he and Aston stood, or where his head was, but he knew that getting physical with Aston Hopewell would be a mistake. They'd only end up hurting each other.

After a shaky breath, he raised a hand in front of him, and as he suspected, it was trembling. He expelled the breath and sucked in another one. It took him about twenty deep breaths before he was calm enough to begin walking back to the bar.

Sam was barely finished with his next round before Reed noticed his off-kilter demeanor.

"Ugh," said Reed. "You're so damn broody now. I'm never settling down."

"You're young, Reed," Sam said. "You have time."

"What about you, Sam?" Tate asked, "How you doin' with life after, uh, you know..."

"Ever?" Sam asked. "You can say her name. I'm not gonna crumble. Life after a nine-year relationship? It's...freer than I would have expected."

"Freer?" Tate asked, wrinkling his forehead. "How so?"

"It's hard to explain."

"Try," Tate begged. "I'd really like to know."

Tate's voice had dropped, and his tone took on a level of seriousness Sam had never heard from him. Sam looked at him, surprised, but Tate's expression gave nothing away.

"It feels like I can finally see the road in front of me the way it should be laid out," Sam answered. "I was all set to travel down one fork in the road, but now I can see that way would have been a dead end. So now I'm going to go a different way, and it will lead me to the life I'm supposed to have. Hopefully."

"Whoa," Blaze rumbled, his big voice carrying through the restaurant. "That's deep, bro. Can we stop talking like bitches now?"

A collective laugh went up around the table, and Sam tilted his beer back against his lips.

"Wait a minute," Finn interjected. "One more bitch question. So this new road, Sam…does it have another girl standing at the end of it?"

Sam cocked his head to the side, considering. He rubbed his scruffy chin. "Maybe. Eventually."

"So, you bringing a date to the party tomorrow, Tate?" Reed asked quickly.

"Hell, no, dude. There's going to be too much ass there to narrow it down by bringing a date."

"So true," Reed agreed, bumping fists with Tate across the table.

Sam looked around, glad he'd found the camaraderie this group offered. He'd always had Hunter in the past, but he was too busy with Ever to ever really make friends with the guys on the football team. This felt nice and normal. And fun.

She wasn't sure what Sam had been thinking the other night, but Aston hadn't been able to get that kiss out of her head. She'd never been kissed like that, ever.

She sat back on the lounge chair, fanning herself with the little red, white, and blue flag fan they'd passed out to all the women at the Fourth of July pool party. The daylight was waning, and she was exhausted from a day of shaking hands with her dad's business acquaintances. She'd made the rounds with her dad and Sam, while Reed had been free as a bird to drink and do cannon-balls into the pool like a party animal. Which was what he always was.

She huffed a sigh and cut her eyes toward Reed. It was like he was the Energizer bunny. He hadn't taken a break all day, and she swore he must have been on his tenth Corona.

"Aren't you tired yet?" she called out to him with irritation. He was standing at the edge of the pool, about to jump in.

He glanced at her, grinned, and sauntered over. "What, sis? Did you say the *T* word?" He reared back and crouched, about to pounce.

"Reed," she warned in a deadly voice. "I swear, if you—"

He sprung. He grabbed her around the waist and dragged her to the side of the pool. Then he hoisted her into the air and flung her with a roar into the water.

She pushed to the surface, spluttering and coughing. Reed stood at the edge of the pool, doubled over with laughter.

"You know better than to ask me if I'm tired on a day like this," he managed to choke out. "I *live* to party!"

She propped herself up against the side of the pool on her elbows and pushed her now-soaked hair out of her face. "Asshole."

"Wow, and she's not talking about me for a change," Sam drawled, sidling up next to Reed.

She glared at him. "Only because you weren't the one who threw me in the pool."

She pulled herself out and sat on the side, wringing out her inky hair. She glanced at Sam, and noticed his eyes on her wet skin. She stretched out her legs to gauge his reaction, and his eyes widened slightly. She watched his pupils dilate as he drank her in, and when he caught her eye his gaze darkened under spiky lashes. She quickly looked away.

"Idiots," she grumbled.

Ashley walked over, a pink cocktail adorning her hand. "What the hell happened to you, A?"

"Reed," she spat.

Ashley laughed. Then her face quickly sobered as Reed took a step in her direction.

"Reed." Her voice held a note of warning. "Don't you *dare*. Finn's right over there and he will murder you."

Reed glanced over at Finn. "That's probably true. Oh well, there's plenty of gorgeous ladies here just waiting to be flung into the pool and rescued by yours truly."

He went moseying off toward a group of girls just arriving, decked out in bright cover-ups and searching for the cooler.

"Do you need help?" Sam asked Aston.

"Not from you," she answered coldly. "Where's Tamara? I'm sure she can think of some way to keep you busy."

A shadow crossed his face. "Fine. I'll find her."

He walked away, and Aston groaned in frustration.

How long was it going to take Sam to get back to being him-self? Losing Ever and his brother in one fell swoop had been tough, she was sure of that. His heart needed to heal so that he could move forward. But she missed the Sam who'd thawed the frostiness she'd shown him when they'd met. She missed the Sam who'd charmed her with his sweetness and his genuine heart, who always tried to save her whether she needed it or not.

She wanted that Sam back.

"What's up with you two? You're still pissed that he kissed you?" Ashley asked. "If you're honest with yourself, you're not really mad at him at all, are you?"

"I'm mad because…of the *way* he kissed me. I stayed up at night, Ash, thinking of what it would feel like if that ever happened. And he ruined it by being an *ass.*"

"Fine, but can you tell me this? Was the kiss freaking amazingly hot?" Ashley had turned on her sneakiest smirk.

"Shut up, Ash," Aston growled. "It's getting dark. This party's finally about to get started. I'm getting a drink."

When she and Ashley were settled in lounge chairs and Aston was on her third cocktail, she finally began to feel the tension drain away from her body as she loosened up. The alcohol was working its way through her system, lowering the walls and inhibitions she worked so hard every day to build.

She welcomed the change. She was sick of feeling so in control all the time. Why should she be the only one who ever kept it together around here?

She sipped her drink, holding the straw on the side of her mouth. She stared with hostile eyes at Sam and Tamara cuddled up on one lounge chair nearby, and she gagged.

Looking around, she saw that her parents and the rest of the over-thirty crowd were long gone. Every year, when the afternoon portion of the Fourth of July party ended, her parents went into Charleston for the night. They stayed at a hotel and met up with friends to watch the fireworks.

But, at the ranch, the party raged on.

She stood up. She'd lost her cover-up long ago, and was now wearing only the tiniest black bikini she'd found at the store and her black, red-soled peep-toe wedges. She tottered along the edge of the pool, headed for the bar.

She managed to make it to the tiki-themed counter and asked the man working behind it to make her fourth drink of the night, a Blue Hawaiian. While she waited, she watched in amusement as Tate and Reed played chicken in the pool with a couple of girls she recognized from around town.

"Wow," Sam said as he pulled in next to her. "Not taking it easy tonight, I see."

"Really? You're stalking me now?"

He stared dolefully at her. "Why does this conversation seem familiar?"

"Because you make it a habit when I least want to see you or talk to you?" Her smile was sugary sweet, while her voice was filled with bite.

"No. But I think you need to take it easy on the liquor. You never drink this much. You're going to regret it tomorrow."

She brushed his warning off with a flick of her hand. "Thanks, Dad. You can go back to your date."

"Look," he blurted out. "About the other night…I'm sorry. I'm sorry I kissed you. You weren't expecting it and neither was I.

I just…I'm just sorry, okay? Can we move past it?"

She stared, startled, into his chocolate eyes, so somber and pleading her to forgive him. She felt herself begin to thaw, and quickly turned away. It was only the alcohol, working its magic in her brain. His apology was belated. He'd been treating her like a stranger for weeks, and she was over it.

She ignored the tiny voice in her head that told her the only thing she was sorry about was that he hadn't kissed her because he'd wanted her. He'd only done it to prove a point.

"Leave me alone, Sam!"

She grabbed her drink and started toward her lounger. When she looked back, she saw that Sam had once again settled onto his chair with Tamara. But his eyes were fixed securely on Aston. He stared at her as she picked her way back to her seat, walking close to the edge of the pool.

With a sharp twinge of pain, Aston's ankle twisted in her wedges. She cried out as she lost her balance. She had a glimpse of blue mood lighting and rippling water just before she crashed into the water.

Surfacing with a splutter, she cleared her hair from her face and coughed.

"Aston!" shouted Ashley. "You okay?"

"Ugh, I'm fine," Aston said, disgusted with herself. She could hope that Sam hadn't seen her fall, but her hopes weren't high that it was the case. "But now my wedge is on the bottom of the pool. I'm getting it."

Because she wasn't leaving one-half of her favorite pair of shoes underwater.

Feeling a twinge of pain in her ankle, she dove beneath the surface and kicked down into the eight-foot depths. The pain in her ankle reminded her to kick one-legged. Her shoe lay directly next to the white, grated access hatch.

Like Reed, Aston had been swimming since she was a little girl. So a tweaked ankle and a buzz weren't going to stop her from getting her wedge.

But, once she grabbed it and began her ascent, she discovered that her long hair getting caught in the access hatch just might stop her from ever being able to wear it again.

Seventeen

Sam may have been sitting with Tamara, but his eyes were on Aston's every step. He saw how much she'd had to drink. His eyes were on her lithe, graceful body as she wobbled where she usually glided. Why was she walking so close to the pool?

So his eyes were the first to zoom in on her ankle as it twisted beneath her. It was as if the scene were moving in a blur, slower than real time. His eyes rose to her face, and he was on his feet as it contorted in pain. He wished in that moment that his chair was closer, because she was already tilting toward the water.

When she surfaced just seconds later, the sigh of relief caused his entire torso to sag. She was okay. Of course she was okay.

She was Aston.

He heard her say something to Ashley about getting her lost shoe as he settled back onto his chair. Her long, dark tresses disappeared beneath the surface of the water.

He half-listened as Tamara talked excitedly about the upcoming fireworks display while he waited for Aston to resurface.

He waited.

Aston didn't appear. Panic coursed through him once again.

He had closed the distance by half when Ashley screamed.

"She's stuck! Ohmygod, she's stuck at the bottom!"

A collective gasp went up around those sitting closest to the pool, and he didn't pause before he dove into the deep blue water.

His heart battering his chest like a jackhammer, Sam propelled himself to the bottom of the pool. Aston glanced at him with alarm as she tugged furiously on her hair.

Her hair. Oh, God, her hair was stuck in the drain. He tugged, to no avail, because the drain's small amount of suction was enough to keep a piece of her long, thick mane wrenched firmly inside of the hatch.

Blind panic filled his senses as he tugged harder, eliciting a scream from Aston that sent tiny air bubbles rushing for the surface of the pool. His chest was burning, and he rose quickly to the surface to take a breath.

When he plunged back below the water, a splash beside him told him he was no longer alone. Reed swam beside him as he kicked back toward where Aston was now floating limply next to the drain.

Sam and Reed exchanged glances, and Sam gestured wildly toward Aston's hair. They both worked, tugged, and pulled, to no avail. When they surfaced again for a breath, someone shoved something sharp into Sam's hand.

He rushed back down with the knife and didn't hesitate as he chopped off the chunk of Aston's hair trapped inside the access hatch. Sam hooked one arm around Aston's abdomen and stretched the other out in front of him as he kicked for the surface of the pool. Her dark hair billowed out behind them as he made his way toward safety.

"Aston!" Reed shouted as he flanked Sam's side. "Sam! God, is she okay?"

Sam didn't know if Aston was okay. As he pulled her out of the water and lay her down on a lounge chair nearby, he was terrified by her still features and limp limbs. He began to shiver, an odd reaction in the hot and heavy night air.

But he wasn't reacting to the weather.

"Aston!" he shouted, kneeling next to her. "Come on, Princess. Stay with me!"

The crowd of partygoers pressed in behind him as he tilted her chin upward and blew breath into her empty lungs. Her chest rose and fell as he repeated the motion, her lips cold and blue. He reared back, panting, and used his hands to pump compressions against her chest.

"Breathe, baby," he whispered as he tried to force life into her limp body.

Reed brought two trembling hands to his head and kept them there. "Sam...her lips are blue. Is she breathing yet?"

Sam shook his head roughly, feeling the lump in his throat grow to an alarming size as he stared down at her closed eyelids.

"Call an ambulance," he spat.

"Already done," Finn answered from somewhere behind him. "They're on their way, Sam. I can help with compressions."

Finn moved forward until he was on the other side of Aston's chair.

"Come on, Princess. Breathe!" Sam roared just before he exhaled two more breaths into her.

Nothing. The horror building in his chest was a black hole sucking him into a bleak world where Aston didn't exist. If Aston died here tonight, like this...

He pressed more compressions to her chest, working doggedly to force her to begin breathing again on her own. Her body was so still, so goddamned still. She was the strongest fucking girl he'd ever met. She had more life in her, dammit.

He bent to place his lips over hers yet again, when her eyelids fluttered and her chest heaved. She spluttered and coughed, and he cradled her in his arms, turning her body over to the side to dispel the water she had swallowed. All of the blood came rushing back to his extremities, causing a violent shudder to overtake him, and he buried his face in her hair as he thanked God for bringing her back to him.

"Oh, my God," Ashley's face was streaked with tears. "Aston!"

Sam tucked one hand behind her neck so she could sit up with his assistance. Her open blue eyes staring into his were the most beautiful sight he'd ever seen.

"Hey, Princess," he whispered, rubbing gentle circles on her back as she sucked in raspy gasps of air.

Sirens screamed in the distance.

Reed was staring up into the heavens, his lips moving in a silent, wordless prayer. When he looked at Sam, his eyes were bloodshot.

"Sam...you just saved her life."

Aston was still focusing on Sam, as if she were afraid to allow her eyes to leave his. Sam would let her stare at him all night if that was what it took for her to feel safe. He didn't remove his gaze from hers as paramedics rushed onto the scene.

"Sam?" Aston croaked.

"I'm right here," he responded. He didn't think he could say much more than that just then. Safer not to try. All the emotions bottled up inside him might just come flying out.

"My ankle hurts."

He laughed, a bark that was close to madness, and he gently cupped her face with both hands as the paramedics began firing off questions to the group.

"I know, Princess. You're going to get all fixed up now. Okay?"

"Okay," she whispered, leaning her forehead against his. "Don't leave me, Sam."

"I'm right here," he answered.

He stayed beside her as the paramedics took her pulse and listened to her lungs.

"You need to be monitored at the hospital," the woman said, glancing up at Aston. "They have to check for near-drowning aftereffects."

"No," Aston answered.

"Aston," Reed protested.

Aston shot him a look, and her brother clamped his lips together. His frustration was displayed plainly on his face.

"Well, if you're not going to the ER then you need to be watched tonight, just in case. And check in with your doctor tomorrow. Your lungs sound good, and your pulse is strong. You're a lucky young woman."

The other paramedic, a younger man, was wrapping her ankle.

As his nimble fingers worked, Sam watched his eyes travel up Aston's shapely leg.

A flash of anger shot through him at the mere thought of this guy thinking of Aston in any way other than someone who needed to be patched up. There was no reason for his eyes to wander any farther than her ankle.

Sam cleared his throat. When the guy glanced up at him, the look Sam gave him convinced the paramedic to keep his eyes on the ankle tape he was using.

Sam looked around the yard. Most of the party had cleared out, except for Aston's close friends. When he looked back at Aston, her blue eyes burned steadily back into his, and his stomach flip-flopped. He told himself that it was because he was thoroughly relieved that she was safe.

Finn and Tate walked the paramedics out of the yard. Sam saw them go out of the corner of his eye, but his focus was still firmly planted on Aston.

"I'll stay in your room tonight," Reed piped up.

Aston nodded, and glanced at Sam.

"I love you, A," said Ashley, bending down next to her friend to give her a gentle hug. "We'll come check on you tomorrow, okay? Call me when you get back from the doctor."

Sam looked down to see he was still holding on to Aston's hand. He squeezed it gently, rubbing his thumb along the soft lines of her palm. He felt her shiver, and heat spread like lava throughout his body. Now that he was no longer afraid for her life, the closeness they currently shared was working its familiar magic on his body.

"Reed," he said softly. "I'm going to carry Aston upstairs. She doesn't need to be walking on her ankle."

Reed studied Sam for a moment, his glance bouncing back and forth between him and Aston like a yo-yo. "Okay."

He bent down to kiss his sister's forehead, and then turned and strode toward the kitchen door. As he entered, he left the door wide open for Sam's entry with Aston.

"You don't have to do that," she whispered.

"Do what?" Sam's heartbeat picked up its pace, now that he was alone with her. Suddenly everything felt different.

She was the strongest girl he knew, but for a few moments she'd needed him. She hadn't had a choice in the matter.

"Carry me. I can hobble, you know."

He bent down, brushing her ear with his nose. "Don't be so…so Aston for a minute. Okay, Princess?"

She stilled and her chest rose and fell as she inhaled a deep breath.

His voice dropped even lower as he murmured in her ear, "You don't always have to be made of steel. Let me be strong for you. Just tonight."

He lifted her, one arm cradling her shoulders while the other wrapped around the backs of her knees. The proximity of her body to his sent a jolt of *need* through him, and he shuddered. He knew she felt it, too, she gazed at him with those wide eyes that only hardened the current swelling in his trunks. She slid one arm around his neck, trailing her fingernails against his nape, and the hair there stood on end in response to her feather-light touch. Her other hand pressed gently against his bare chest, and he wanted nothing more than to lay her back down on the lounge chair and cover her body with his. He stilled himself, because that kind of thinking was going to land them both in a world of trouble.

He just couldn't bring himself to care very much, after what had just happened in the pool tonight. The threat of losing her altogether had nudged something loose inside him.

Shaking the thought from his head, he carried her through the kitchen, up the stairs, and along the upstairs hallway to her bedroom.

When they entered, he gently laid her down on her bed and stayed close, sitting on the edge of the mattress beside her. As he stared down into her deep blue gaze, her eyelids fluttered.

"Sleep, Princess. You've been through hell tonight. Just sleep."

Her lids fluttered again before they shut completely, her thick black lashes resting against her cheeks.

Her beauty took his breath away, and he couldn't move a muscle to leave the room.

He heard her stir some hours later, and he rose from the chair in the corner of the room. He'd told Reed he would stay with her, but Reed had been checking on her every hour or so nonetheless.

Sam couldn't blame him. Aston occupied such a huge space in all of their lives. Sam was now no exception.

He moved until he was standing beside her, and her eyes widened when she saw him.

Sitting down beside her, he took her hand gently in his.

"You're here." She breathed.

"Where else would I be?" He lifted her hand to his lips and breathed her in.

He touched her face, brushing a damp strand of hair off of her cheek. She stared up at him, waiting.

"I thought…" he began. He stopped, gazing down at her, and then his words came out in a jumbled rush he couldn't halt with sense or reason.

"When you fell, and I saw you go into the water, it was terrifying. Then you didn't come up again, and I lost it. I've only been that scared a couple of times in my life, Princess, and the thought of losing you had me shaken. I don't want to lose you."

"Sam," Aston said softly, her voice sounding so forlorn he wanted to push it back inside her so that she could say his name again without sounding so sad. "You have to actually *have* someone in order to lose them."

"That's true," he answered, and a tiny little piece of his heart fell into her lap.

He trailed a hand along her bare leg as she lay on her side, her head angling toward him at his touch. His hand responded on its own to the smoothness of her skin he'd always suspected was there but had never been able to stroke.

She sucked in a breath as his straying fingers climbed. Her leg trembled beneath the rough skin of his palm.

"And I don't have you," he continued sadly.

His hand crept higher on her leg, now grazing the way-too-soft flesh of her midthigh. "Jesus *Christ,* Aston. It's not because I don't want you. I just know it'd be wrong. I was with Ever for so damn long…it was wrong to want you like I did. And now that

I'm free, I can't let myself jump into something that could end up breaking me."

She reached out and allowed her fingertips to graze his chest, so softly she barely felt the fine hair on his skin against her fingertips. Fueled by the jump in his muscle, her fingers squeezed his rock-hard pec gently and he froze. A slender index finger traced a light circle around the nipple, and the hand on her leg gripped her tighter.

"Sam." She breathed. "I'm not going to break you. I'm going to put you back together again."

He made a fatal mistake; he allowed his eyes to run the full length of her bikini-clad body, taking in the soft curves of her legs and her hip, and the perfect cinch in her exposed waist. His eyes traveled up to the swell of her plump breasts, and then he could no longer remain a spectator. Aston was a contact sport, and Sam knew exactly what to do when he was called into a game.

His lips were covering hers, because he couldn't stop himself anymore. He didn't *want* to stop himself anymore. He let his hands stroke every inch of her exposed skin, he couldn't touch enough places on her body fast enough or thoroughly enough. And as his brain caught up to the massive desire currently building somewhere deep in his gut, he had a thought that maybe he should stop this before they got carried away.

He opened his mouth to say it aloud, but then her hands were up and tangling in his short hair and all that reasonable thought he'd suddenly acquired flew right back out from the place it came. She moaned against his mouth, *moaned,* and he prodded her lips with his tongue, wanting her to open up for him. Needing her to open up for him so he could feel the heat he knew existed inside her mouth. She did almost instantly, and their tongues began to gently taste and explore each other for the first time.

Kissing her was everything he thought it would be when he'd dared to fantasize about it. Sparks of electricity were igniting small fires all over his body, and the ache in his trunks was almost painful at this point, the throbbing sensation begging him to relieve it.

She tugged him closer, and he willingly leaned against her, closer, to meld his body against hers. They were chest to chest, and the delicious feel of her chest crushed against him was exactly how he pictured heaven would feel. The vibration of the sound she made against his lips as his hand skimmed up her side and cupped one of her breasts sent his mind spinning to the moon and back again.

So close. She was so close and she tasted more than good, like candy and ice cream and every other decadent thing he could think of and…she wanted him. He could feel the heat between her thighs through the thin fabric of his swimming trunks, and the thought of her sizzling against him made him almost crazy with the need he could no longer contain. They'd started this, now he was damn well going to finish it. The fact that he was kissing a girl who'd nearly drowned hours before wasn't lost on him, but the look of focused clarity in her eyes was enough to let him know that she knew exactly what she was doing, and she wanted it.

"Aston," he groaned against her mouth as he tore his lips away to trail kisses around her jawline and nip at the soft skin underneath her ear. One of his hands continued to palm her breast, his thumb circling her tautly erect nipple. Her nails clutched his bare skin again, and he hoisted one slender leg up around his waist to feel more of her direct heat.

A door suddenly closed farther down the hallway, and they both froze, lips hovering millimeters away from each other.

"Did you close my bedroom door?" Aston asked in a breath, her eyes still closed and her hands crawling down the front of his swimming trunks.

"No," he groaned. His breath came in heavy gasps as her fingers grazed against his painfully swollen erection. He tried, and failed, to gain control of himself. She was making him lose his ever-loving mind.

"Dammit," she cursed. "Don't leave, Sam. Close the freaking door."

Sam held her against him, and she wiggled her hips in a way that nearly ripped a yell from his mouth. He buried his face in her neck to squelch it, and he breathed in her scent again as he willed his pulse to slow down enough for him to disentangle himself from her.

"We're in your house," he mumbled against her neck. "Reed's coming to check on you."

He sat up, and she objected, the disappointment she felt also filling his limbs like hot, heavy lead.

"Do you two want me to come back?" Reed asked from the door, a smug smile tugging at his lips.

Sam and Aston both shot him a glare. Reed's smirk grew wider.

Sam gently set Aston back against her pillows, removing her leg from his waist and sliding away from her.

"I got her upstairs safe and sound," he said lamely.

"Yes, I can see that, Sam. I'm sure my sister is very grateful." A deep laugh bubbled up from Reed's throat.

Sam glanced down at Aston, and the sight of her almost sent him right back into her arms. She was flushed from the heat of their encounter, and her eyes sparkled with a bright ferocity that showed him just how much of a tigress she'd be if he'd gotten her naked. Her lips were plump and wet, and as he watched, she slid her tongue over them slowly. He had to bite down on his lip painfully, and shifted in his seat to adjust himself in his new, painful state of need.

"Shut the hell up, Reed," Aston grumbled. She reached out her hand and squeezed Sam's. "Thank you. For saving my life tonight."

"You're welcome, Princess."

He bent down and kissed her cheek, letting his lips linger against her skin for a brief moment. She rubbed her cheek against his rough chin, and he sighed with regret.

"I'll call you in the morning," he whispered.

"You'd better."

When Aston awoke the next morning, the throbbing pain in her head made her want to close her eyes and drift back to sleep. She groaned.

"Here," Reed said from beside her.

He'd gotten up from the comfortable armchair in the corner of her room to hand her a glass of water and two pills.

"Did you sleep at all?" she asked groggily as she sat up to take the medicine.

"A little," he answered, studying her. "Are you okay?"

"My head hurts like a bitch," she answered. "But I don't think I'm going to die anytime soon."

"That's a relief," Reed said. "Even though it would have been nice to add that BMW to my side of the garage."

She slapped his arm. "Thanks, little bro."

"So, we gonna talk about you and Sam now?" Reed grinned like a schoolboy.

Her mind flashed back to the kiss from last night and her face burned hot. "No."

"Are you sure? Because I'm pretty sure I interrupted something when I came in." The smirk was back.

"Reed," she warned.

"Aston," he replied. "Okay, I'll drop it. I'm guessing you don't want me to ask Sam about it, either."

"If you do, I will kill you in your sleep," she answered.

"Noted."

Aston's visit to the doctor later that day confirmed popular suspicions: She had no lasting effects from the near-drowning. The doctor instructed her to return if any new symptoms arose.

Her ankle, however, was badly sprained. It required an air cast and instructions to keep off of her feet as much as possible.

"See?" she told her father and Reed. "I'm fine. No harm done. Now I can relax the rest of the day, and get back to work tomorrow."

"No, you won't," Gregory admonished. "You won't be back at work this week. Sam can handle it while you're gone. You wouldn't want to step in and help, would you, Reed?"

"Hell, no," Reed answered, shocked.

"See," Aston said, shooting Reed an amused glance. "You need me, Daddy."

"Of course I need you," Gregory answered. "But I can live without you in the office for a week. Rest, baby girl. Get better."

"Right," Aston answered. She was unable to hide her exasperated tone. "Because since Sam is a man, he's better at my job anyway, right?"

Gregory leaned over the couch where Aston sat splayed out and kissed her cheek.

"Those are your words, honey," he answered. "Sam may rise in the company one day. And I hope you'll be by his side." He winked.

Aston's mouth dropped open. "You want me by his side? In what way, Daddy?"

"In whatever way you two see fit," he answered. He squeezed her shoulder and left the room.

"Don't say it," Aston instructed Reed, whose head was swiveled toward her.

He feigned a zipping motion at his lips and rose. "I gotta go, sis. Amy's waiting for me at the beach."

"Who the hell is Amy?"

"Don't worry about it," A wide grin spread across Reed's face.

With her family gone, Aston's thoughts strayed to Sam. She snuggled on the couch cushions, sinking deeper into the fluff, and remembered how delicious his lips had felt on hers the night before. And when she closed her eyes all she could see was the ravenous look in his chocolate ones as he gazed at her on her bed.

Shivers rocked her body as her hand reached out for her phone. She couldn't spend another minute alone on this couch.

The phone jingled happily as she picked it up, and Sam's name flashed across the screen.

"Sam?" she answered breathlessly.

"Hey, Princess." Sam's deep, husky voice sent a tingle of longing from her heart to her belly. "How was the doctor today?"

"Good," she answered. "I've got a sprained ankle. So I'll live. I have to rest it this week, though."

"I'm so sorry this happened to you." Sam's voice was low. "Can I come see you? Do you need some company?"

"Yes," Aston immediately replied. "Are you on your way up?"

She could hear the motion on Sam's end of the line. And the smile in his voice. "Already halfway there."

"Well, that's presumptuous, Waters." She was unable to keep her mouth from forming an answering smile.

"I guess it would be, if I wasn't completely sure you would say yes." He chuckled, and ended the call.

She sighed and flopped back on the cushions. She couldn't remember a time when she'd felt this excited about seeing a guy. Her relationship with Princeton just wasn't like this. It hadn't been so…intense.

It finally felt like…they'd reached a turning point. A swarm of wings took flight in her stomach at the thought.

A light knock echoed down the long hallway outside the great room, and the front door opened and closed. Sam's footsteps thudded on the wood floors and when he appeared in the doorway, her heart melted.

He wore a pair of the newer jeans he'd bought while shopping with her and they fit more snugly on his hips than his old ones did. The army green T-shirt made his eyes glitter, and her gaze wandered from them to the full lips that she very much wanted back on her body right now.

"Hey," she squeaked, pulling the pillow she hugged closer to her body.

"Hey yourself," he answered.

He sat on the opposite end of the couch and she exhaled in relief and regret. She wanted him closer, but if he was closer the territorial lioness inside of her might be forced to pounce.

His hands fidgeted in his lap, then settled upon his thighs, fingers splayed. He cleared his throat, not looking at her.

"So, Aston," he began.

She waited. If he was going to tell her that last night was a mistake, she would let him get it out. Then she'd have to ask him to leave in order to put herself back together again.

"Last night...last night I lost control. I didn't mean to. I respect you too much to ruin our friendship."

"Sam..." She slid over on the couch. She stopped right next to him, her thigh grazing against his.

He eyed their legs, assessing their proximity. When he met her eyes again, firelight flickered dangerously in his.

She nodded. "The feelings I have...I've tried to ignore them. I've tried to forget they exist. I work with you and try to keep things totally professional. But then, I hang out with you at night and can't force my eyes away from you. I went from not trusting you in the beginning to being someone who believes in you, Sam. I can't get you out of my head."

She rested a small hand timidly on his thigh, and his muscle tensed beneath her touch. She liked the feeling of security the sheer size of him beside her provided. She liked his reaction to her. Maybe it meant that he'd be able to let this happen.

Let *them* happen.

"I…I can't feel anything for you," he said, his voice desperate and pained.

The hope she'd allowed herself to feel was instantly extinguished, leaving a chilly emptiness in its place.

"I just can't, Aston. Yeah, I feel drawn to you, and it confuses the hell out of me. It wasn't like that with Ever. With you, I feel free to be who I really am, who I can one day be. When I'm with you I see a whole world I never knew existed. But…I think it's just physical. We can't be more. I don't have any more to give."

Now Aston's eyes flashed, with anger. "You're lying to yourself, Sam." She squeezed his thigh, and his muscle jumped beneath her hand. "You're telling yourself, for whatever reason, that you can't have this. I don't know what you're afraid of. But ignoring this…ignoring what we have, is a mistake."

His eyes locked on hers, and she made a snap decision. She leaned forward and melded her lips against his. Immediately, he groaned in response and pulled her head closer with a firm hand on the nape of her neck. She kissed him fervently to convey the emotions she was feeling, and to unlock the ones he was hiding deep inside his heart.

His tongue nudged inside her mouth and tangled with hers. She sighed against his lips and tilted her head, allowing him to deepen the kiss. His arms went around her, strong and steady, and she sank into them as his mouth moved against hers.

"Sam," she whispered against him. "Please don't deny this."

He struggled; he pulled away a fraction, and then his arms tightened around her and he pulled her close again. He was torn. She could convince him to give them a chance. She kissed him harder. His large hands found their way under her tank top, and she shivered in response to his touch. Those strong hands covered her inconvenient bra, cupping her breasts almost roughly, and she immediately leaned into him to achieve more closeness. She wanted more; more of him, more of his hands on her body.

Footsteps echoed down the wood-floored hall and Sam pulled back from her immediately. He closed his eyes and shook his head, and then released a frustrated sigh. He rose from the couch and moved to stand against the window. When his eyes found hers again, the ache in them was visible.

"Sam," she whispered. He held up a hand to quiet her.

"Oh, hello, Sam," Gregory said brightly as he strode into the room. "Here to keep Aston company?"

"Yes, sir," Sam answered, his voice clipped. "We've become good friends."

"I figured as much," Gregory answered. "I'm glad to hear it. I'm more than grateful to you for last night, Sam. Saving my daughter's life is something I'll never forget, and I'll always be in your debt."

"Sir," Sam declared. He scrutinized Aston. "I'd save her life a million times over."

If his statement took Gregory aback, he didn't acknowledge it. He simply nodded and smiled faintly.

"I'm also glad you're here, Sam. I wanted to let you know that some business has come up in Europe, and I'm going to have to travel to Belgium in a couple of weeks. I want you and Aston in the office in Charleston while I'm gone. I know you can manage it. Also, Sam, I'd like to talk to you about your future a little bit more when I get back. I've been thinking that you could stay on at Hopewell Enterprises while you attend college in Charleston this fall."

"College in Charleston?" Sam asked. "But I'm not—"

"We have some time, son. You can think about it. A company scholarship would provide anything you needed, of course. Tuition, books, all fees would be paid for. If you plan to be an asset in my company in the future, it behooves me to help you, Sam. And…I just want to."

Sam stared at Mr. Hopewell and Aston stared at Sam.

If he took the offer, he'd be staying in South Carolina…for good. The emotions that swirled around her heart were slowly warming her body from the inside out. She wanted Sam here, more than she'd known. She wanted him to take the scholarship. She wanted him to stay.

And she was beyond grateful that her father had seen the potential in him when she hadn't. She'd never been so happy he hadn't listened to her in her life.

"Mr. Hopewell." The emotion in Sam's voice was apparent

in the thickness of his tone. "What you're offering…is insane. You're offering to send me to a four-year school? Here? And I could keep working? I never expected…" Sam sank down onto a chair near the window and dropped his head in his hands. The trembling in his arms was visible to Aston from her seat on the couch.

She wanted to go sit with him and put her arms around him, to let him know that it was okay. He could take this offer and not feel guilty, or suspicious, or used. Her father wanted Sam because he was amazing. Just like she did.

But Sam wasn't ready to hear that yet. He may never be ready to hear it. Not from her. And patience wasn't a virtue Aston had ever mastered.

A sudden hope of waiting Sam out lit a fire inside of her, hotter than her ambition for success in school or business.

She would wait for Sam. As long as it took. Because he was worth it.

For the first time, she recognized that he didn't know he was worthy of all the good things piling up around him. He thought he'd left his worth back in Duck Creek with Ever. He was lost; he was drifting.

She just needed to show him that his value was inside of him, and it was visible to everyone he met.

He was worthy. It wouldn't be easy to make him see it. First, she needed to make him see *her*. Then she could focus on proving to him that his life could be wherever she was.

Eighteen

Sam tossed the football across the thick green lawn of the south pasture on the Hopewell property. Reed caught it and tossed it back with a *whump* in Sam's capable hands.

"You gonna take it?" Reed called.

Sam threw again, a perfect spiral in a graceful arc. Reed caught it in a running jump.

"Tell me again why you never played football," Sam yelled.

"Do you see this face?" Reed asked.

Sam laughed and grunted as he caught Reed's bullet of a pass.

"You didn't answer the question," Reed reminded him. "Are you going to take the offer my dad made you a few days ago?"

Sam sighed and held the ball in his arms, staring down at the white laces. Reed walked over to him and sat down in the grass, grabbing a stray piece of straw and chewing on it.

Sam plopped down next to him. "I don't know."

"What's not to know?"

"I...I don't know if I'm going to be able to fill out paperwork for that."

"What? That's the craziest reason I've ever heard. Not what I expected. Why the hell wouldn't you be able to fill out paperwork?"

Sam didn't look up at him, just kept gazing down at the ball, the grass, anywhere else.

"Sam? Is this about the trouble you got into back home?"

Sam nodded. "Yeah, man. It's big. I don't think I can enroll in school in a couple of months. It won't be worked out by then."

"Let my dad help you. Whatever you did—and I hate that you won't tell us—it has to be fixable," Reed said. "Power and money can go a long way."

"Maybe," Sam answered absently. "What are you going to do this fall, Reed? I haven't heard you talk about college. Are you going off somewhere?"

Reed fidgeted, scratching his head and staring off into the distance. "I've been accepted to a few places," he finally answered.

"Okay," Sam said slowly. "Which one did you decide on?"

Reed blew a breath out that lifted his dark hair in the front. His hair was the exact same shade as Aston's, the tips sun-bleached.

"My mind isn't on college right now," he admitted.

"Why not?"

"Because there's other stuff I want to try first."

"Like what?"

"Like music."

"Really? I've never even heard you play. Or sing."

"Let's just say that in my family, academics are the fucking universe. A career in music wouldn't sit well with them. Well…maybe my mom would understand. But her opinion isn't worth much."

"Does Aston know?" Sam asked.

Reed shook his head slowly. "She knows I can play the guitar, and that I love to sing and write songs. But she and my parents just see it as a hobby. She wouldn't get it…as hard as she's worked at school and being smart her whole life. She wouldn't have a clue."

"I disagree," Sam argued. "Aston loves you. If you told her about this, she'd have your back."

Reed aimed a pointed gaze directly at Sam. "Then why haven't *you* opened up to her?"

Sam opened his mouth to answer, and then closed it again. He didn't have an answer for Reed, because he didn't know himself why he couldn't open himself up to her.

Ever had hurt him. No, she'd taken his heart out of his chest and squeezed until mere ashes fell from her fingers. But Aston wasn't Ever.

Somehow, he still couldn't seem to trust her enough to open his heart again so soon, so fully. Because Aston Hopewell deserved nothing less than all of him. And he just wasn't sure if he was ready to give it to her. If he would ever be ready.

When Sam didn't respond, Reed continued, "Everyone on the island's heard about her and Princeton's breakup by now. If you want a chance with her, I wouldn't wait too long."

* * *

The following week, he headed to the office bright and early. He bustled around the room following the day's to-do list while he waited for Aston to return from an errand she'd run to the main office building across the bridge. Her ankle had healed nicely during her week of rest, and now her limp was barely noticeable.

Sam sat down in the office chair, ready to type up a report on an energy source acquisition on which Hopewell Enterprises was currently embarking. The French doors opened and a man who looked vaguely familiar strode inside.

"Can I help you?" Sam stood, coming halfway around the desk.

"Yeah, I'm Brett Nash. I think I met you a couple of times at Sunny's. I'm here to see Aston."

Sam leaned a hip against the desk, studying Brett. He did remember him from Sunny's; that was why he'd looked familiar. Brett was about his age, with long blond hair tied in a ponytail. He dressed like many of the other guys on N.I: polo shirt and khakis, with brown leather flip-flops.

Sam frowned. "What about?"

"Uh," Brett stammered. "Is she here?"

"Nope," Sam answered. "Guess you'll just have to deal with me. Is it work-related?"

The half-smile that turned up Brett's lips caused Sam's stomach to clench. "Definitely not work-related. I can wait for her outside if you think she'll be back soon?"

Sam heard the heavy oak front door open and shut, and Aston appeared in the doorway.

"Brett?" The pleasant rise in her voice aimed at Brett was like a punch to Sam's gut. "What are you doing here?"

"Hey, gorgeous," Brett said.

Sam's fists clenched under the desk, and hot fire rushed to his face. *He'd called her gorgeous.* The desire to smash Brett's face in and drag Aston off to the tack house was overwhelming. He turned his back, walking around the desk to sit in front of the computer. He clenched his muscles, willing himself to stay firmly planted in the chair.

"I wanted to know if you wanted to take the day off, and join me at the beach." Brett's one-hundred-watt smile matched his white-blond hair and his bright white polo.

"Uh," Aston stammered. "We're actually working on something here today that needs my immediate attention."

She stole a glance at Sam, which he didn't return. Her eyes narrowed and she looked back at Brett.

"You know what? Sam will be just fine on his own here. You can just wait by the door while I go upstairs and put on my suit. Okay?"

"Yeah, okay," answered Brett. Sam pictured him rubbing his hands together with anticipation at seeing Aston in her bikini. His stomach lurched.

"Be down in just a sec," Aston promised before limping out of the room. Her light footsteps echoed on the hardwood staircase. He imagined her trajectory: down the hall, turn right into her bedroom, shoot left to the walk-in-closet...

A soft *click* met his ears, and he looked up to see Brett standing just beyond the now-closed French doors. Sam guessed Brett supposed his conversation with Sam wasn't worth a proper closing.

He watched, through his eyelashes, as Aston came back down the stairs. When she arrived on the third step from the bottom, where she was clearly visible from the office, he jerked to a standing position, as if a puppet master had yanked his strings.

He cleared his throat loudly, and Aston glanced in his direction. There was so much he wanted to say. To ask her. Like why her cover-up was so short and sheer. Like why the bright red bikini she donned underneath was so tiny.

He needed to get himself together. If he came around the desk, Aston would see very clearly how badly he wanted her to stay with him rather than going to the beach with Brett. Instead, he raised a hand in a wave.

She nodded at him dismissively, and with a bang of the front door, she and Brett were gone. Sam now had the entire day to brood about what they may or may not be doing together on their date in the sun and surf.

He was still grimacing later as he pulled up to Sunny's on his bike and took off his helmet. He scanned the parking lot, seeking out Aston's car as he told himself he was making sure Reed was already inside.

Aston's car was missing, and he sighed as he headed inside. His boots crunched on the gravel as he plodded across the lot and opened the large wooden door of the bar. He was an hour later than the rest of his friends. He'd actually been debating whether he'd come out tonight at all. He wasn't really in the mood for Reed's ever-present addiction to women, and Tate's inevitable stupor after chasing five shots of tequila with salt and a lime.

He was surprised to find his friends all out on the dance floor. Sam stopped at the bar to ask Kelly for a shot and a beer as he leaned his back against it to watch everyone letting loose to the music of a Zac Brown cover band.

Reed spotted him and whispered into the redhead's ear that was shimmying against his groin. He jogged over to Sam, weaving around a couple sucking the life out of each other's faces. With a grin, Sam realized it was Tamara and a guy he'd never met.

"What's up, buddy?" Reed asked, his speech slightly slurred. "Thought you might have bailed on us tonight."

"Thought about it," Sam answered as Kelly slid his Cuervo across the bar. "Thought about it real hard."

"What's up?" Reed asked, furrowing his thick brows as he scrutinized Sam's frown. "You stressed about something? Wouldn't be my sister, would it?"

Reed's knowing grin and the gleam in his eye irritated Sam tonight. He didn't want to talk about Aston. He chased his Cuervo with a long swallow of Michelob.

"Not in the mood," he replied.

"Whatever, dude," Reed said. "Grab a girl and get out here. That long fucking face is gonna get old fast."

He sauntered off, back toward the waiting redhead, and took his place behind her as she resumed dancing.

Sam shook his head and held up a finger to Kelly, indicating one more shot. And as he downed it, Aston walked in with Brett.

Sam rolled his eyes and groaned, leaning over the bar. Kelly noticed and came over, wiping her hands on a stained rag.

"You want somethin' else darlin'?" she yelled over the thumping music.

Sam shook his head. "No, thanks."

"Uh-huh," Kelly said, swinging her blond hair over her shoulder. "Ain't nothing in here you can't have, Sam Waters."

She winked at him and moved to the other side of the bar, where two coeds were singing along to "Toes."

Sam turned, beer in hand, and headed to the quieter, more remote area of the bar. He wanted to be as far away as possible from the dance floor when Aston hit it with her date. But something kept him hovering around the pool table, where he still had a view of the dancers.

"Waters!" Blaze's booming voice echoed against the glasses behind the bar as he pulled out a stool and sat next to Sam's place at the bar. He indicated to Kelly that he wanted a beer, and then turned to survey the dance floor. Aston and Brett now had drinks, and were making their way to the dance floor.

Sam focused on Blaze. "What's up, man?"

"Not a damn thing. What's up with you? Why does your face look like you wanna murder someone?"

Sam couldn't run from the question anymore. "Because Aston went out with Brett today, and now they're here together. So, yeah. I wanna smash his face in. Just a little bit, though."

Blaze roared with laughter. "At least you're finally honest. I don't get something, though."

"What's that?"

"You're a pretty straightforward dude. You want her? Why not tell her?"

"And say what?" asked Sam, running a hand through his hair. "I don't want you to date other guys, but I'm too much of a fuckup to date you myself?"

Blaze shook his head. "There's a lot of fuckups in here, and you ain't one. Hunter and Ever? Not your fault. What's the real reason you aren't with Aston?"

"Blaze," Sam said, his brow furrowing as he remembered the hurt he'd felt when he caught Hunter and Ever kissing. "Ever really messed me up. I gave everything to that girl. That's all I got. Aston deserves more than I can give. She's...she's everything. I'm not the one for her."

"Okay, Sam. Let me ask you this. Did you feel like shit after you found out about Ever and Hunter?"

"Like complete shit, dude. What do you think? I've never been that pissed. Except when her father hurt her. I never thought my brother would screw me over like that. I thought she and I were it, and that we were going to be together for the rest of our lives. I had prepared for that. Then it just ended. I'm still trying to figure out what the hell I'm supposed to do now."

"But you're not spending your nights crying over her? You're not thinking about how you're going to get her back from your brother?"

"Hell, no. It's over."

"Then she wasn't it for you." Blaze sat back, interlocking his fingers over his massive chest, flashing a serene smile like he'd just morphed into Yoda.

"What?"

Blaze leaned forward. "If you really thought in your heart that Ever was the girl you wanted forever with, you'd fight. And you're not doing that. So she ain't it. And if you're wondering how you're going to fill your time from now on…" His eyes glossed over the dance floor until they landed on Aston.

Sam's eyes followed, and when they found Aston, his heart thumped wildly. She was dancing with Brett, a little too close for his liking. She was swaying to the beat while his arms pulled her up against his front. Sam's anger hit a fever pitch at the sight of Brett's hands on her. He was a nice guy, always had been.

But every nice guy had a limit.

"You're right, Blaze," Sam said. "Fuck, you're right. I didn't see it before. What the hell am I going to do?"

"Well, first, you might wanna go get Brett off of your girl."

Sam moved then, without another thought or another word to Blaze. He wound his way across the floor, squeezing around dancing bodies until he was standing right in front of Aston.

Her eyes widened. Her arms, which had been snaking up around Brett's neck, dropped to her sides. "Sam? What's wrong?"

He leaned in so she could hear him over the music. "What's wrong is that you're dancing with him and not me."

A shadowy mixture of emotion crossed her face. She stared at Sam. "Go away, Sam."

Sam watched her for a moment, and then turned to Brett. "Excuse us."

Brett looked unsure. "I don't think—"

Sam stopped him with one look. He towered over Brett, really.

And Brett didn't know that Sam wasn't a violent guy. Brett's face changed, and he stepped away from Aston. "I'm going to go sit down, Aston. Catch up with you later."

Sam didn't give him a second look as his eyes locked with hers. "Dance with me. Your partner left the floor."

Aston shook her head, her lips parting to speak. But she closed her mouth quickly when Sam's hands pressed into her hips, moving them along to the beat of the music the band was playing. His hands slipped just beneath her top, and settled onto her hot, bare skin. He sighed, remembering how all the softness of that skin felt underneath his hands the night of her pool accident.

"I'm…surprised you did that," she said, meeting his gaze with her steady one.

"Tell me how surprised you are later. Right now I just want to feel you against me," he whispered into her ear.

She shuddered in his arms, and his hands ran up her sides. As his thumbs settled into the soft crease beneath her breasts she sighed and closed her eyes.

"I really don't like this outfit," said Sam. "It shows too much skin."

He leaned down and placed his lips against her shoulder, brushing them across her skin.

She opened her ice-blue eyes and locked on his. "I thought you liked my skin."

"I love your skin," he growled, pressing his lips to the other shoulder. "That's the problem. I don't like everyone else seeing it, too."

"That's very possessive of you, Sam," she said, letting her head drop back. "You don't own me."

Sam placed his hands on her shoulders and then ran them down her arms. "No, I don't. But I'm scared that you might own me, Princess."

Her head snapped up and she studied him. "What are you saying, Sam?"

The song ended and Sam stepped back from Aston, taking her hands with him.

"I don't know what I'm saying. All I know is seeing you with him today made my blood boil. It also made me go crazy back at home, worrying about where he was touching you and whether he was making you laugh. I want to do those things."

She glanced down at their hands, and then back up at his face. "So what's stopping you?"

The rest of the dancers on the floor melted away as Sam stared into her eyes. He wasn't ready to tell her what she needed to hear. But he needed her to know something.

"I don't know if I can open my heart again so soon. You're the most gorgeous girl I've ever met. I'm just a country boy from Duck Creek, Virginia. Eventually, you'll figure out the same thing Ever did: I'm no good for you. And it's gonna hurt like hell. I'm just trying to avoid having my heart ripped out."

He dropped her hands and walked away from her, leaving her standing in the middle of the dance floor all alone.

Nineteen

*H*ere, Mom," Sam said.

He handed his mother a wad of cash he'd earned working at the garage in town. He handed over most of the money he earned to his mother for bills and food. He kept a small amount from each paycheck for himself, which went directly into his savings account. He'd saved up quite a bit by this point, considering he'd been working since the age of twelve.

"It's about damn time," his mother snapped. "Is this all you've got?"

"That's enough," said Sam firmly. "It will pay the electric and buy some groceries. If you need anything else, just let me know."

He headed back toward his bedroom. He only stayed here because he knew that without him she wouldn't make it. She barely kept a job, and he had to make sure she was eating right and making it to *work on time. She lived half a life, and without Sam around she would just cease to stop living at all.*

Not that she appreciated the fact that he stayed. Hunter hadn't stayed. He'd gotten a house of his own. It was only across town, but still. He'd moved out. Sam hadn't.

He stripped off his shirt on the way back to his bedroom, eager to change out of his oily work clothes.

"Wait," his mother said.

He turned around with a sigh, waiting on the berating that was surely coming.

"Why do you bother?" she asked seriously. "You know how I feel about you. Why do you give me money?"

"Because you're my mother," he answered simply. "And I love you."

Her eyes wandered down to the tattoo on his stomach. "Ugh. I hate that thing. Of course you had to become a tatted-up meathead, just like your good-for-nothing father. What does it even mean?"

And there it was. He'd gotten his tattoo last year. The Old English letters stretching across his abdomen read RISE. *It reminded him every morning of what he had to do in order to survive the day. All he had to do was rise. If he did that, he could make it through one day and move to the next.*

He headed back to his room, slamming the door behind him. As soon as it was shut, he heard the front door open, and Hunter's voice boomed through the tiny trailer. His mother's gleeful response made him grimace. She never sounded like that when she talked to Sam.

Hunter made his way back to Sam's room and threw the door open.

"Hey, little bro. She drive you to drink yet?"

"Not yet. Day's not over, though." Sam's wry response was the way they always greeted each other.

Sam's cell phone began buzzing on his bed, cheerfully singing "Home" by Phillip Phillips.

"Ever," Sam said, more to himself than to Hunter.

He picked it up. He heard her screams before he had a chance to say hello.

"Ever! Ever, sweetheart!" Sam began pulling his shirt back on and then swiftly opened his bedroom door to run back down the hallway.

"Sam! He's going to kill me!" Ever's voice was more panicked than he'd ever heard it.

She didn't usually sound like this. She was resigned to her fate. Beatings every time her father drank. And lately, he drank every single night. They'd known it was getting worse, that it would soon come to a head.

They'd tried to go to the authorities, but Ever's father was a good ole' boy, just like the sheriff. No one would help; no one would listen. In Duck Creek, a family's business should stay inside the family.

"Baby, I'm coming," Sam said. "Stay with me. Are you in your room?"

He pulled on his shoes and he went flying out the front door with Hunter right behind him. They began to sprint across the field that separated the trailer park from Ever's house.

She didn't answer. Now all he could hear was her screams.

"Ever!" he yelled. "Get it. Get it now. Use it if you have to!"

A few months ago, Sam had asked Hunter to purchase a gun for

Ever. He gave it to her because she was the only person he knew who'd have use for a pistol. It was in a box under her bed, and he'd showed her how to load it and take the safety off. They'd been doing target practice in the cornfield, making targets out of soda cans and beer bottles. She knew how to handle it.

But he knew she wouldn't want to. The last thing she'd ever want to do is use that gun.

Hunter and Sam heard the shot ring through the night when they were halfway there. They froze, and the line went dead in Sam's hand.

He sprinted the rest of the way and took the steps up to the front door two at a time.

When he burst through the entrance he found her. She wasn't crying anymore, she wasn't screaming. She was lying next to her father's dead body, which was bleeding out on the living room floor.

Sam crouched next to her and gathered her into his arms.

"Ever," he breathed into her ear. "You're safe, baby. He can't hurt you anymore."

She looked at him dully. "I killed him. He knew the sheriff, Sam. They were like brothers. I'm going to jail for this. I know I am."

"No," Sam said firmly. "You're not."

She pulled back and met his eyes. "But—"

"You're not going to jail," he repeated. "Because we're going to tell them that I shot him."

"Sam!" Hunter's voice came from the door, where he still stood staring. "No. You aren't doing this."

"Yeah, I am," he said, his eyes still locked with Ever's. "You know it's the only way to keep her safe. And she deserves that after every-

thing that bastard put her through. Should have been me who killed him anyway."

Hunter's sigh from the door echoed around the room, and Sam knew his brother would do what he asked.

He tossed his keys to Hunter. "Go get my bike. Park it by the highway, through the woods. I'll meet you there in twenty minutes."

He turned back to Ever. "We're going to do this, sweetheart. And everything is going to be okay. You tell them that you called me when your dad came banging on your door and I came over. Tell them I brought my gun. We struggled, and the gun went off. It was me. I killed him. That's your new truth, okay? Do you hear me?"

She nodded numbly. "But where will you go?"

"I'll go…somewhere far away. I haven't figured that part out just yet, Ever. I'm thinking on the fly here. But this much is certain. When things clear up here, I'll send for you, and we'll be together. Somewhere else. Not in Duck Creek. Okay?"

She nodded again and flung her arms around his neck. They sat that way for a minute, just squeezing the strength out of each other, neither wanting to let go.

"You've always protected me," she whispered into his neck. "God, Sam. Always."

"Always will," he said, and kissed her cheek. "Always will."

They slowly rose together, not looking again at the dead man on the floor. They left the house, not looking back, and headed for the woods. For Sam's getaway.

Twenty

Aston parked outside the front doors of the main house and darted out of the car. She ran for the trail past the tree line, heading straight for the tack house. When she arrived at the door, she pounded hard, beating her fists against the wood with a ferociousness that was only matched by the beating inside her chest.

Sam opened the door, rubbing his eyes against the cold light of the moon streaming into the tack house.

"Aston?"

She strode past him into the living room, whirling when she got to the countertop and staring him down. Her eyes were full of fire and angst, and Sam wasn't sure which emotion took precedence.

"What are you doing here?" he asked hoarsely.

"I can't do this with you anymore, Sam! You can't keep any guy from being with me and then walk away. You can't say those things and then leave me by myself. This isn't just about you."

"Aston—" he started, but she held up a hand.

"No. No more explaining why we can't be together. No more telling me about all the reasons we aren't a good idea."

She closed the distance between them with quick strides, until her chest was heaving against his rib cage. He stared determinedly at a spot above her head, his breath coming in shallow gasps.

"You shouldn't be here right now," he whispered, refusing her glare. "I don't want to—"

"You don't want to what, Sam?" she asked.

She reached up and grabbed hold of his stubbled chin, jerking it hard enough that he'd look at her. The pain in his eyes was heartbreaking. She swallowed and steeled herself against it.

"You don't want to talk to me? Who else are you going to talk to?" She reached down for the hem of his soft gray T-shirt and yanked it up until he relented, raising his arms over his head. His eyes now burned holes into hers.

"You don't want to touch me? Fine. I'll touch you." She ran her hands over his chest, feeling his rock-hard muscles twitch as she touched them. She grazed her fingers over the black letters etched out across his stomach. RISE. That word had new meaning for her now that she knew him. After all he'd been through, and she still didn't know the half of it, he'd risen again and again. And now she wanted him to rise to the occasion for *her*, tonight. Her thumbs found his nipples, and she rubbed slow circles around them as she stared up at his face.

Sam closed his eyes, his lips parting. His hands fisted at his sides, as if he were willing himself not to touch her.

"Don't do this," he pleaded softly. "I want you, you know I do. Don't push me, Princess. Please don't."

He groaned as she leaned in and took a swipe at his chest with her tongue. He trembled all over. "I can't."

"You can't what, Sam?" she asked, her voice softening to a sexy whisper. "Can't you see that this is right?"

She reached down for her own shirt, felt the fabric stretch as she threw it off. Her lacy bra was cut low enough that her breasts peeked over the cups as she breathed deeply, inhaling the masculine, woodsy scent that was Sam. She smiled in satisfaction as she watched his eyes find them and darken with his need. She wanted to smell that scent all over her body as his entire being melded with hers.

"*Jesus,* Aston," Sam said in the low growl that told her she was winning.

His arms went around her then. "You're so damn beautiful. I can't handle this. Why are you doing this?"

"Because I can't stay away from you anymore," she said firmly. "I don't want to."

She backed out of his arms, satisfied as they reached out in her absence. She undid the button of her jeans and slid them down over her hips, over her calves, then kicked them off completely.

"*Dammit,*" Sam growled.

He stepped toward her. "Aston, you don't know what you're starting. How am I supposed to stay strong when you're stripping for me in my living room?"

"I'm a big girl, Sam," she said. "I know exactly what I'm doing."

He took another step toward her; only one more step and he'd be upon her.

"I need you to stop me," he begged. "Just put your clothes back on. Sit on the couch and we can talk."

She stuck out her chin, shaking her head slowly. "It's not gonna happen, Waters. I'm all talked out."

She saw every good-guy line he had fly out of his brain and she dripped with anticipation.

He reached out, grabbing her tightly and encircling his arms around her waist. He pushed against her, backing her up until her skin hit wall, his body pressing tightly against hers. The skin-to-skin contact elicited a gasp from her. His lips were upon hers before she could say anything else, and she accepted them willingly. She moaned as his tongue invaded her mouth, and ran her hands over his hair.

"Aston, baby," he said against her lips. "You have no idea how bad I want you."

His hands dropped to cup her ass and he squeezed gently, groaning as he kneaded her soft flesh beneath his fingers. Lifting her, she wrapped her legs around him and squeaked as his rock-hard erection grinded against her hot center.

His lips broke free of hers only to nip at the satiny skin of her neck and kiss a trail along her collarbone. He rocked his hips gently, and the sensation of his jeans rubbing against her and his lips on her skin almost caused her to rocket into space before they'd barely begun.

She couldn't stop the sound of pleasure that escaped her; his lips on her like this, his attention so totally focused on her body...it was delight in its purest form and she couldn't even begin to control her reaction to it.

"You wanted my attention, Aston? Here it is." He tugged her hair gently to tip her head to the side, exposing her slender neck. He focused on the familiar spot where her pulse raced beneath her skin. "This spot. Right here." His tongue darted out from his mouth to lick it, and heat surged from her belly downward.

"You rub that spot when you're thinking...I've seen you do it so many times while we're working. I've wanted to put my lips on it."

"More," she gasped, reaching to unbutton his jeans and shove them to the floor.

He obliged, moving his lips back to her skin and thrusting against her again. The friction he was causing with his motion built a fire deep within her, and his low noises of approval fueled her straight toward oblivion. He continued to grind, moving faster against her until she was calling his name urgently into his hair.

"That's it, Princess," he whispered roughly. "Go ahead and come for me."

That growl of a whisper was all it took to send her over a cliff, and she fell into pieces against him, trembling and shuddering with shaky breaths.

He growled and lifted her easily in his arms. She squeezed her legs tighter around his waist and draped herself weakly around him. He walked, still tasting her, to the bedroom and kicked the door closed behind them.

"No interruptions," he murmured urgently. "I don't want anything to stop us tonight."

"Me either," she answered, dropping her head back so he had better access to her neck.

Sam dropped her down on the bed following closely behind her, not breaking the connection of his lips to her flushed and fiery skin.

He stared down as he held himself steady above her on his hands, and she took in the sight of this huge beautiful specimen of a man hovering over her. He was always so good, such a gentleman, and yet he'd just made her come while screaming his name against the wall in his living room. She shuddered.

He continued to stare, locking in on her eyes and holding her gaze with bated breath. She was afraid to let go of the air gathered in her lungs; if she did, this dream playing out in front of her eyes might vanish.

She'd never wanted someone inside her as badly as she wanted Sam inside her right now. The way he'd moved against her in the other room until she fell apart made her body sing with anticipation of having him fill her up completely.

"I dreamed about this," he whispered, holding her eyes with his own. "But the real you is so much better."

He bent his head, kissing the swell of her breast as it plumped out of the top of her bra. He held his lips still against her skin, and she breathed heavily underneath him. He seemed frozen by the sound of her violently beating heart hammering against her chest.

His *eyes*. That mad, flaming passion in his liquid-brown eyes was in reaction to *her*. It was unfathomable; it caused her own heart rate to speed up in response.

"I know how much you like to drive," he murmured against her skin. She lifted up as his arms went around her, assisting him to remove her bra, exposing her to him fully. Time stood still as she watched him, slowly, so slowly, take her nipple into his mouth. Her eyes squeezed tightly shut and the softest of moans escaped her.

It was his turn to close his eyes.

"Princess," he said softly. "If you keep making those sexy little noises, I'm gonna come all over this bed. I don't want that to happen, because I wanna come inside of you."

She gasped at his words, this bad-boy side of Sam was doing crazy things to her body and her mind.

"What," she gasped. "Were you saying about me driving?"

"Well," he said as his nose brushed against her stomach. "Do you want to take control here? Because I'm very happy to let you"—he grabbed the backs of her thighs and prepared to roll her over—"let you take the wheel."

He stared down at her, waiting for her response.

She contemplated letting him roll her over so that she could take over the moment, and normally that would be exactly what she wanted to do. But the memory of the moments before, out in the living room…she wanted him dominating her all night long.

She looked at the man she'd been waiting months for, and for the first time in her life, she *didn't* want control. She shook her head, never breaking his gaze.

"I trust you, Sam," she whispered.

His eyes softened at the corners and he pulled her body suddenly against him so her shape melded perfectly with his much larger one. He lowered his head to hers, taking her lips hostage again and kissing her with a desire she never expected to feel from him. A desire she never expected to feel from anyone, ever.

He reached between them tracing a trail along her stomach with his fingers, stopping at the edge of her panties, completely taking her breath away. Her heart stopped as his fingers stilled, and she whimpered softly in anticipation of their continued journey.

"I've wanted to touch you for so long," he whispered. "*So* long, Princess. The fact that you want me, too…it blows my mind. It makes me crazy. Just like…just like the sounds you're making right now are diving me up the *goddamned* wall."

His fingers continued their exploration, one aching millimeter at a time, skimming along the top of her panties and feeding the fire that was almost burning his fingers.

"Do you want me to take these panties off and touch you? Really touch you?"

She could only nod furiously.

He picked up the fabric and let it snap back, eliciting a gasp from her that almost rendered him speechless. He raised an eyebrow at her, and she knew that he wanted an answer.

"Yes," she moaned. "God, yes, Sam. Please touch me."

He closed his eyes briefly.

"Say that again, Princess," he said, his voice rough.

"Sam," she whispered. "Touch me. I want you to."

With a groan, he reared up so he could pull her panties down her legs and toss them aside. His fingers slid along her folds to find hot wetness. He pushed a finger inside her and she sighed with the anguishing pleasure of his touch. She'd been touched before, she'd made love before; but no experience she'd had with Princeton compared to the sensation Sam's touch gave her.

"Princess," he whispered, in a strained voice as he withdrew his finger slowly. "I wish I could do this all night, but I need to be inside you. Now."

She nodded, meeting his gaze. She knew this moment would change everything. She welcomed the change. As he lowered himself over her, a flash of anxiety met her with a paralyzing force. What if she wasn't what he was expecting? She strived for perfection in all aspects of her life. She needed it. But when he gazed down at her the expression in his warm, dark eyes was that of desire and wonder, and she accepted him without further hesitation or worry.

When he reached for the nightstand drawer, she stopped him. "We don't need them."

He raised his eyebrows in question.

"I'm on the pill. We've each only been with one other person, right? We don't need them."

She wrapped a firm hand around his dick, causing him to cry out a string of curse words that made her smile. She stopped breathing as she guided him toward her entrance, and they both groaned as he achingly slid inside her.

They began to rock together, slowly at first as they learned one another's rhythm. Sam raised a hand to her forehead to brush the hair out of her eyes, and his lips stole hers once more. This kiss was sweet, with longing, and tender. His lips told her everything his words couldn't. She'd never forget this, even if he ran after it was all over.

Even if he told her she was a mistake. She'd never recover, but she'd never forget being with him like this, either.

She wasn't sure if it was his rhythm, or the proximity of those eyes, or the smell of him mixed with the smell of her...but she was going to come again, and hard.

As the pleasure building inside of her rose, Sam moved faster over her with grunts of encouragement and she closed her eyes, holding on to his shoulders as she climbed higher on the best roller coaster she'd ever ridden. At the crest, he buried his head in her neck and she plummeted, screaming out his name and wanting to do this ride again. Over and over until she could no longer stand.

The need for coffee pulled Sam out of bed. He glanced back toward the bedroom, where one of Aston's long legs stuck out from under the sheet. He gazed at her leg a moment, the memories of last night making him smile.

Today was Saturday. He could watch her bare leg all damn day today if he wanted to. The thought put a satisfied grin on his face.

He tore his eyes away from her and grabbed two large mugs from the cabinet above the coffeemaker. He realized he had no idea how Aston took her coffee. Oh well, he'd just bring a little of everything. He poured the steaming coffee into her mug and grabbed a carton of creamer from the refrigerator. He also took hold of some sugar packets and carried the whole arrangement into the bedroom on a tray.

He sat the mug on the nightstand next to her, then kneeled beside the bed. He just watched her as she slept, the rays of sun streaming in the window landing on her face as she breathed in through her parted lips. Her dark tumble of hair splayed on the pillow under her, and her arm was slung across her bare chest.

She was the single most gratifying sight his eyes had ever taken in, and the fact that she was lying in *his* bed caused his heart to beat faster than it should. As did the thoughts from the night before.

Aston stirred, turning her head toward him. Her mouth stretched open in an adorable yawn, and Sam couldn't prevent the corners of his mouth from twitching into a smile.

"Sam, stop it," she admonished. "I don't have to look to feel you staring at me. It's embarrassing." She peeked an eye open to look at him. "For you. Not me."

He chuckled. "Good morning to you, too, Princess."

He reached out to brush the hair away from her face, and her body tensed in response. He let his fingers trail down her cheek, stopping to grab hold of her chin. He leaned in and planted a kiss on her full lips.

"Don't tense up with me this morning," he whispered. "Last night was incredible. Everything's different now. Whether we're ready or not."

Aston opened both of her eyes. "I know that, Sam. I just didn't know if it was going to be a good change for you."

He continued to stare at her, transfixed.

"I've never tackled anything, Sam, that I didn't think was going to be a success. This is no different. We can do this. I know we can."

"You've been awake for five seconds. Don't you want some caffeine before we conquer the world together?"

She finally smiled, letting the gesture brighten her entire face. "You brought me coffee?"

He reached out for her mug, handing it to her as she sat up. The sheet fell away from her body, and Sam experienced an immediate reaction in his groin. His boxer briefs did nothing to camouflage him, so he stayed kneeling. He kept his eyes trained on Aston.

"Let's go to the beach today," he said.

"You can't handle me all day in a bikini, Waters," she said.

"We'll never know if we don't try."

She nodded, keeping her eyes glued on him as she sipped her coffee.

"If I don't get up now and take a shower, I'm not going to let you leave the house today, much less put on clothes."

He rose, turning toward the bathroom. He turned back and bent, capturing her lips with his.

He kissed her deeply, toying with her lips until they were swollen, and then gathering the bottom one into his mouth to suck it lightly. His tongue tangled with hers, and then urgently, deepening the kiss as his hands went up to cup the sides of her face.

When Sam pulled back, he stared into her shocked blue eyes. "Everything *is* different. I know that, and I want it."

As he strode toward the shower, he mumbled to himself.

"Two sugars, spoonful of cream."

"What?" Aston called from the bed.

"Your coffee. I'm memorizing how you take it. Because I plan on making it for you a lot."

Sam hummed to himself in the shower, already missing Aston's body pressed against his. But they had time for that.

Today he'd come clean with everything. It was time to let go of the past, move on, and really start living again. He was going to tell Aston the truth about Duck Creek and about Ever's father. Tonight. He knew he'd have to go back, set everything straight with Ever and the sheriff. He would do that.

Whatever it took to start this life he now so desperately wanted here in N.I.

An hour later, Sam was enjoying the feel of Aston's arms around his waist and her thighs snugged against his as they rode his motorcycle to the beach. His extra helmet fit her perfectly, and the sexiness with which she donned it and a leather jacket on top of her bathing suit cover-up left him speechless. When he parked in a small lot outside a private stretch of ocean where Aston had instructed him to go, he helped her off the bike with one hand.

"Did anyone ever tell you that you're made to be a biker chick?" he asked her.

"Nope," she answered. "That's my first time on one of these things."

"You're kidding," he said. "You like to walk the line between wild and perfect. I assumed you'd been on the back of tons of bikes, or driven one yourself."

"You assumed wrong. I was with Princeton forever, remember? I wasn't jumping on the back of guys' bikes."

Sam nodded and wrapped an arm around her while they strolled onto the sand. "Good. I'm glad I was your first."

They spread out a large blanket Sam had stowed in the storage compartment of the motorcycle, and stretched out on top of it. Sam stared out at the waves crashing onto the silky golden sand.

"I'd never seen the ocean before I came here," he admitted.

"Really? That's crazy to me. I can't imagine that. I'll always want to live by the ocean. I need it like air."

"It's beautiful," answered Sam. "I understand why you want to keep it close to you."

"It's not the only thing I want to keep close to me, Sam," she said, reaching out for his hand.

He intertwined their fingers, stroking the back of her hand with his thumb. "Last night was the best night of my life."

"Yeah?"

"Yeah. I know I came here for a reason. I thought it was to lie low while I figured things out. But now I know that every road, every crazy twist and turn my life has taken in the last few months, has led me here. To you."

She smiled, meeting his eyes. "I'm glad you realized that, Waters. Because I feel the same way. We're going to be good together. Meeting you has changed things for me in a huge way. I thought my life was headed in one direction, and I was going after it with a single-mindedness that didn't leave much room for anything else. I never pictured my future together with Princeton, not really. I just assumed we'd be together forever. When you walked into my life, as hard as I fought it at first, I knew I couldn't stay with him. That forever in my mind had changed. Now I can't wait to share my future with you. We're going to do such amazing things together. Even my dad agrees."

Sam laughed. "He's saved my life. I still don't understand why he puts so much faith in me. Dating his daughter might be a different story, though. I have no idea how he's going to feel about us."

"I already know how he feels. He didn't come right out and say it, but he likes the idea of us together. I got the distinct impression that he saw it coming before we did."

Sam nodded thoughtfully. "Maybe you're right."

He leaned across the blanket and kissed her, capturing her lips completely with his.

"I have some things to tell you about," he said when he pulled back.

"You can tell me anything," she promised. "After I enjoy my day at the beach with you. Let's go cool off!"

Shoving him aside, she took off for the waves, giggling. "Ready, set, go!"

He caught up with her quickly, gathering her into his arms and continuing to run for the water. She squealed, twisting in his grasp.

"Stop squirming around," he said. "Or I might drop you before we get to the ocean."

"Waters!" she screamed. "Stop!"

He threw her unceremoniously into the rollicking waves, diving in after her as the cool water cut off her screeches.

They both rose from the froth with a breathless gasp.

"You monster!" Aston cried, smoothing her dark hair back from her face.

"You liked it," he said, playfully splashing her as he slid toward her.

His hands found her hips under the water, and he pulled her toward him. She reached for him, running her hands over his hair and settling her arms around his neck.

"I like a lot of things," she whispered.

Their lips met, and it was salty and sweet and a little electric all at the same time.

She pulled back, a mischievous smile tugging at her lips. "If you've never been to the beach before you came here, then you probably haven't..." she trailed off.

His eyebrows shot up at her insinuation. "No, I haven't."

She let her arms fall from around his neck and found the elastic to his board shorts underneath the water. He tensed as she tugged.

"You're so bad," he murmured, nibbling at her earlobe with his teeth.

"Am I?" she asked, the picture of innocence. "Do you want me to stop?"

She took his very willing erection into her hands.

"No," he choked out. "Don't stop. I love it when you're bad."

"Good," she said. She guided him slowly toward her, wrapping her legs around his waist. "This is going to be fun."

He grunted when she pushed herself onto him and began to take him for a ride. He let his head fall back.

"Holy hell," he muttered. "You're gonna kill me."

Twenty-One

It was dark when Sam's Harley roared into the long drive at the Hopewell ranch. He killed the engine when he saw Reed standing by the side of the road, waving his arms frantically.

"What is it?" Sam yelled, jumping off the bike. "Are you okay? Is someone hurt?"

"No," Reed said breathlessly. "Fuck, Sam. You weren't answering your phone. Dad is keeping them busy up there, but—"

"What are you talking about? I left my phone at the tack house. Keeping who busy?"

Aston pulled off her helmet, grabbing her brother's shoulders. "Reed! Is Daddy okay?"

Reed shook his head, trying to catch his breath. "He's fine. You guys don't understand."

He cut his eyes back to Sam. "The sheriff's department is here. Dad had to let them go through your stuff at the tack house. It's about something that happened back in Virginia."

Reed's eyes were huge. Sam could tell he was scared, so he stood up straighter and grabbed Reed's shoulders.

"Reed," he said firmly. "It's going to be okay. It's just a misunderstanding. I can explain it."

"Explain what, Sam?" Aston asked.

Before he could speak, they heard the gravel crunching in front of them. Sam looked up, and the sheriff he saw at the house two months ago now marched toward him with several armed deputies.

Their guns were drawn, and pointed at Sam.

"Freeze!" the man in front shouted. "Don't move. Put your hands in the air, and back slowly away from Miss Hopewell."

"Luke!" Aston screamed, stepping forward. "What the hell are you doing? Why are you here for Sam?"

The sheriff glanced at her. "Step back, Aston. Now. This man is wanted in Virginia."

"Wanted?" Aston gaped at Sam, her mouth dropping open. "If he's wanted, then there must be some sort of mistake."

Gregory Hopewell came jogging up, pushing past the sheriff stopping adjacent to Sam, Reed, and Aston.

"Look, Luke," he told the sheriff. "We've known each other for years. You need to take my word on this. Sam is a good kid. He works for me. Put the guns away, and let's go inside and talk."

"Can't do that, Greg," Luke answered, never taking his eyes off Sam. "Someone called in a tip to check him out, and we found an APB on Sam Waters. We're told this man is very dangerous. I have to follow orders and bring him in to be transferred."

Sam placed his hands on Aston's shoulders and moved her behind him.

"Okay," he said, putting his hands up. "I'm doing this. I'll go with you."

One of the deputies rushed forward and grabbed Sam's wrists, pinning them behind his back with some force. Sam winced.

"Stop!" Aston screamed. Tears streamed down her face, and her hair whipped wildly around her head. One shoulder of her cover-up drooped, exposing the skin there. "He didn't do anything!"

Gregory placed his hands on Aston's shoulders and shot a grim look at Sam. "I know you want to clear this up, Sam. But don't say anything. We will get a lawyer down to you right away, and this will all get cleared up."

"What'd he even do?" Reed shouted.

"Sam Waters," Luke began. "You are under arrest for the murder of Graham Allen."

Aston collapsed against her father. "No, no, no! What? Sam?"

She buried her face in her father's collar while he murmured in her ear. Reed just stared at Sam, shaking his head.

"You have the right to remain silent," Luke continued.

"Shut up," Sam told him. "Aston. Princess, listen to me! I told you, this is a misunderstanding. Remember when I told you earlier there was something I wanted to talk to you about? This is it!"

"That's convenient," one of the deputies muttered.

"Look at me, baby," Sam pleaded. Aston's eyes, red-rimmed

and bloodshot, met his. "You are my future. I promise you, I will clear this up. And then we will be together. Just hold on for me, Aston. I want you. Hold on for me."

The deputy who handcuffed Sam began dragging him toward the car. Sam bent his knees, trying to release the deputies hold on him so that he could turn around and look back at Aston.

"Sam!" Gregory shouted. "Go with them. Just go. I know you're innocent. A lawyer is on the way. Go, son."

"Make her listen!" Sam shouted as the deputy shoved his head down and into the cruiser.

He watched Aston sob into her father's shirt while the sheriff's cruiser drove away. His heart clenched so hard he thought it was going to arrest, ceasing to beat. None of this mattered; the truth didn't matter—not if he lost Aston. He wanted a life with this woman. A forever. He had it all right there in his grasp. And then his stupid sacrifice had to catch up to him before he could make it right.

"He murdered somebody, Daddy," Aston said again. Settled on the couch in the great room with a blanket and a mug of tea her mother had brought her, she stared off into the stone wall. "He *murdered* someone."

"Aston, stop saying that," Reed snapped.

"Aston." Gregory cut in. "What did you do with Sam today?"

"Why?" Her voice was as dull and glum as she felt.

"Just humor me."

"We went to the beach," said Aston.

"And I know I'm your father, but humor me here as well. I noticed you weren't in your room this morning. Did you spend all last night with Sam?"

"Daddy!" Aston wailed.

"Gross," Reed ventured.

"Aston?" Gregory waited.

"Fine. Yes, Sam and I had an epiphany last night. Not that it matters now."

"It matters, Aston. That's my point here. I know this man. So do you. You probably better than me. He didn't murder anybody."

"But Luke said—"

"He didn't murder anyone, Aston. Search your heart here. When you find the right answer, you can join me at the station."

Gregory left his spot leaning against the wall and strode for the door.

"Call Marshall Cane," he called over his shoulder to Lillian. "Sam needs a lawyer, *now*."

"I'll call him," Lillian answered, following him out of the room.

Reed glanced over at Aston, who was now staring at the doorway through which her parents had just passed.

"He's right, you know," Reed said, his voice quiet.

"I know," Aston whispered. "It's just…crazy and complicated now. Maybe Sam and I aren't right for each other. I mean, of course he's not a murderer. But there's obviously something huge he neglected to tell me here. Right? I can't think of a single thing I've kept from him. And he's kept a gaping secret from me. Does that sound like a recipe for a happy future?"

"Aston." Reed sighed. "You hold everyone to an insane high

standard sometimes. No one can live up to it. You are not perfect. Sam is not perfect. Together? You are perfect. So put your anger aside and just remember that. He needs you right now."

"Reed! I needed him to be honest with me. Do you know what this is about?"

"No," Reed answered. "But I'm sure as hell going to show my support for him, and give him a chance to tell me."

"You're going to the station?"

"Damn straight. Do you want to come with me?"

Aston thought about Sam's face when he was being dragged to the sheriff's vehicle. She was all he was worried about. He could be about to lose his freedom, and he was worried about whether or not she was okay. She owed it to him to be there for him. Maybe he didn't tell her the truth right away. But he'd planned to. They had been through a lot in the short time they'd known each other, and she hadn't always been open to hearing him out. And he had experienced a complete heartbreak with Ever.

Of course she was going to be there for Sam now. He needed her.

"Yeah," she answered. "I do. Let me shower and change first. Then we'll go."

When they arrived at the station an hour later, Gregory greeted them.

"Glad you made the right decision," he whispered in her ear. "I wouldn't have fought for him if I didn't believe in him."

"Me, too," Aston said. "Where is he? Is he okay?"

"Greg." Luke appeared behind a tall counter. The sheriff's department was brightly lit, with clinical white walls and a gray cement floor. Aston pulled her hoodie tightly around her, shivering with the coldness of the place.

"We're getting him on the road," Luke said.

"What the hell, Luke?" Gregory shouted. "Why are you rushing this? He barely got to talk to Marshall!"

Luke shook his head. "Because there's a murderer in my county, Greg. And I want him out."

Aston's stomach dropped, and nausea rocked through her body. "You're sending him back to Virginia? Tonight? I thought that wouldn't happen until tomorrow at least."

Luke shook his head, refusing to meet her eye.

Marshall Cane strode out from the back of the building, coming up behind Luke at the counter and then opening a countertop to enter the waiting area. His short white curly hair was in perfect condition, his gray suit impeccable. Even at ten o'clock at night.

"They're loading him up," he announced. "He'll be back in Virginia by morning. I can represent him, Greg. It will be an open-and-shut case, if what he's told me is true. It was a bad situation, but I can definitely help him."

Gregory Hopewell sat down with a large exhalation, the relief evident on his face.

"Can we see him?" he asked Luke.

Luke shook his head. "It's too late."

Aston stood, yanking Reed's arm with her as she went. "Come on, Reed."

"Where we going?"

"We're going to Virginia. Tonight."

Twenty-Two

WELCOME TO DUCK CREEK, VIRGINIA. WHERE EVEN THE DUCKS WELCOME YOU HOME. The worn wooden sign hung askew on its pole, rattling in the dry wind that brushed against the green landscape. Aston watched the tall yellow wildflowers ruffle in the breeze, stretching out for miles in each direction off the two-lane highway. She could see the mountains in the distance, rising starkly against a cornflower blue sky.

"It's beautiful here, in a lonely kind of way," she murmured to Reed as she drove along the highway.

"Whatever," Reed answered wearily. "If you like middle-of-nowhere, shoot-me-in-the-fucking-head kind of beauty."

"We had to come," Aston answered. "At least I did. And I needed help driving."

"No, I'm with you, A," Reed replied. "I want to be here for Sam, too. He's already like a brother to me."

Aston smiled at him. "I know. He's probably a better big brother than I am a big sister."

"I wouldn't say that," Reed answered, squeezing her hand across the console. "It was just nice having another guy around. Sam's a good listener. He just is who he is—none of the pretentious bullshit you usually find in N.I."

"Do you think he hates me?" Aston asked quietly. "He left thinking I didn't forgive him. I didn't give him any indication that I believed him."

She'd thought about that the entire nine hours it had taken them to arrive in Virginia. It was tearing apart her insides to think that Sam had left thinking she might never speak to him again. He would be in agony, worrying about her and their ruined future. The thought of Sam in pain caused ripples of distress in her chest.

"I think he loves you," Reed said simply. "And he's going to be happy to see you."

"I hope so," Aston said.

As they entered the town limits, Aston looked to the right and saw fields dotted with small clapboard or brick houses and trailers. She looked to the left and saw sporadic businesses spread out between narrow streets and wide-open spaces. She tried to picture *her* Sam growing up here, running across these fields with Ever and his brother, and couldn't. Sam was so much bigger, so much *more* than this place.

The GPS led her winding down the deserted streets of Duck Creek until she reached a squat brick building with a sign on the faded front lawn. The sheriff's office where Sam was being held.

She and Reed walked into the front door, and the deputy sitting behind the desk looked no older than Aston. He rose when he saw them, wide eyes roving over them as they approached the counter.

"Can I help you?" he asked, his gaze only meeting Aston's. He made no excuses for raking his eyes up and down her body slowly, appreciating the view.

"Yeah, Casanova," Reed snapped. "Eyes over here. We're here to see Sam Waters."

The deputy's eyes grew even wider, and he frowned. "Sam? What do you two want to see him for?"

"Look, you—" Reed was sleep deprived, and that wasn't going to bode well for the deputy.

Aston stepped forward, cutting Reed off. She smiled at the deputy sweetly, and his eyes riveted to hers, glazing over a bit. "He's a friend of ours. He's been living with us in South Carolina for the past few months, and we'd really like to see him. Do you think you could arrange that?"

"No, he can't." A tall, sturdy man in a cowboy hat came down the hallway behind the desk. The deputy looked abashed, glancing from Aston to the man who was clearly the sheriff, and back again.

"Why not?" Aston asked.

"Because it ain't visiting hours, that's why," he answered shortly.

"But we've come all the way from South Carolina," she said sweetly. "Can't you just—"

"No," he cut her off with a swipe of his hand. "I don't know who you are, young lady, but none of your sweet talking is gonna fly around here." He gave the deputy a pointed look. "I don't know why you're here or how you know Sam, but I'll tell you this much. He's in a whole heap of trouble. You look like you don't need to be mixed up in that. So just get going."

Aston set her chin in the way she did when someone told her she wasn't going to do something.

"You know what?" she said with venom in her voice. "I'm going to just give his lawyer a call. And then we'll see how long he's going to be sitting in your cell."

"No need," the sheriff said wearily. "His lawyer's already back there with him."

"He is?" Reed asked. "We'll just wait, then. If you don't mind."

"I don't mind," the sheriff said gruffly. "I'm going out on a call, Brandon. Keep everything on the straight and narrow around here."

Brandon nodded. "Yes, sir."

Aston and Reed settled down on one of the hard plastic chairs to wait for Marshall. When he finally emerged, his face was tired. He must have driven all night, too.

"Aston, Reed." He greeted them with a small smile.

"Is Sam getting out now?" she asked him, not beating around the bush.

"Eventually," he said. "The sheriff wants to play hardball. He knows damn well Sam is innocent. He wants to speak to Sam's ex-girlfriend again and see if their stories match. She'll be here in a little while."

Aston closed her eyes briefly. "I need to see him, Marshall."

Marshall turned to Brandon. "Any consequences for this, your sheriff can take them up with me. My client has been treated unfairly. He's going to have a visitor. And his lawyer will be present."

Something about Marshall's tone told Brandon not to argue, gun and badge be damned. He sighed.

"Come with me." He reached out to click a button that unlocked a door leading to the back of the facility.

"I'm Brandon," he informed Aston as they walked down a long hallway with gray cinder block walls. "I actually graduated from high school with Sam. And Ever. You know his girlfriend, Ever?"

He cut a sideways glance at Aston, obviously trying to figure out her relationship with Sam.

"She's not his girlfriend anymore," Aston said. "I'm sure you know that, though."

He stared at her as they walked. "How'd Sam land a girl like you comin' all the way up here from Carolina to look for him? Don't you know he killed someone?"

Their pace was slowing, and Aston sighed in relief. "Are we almost there?"

Brandon gestured forward, and Aston took another step to see a cell, complete with iron bars, located to her right. Sam sat on the low wooden bench inside, his head caught in his hands.

"Sam." She breathed.

"I'll just wait back up front," said Marshall.

Sam's head jerked up, and his soft brown eyes connected with hers. He bolted to his feet, and the sheer size of him overwhelmed Aston. Her eyes filled with tears.

"Princess," he said, rushing to the bars. "Brandon, let her in."

Brandon folded his arms. "I'm not supposed to, Sam. The sheriff wouldn't like it."

"The sheriff's your fucking uncle," Sam growled. "Let her in. Now."

Brandon scowled but held his ground, placing his hand on the holster at his hip and staring at Sam.

"Okay, Brandon," said Sam. "Let her in, or I'll tell Shannon Burke about the fact I saw you making out with Rita Henry in the parking lot when they brought me in."

Brandon's eyes went wide, and he shook his head. He reached for a keypad on the wall next to the bars. He typed in a code, and the door unlocked with a *click*.

Sam wrenched the door open and pulled Aston into his arms. His lips were pressed with relentless force against hers before she could take a breath, and she sank into the kiss with every fiber of her being. One of Sam's hands gripped her nape while his other pulled her hips firmly forward, and her hands roved his broad, hard back, feeling the tautness of his muscles beneath his soft T-shirt.

Brandon cleared his throat behind them. "Looks like you're doin' just fine without Ever, huh, Sam?"

Sam released Aston's mouth but kept a hold of her waist as he stared down into her eyes. "Get the hell out, Brandon. I'm not going anywhere."

Aston heard Brandon's hefty sigh behind her, and his footsteps echoed back down the hallway she had entered with him. But she couldn't peel her eyes away from Sam's to watch his exit.

"You came? You're here?" Sam's hands brushed at her eyes,

catching a tear as it blazed a trail down her cheek. "I can't believe you're here."

She leaned her forehead against his. "Of course I'm here, Sam. I love you. Where else would I be?"

He pulled back, the emotion, already laid out like a map in his eyes, intensifying. "You love me?"

She nodded furiously.

"Oh, my God," he whispered. "I swear I can get through anything, as long as you tell me that again."

"I love you, Sam."

"I didn't kill him."

"I know," she assured him. "I always knew that, Sam. I was just caught by surprise. I shouldn't have let you leave thinking…"

He pulled her to the bench and sat down, guiding her onto his lap. "I thought you hated me. I wasn't even sure if I'd be able to get you to speak to me again after I got out of here."

"Are you getting out?" she asked with lifted brows.

Sam nodded. "Eventually. This is all a misunderstanding that can be cleared up."

"Tell me."

Sam inhaled a deep breath, letting it out slowly as he leaned his head back against the wall. His hands continued to draw slow circles on her back, her arms, her hips.

Then he began to explain.

He told her about Ever's father, and how he'd watched all the horrible things her father had done to her over the years. He told her how he and Hunter got a gun, and he made Ever stash it under her bed.

When he told her about the night Ever's father was finally going to kill her, both of Aston's hands flew to her mouth, and she kept them there, staring at him in horror. But she stayed quiet, listening.

Nausea rolled through her stomach and her chest constricted painfully.

"She pulled the trigger, and just like that, he was gone." Sam's voice was weary, but his gaze was now burning into hers, as if begging her to understand.

Aston took a deep, rattling breath. "Okay, so she killed him. But she had to. Why didn't you guys just tell the police?"

"I wasn't thinking straight. None of us were. I just wanted to protect her from having to go through any more shit because of that asshole. So I told her to tell the cops I shot him. It was easy to believe. Everyone knew what the son of a bitch was like; they'd believe I'd killed him because I couldn't take him beating up on Ever anymore. Hunter didn't like it, but he went along with it and got my bike to a getaway spot through the woods so I could take off."

They sat quietly, Aston leaning her head against Sam's shoulder. She could picture that horrible night, the jumbled mess his mind must have been. Ever must have been in shock, and Hunter was just trying to make it better for both of them. They were scared. She understood. But Sam wasn't a killer, and he shouldn't be sitting in this cell.

"Will Ever and Hunter back you up? Now that...that things have changed between the three of you?"

"They'll be here later today. Marshall called them last night from N.I., explained to them that I was being shipped back home and we all had to come clean or I'd go to prison. They'll back me up."

Aston breathed a sigh of relief. "Thank God."

"Aston," Sam said softly, tilting her chin up with one finger so he could look into her face.

"Yeah?"

"I'm sorry. I'm sorry I put you through this. I should have told you a long time ago. This thing with Ever and Hunter made me crazy, and I couldn't think straight. I think deep down, I always knew I could trust you, but I didn't trust my heart to make good decisions anymore."

She leaned in, brushing her lips against the corner of his mouth. "I know, Sam. But it's over now, and when you get out of here I'm bringing you home with me. And not letting you go again."

"What about Hopewell Enterprises?"

"What about it?" She wrinkled her nose in curiosity.

"Well, I know how you feel about your dad wanting me to be a part of it. Are you going to be okay with everything?"

"That was before I got to know you. Now I know how perfect you could be for the company. And if we're running the company together one day, what the hell do I have to complain about? Right?"

"Promise you're okay with everything?" he asked, dropping a kiss on the soft skin beneath her ear.

"I promise," she answered, shivering.

"God, I love you, Princess."

"You'd better, Waters. I just drove nine hours stuck in a truck with Reed to get to your ass."

His hundred-watt smile was back, and nothing had ever looked so good.

Twenty-Three

Sam placed his hands on either side of Reed's truck. He leaned forward, pressing his mouth to hers.

She pulled back, placing a finger against his lips, and shot him a coy smile.

"So you think you're just gonna come back here, take me to Sunny's, and all will be forgiven?"

Sam had spent one day and one night sitting in the cell in Duck Creek before Marshall was able to straighten the whole mess out. Without a high-powered lawyer like Marshall, it would have taken a lot longer for the red tape to clear. But the bottom line was that Sam had done nothing wrong, and he was released.

Sam had no desire to see either Ever or Hunter, but Marshall had let him know that Ever would likely have to face a judge for her part in her father's death. But it would be a clear-cut case of self-defense.

He pulled back only an inch, far enough away to gaze into her eyes.

"Yep. That's exactly my plan. Is it a problem, Princess?"

"Nope," she answered as her mouth crashed into his.

He kissed her like he hadn't seen her in months, like she was the last glass of water for a man trapped in the desert, like the world would be ending in an hour and she was all he had left.

Her lips were tender and the only thing he ever wanted in a kiss ever again.

She was his; he was finally staking claim on the girl he knew was meant for him, and he couldn't be more satisfied with his decision.

When he pulled back this time, he stepped away from her and lowered his arms, taking her hands in his instead, so as not to break contact completely.

He let go of one hand and began ticking off a list on his fingers.

"She…is a business whiz. She manhandles her drunk *ex*-boyfriend. She changes her own tires…in heels. She yanks wild horses around for fun. She's my personal shopper."

He let go of her other hand and began ticking those fingers as well, continuing.

"You're the girl I want on the back of my Harley…You're the girl who shows me the best spot on N.I. You're the girl who holds my soul in your hands. You're *the girl*…my forever girl."

He grasped both of her hands again, tugging until her body was flush against his and he was staring down into her unfathomable eyes.

"I could get used to that," she said breathlessly.

"Good. Do that," he said, his voice husky.

He pulled her to the doors and flung them open, ready to walk in and see their friends again, this time with Aston tucked under his arm, where she belonged.

The first person they saw was Princeton. He was standing at the bar ordering his drink from Kelly, and when they entered his eyes locked on Aston's.

He slowly appraised her body, head to foot, and grinned. Then his gaze slid to Sam, and his lips became a snarl.

"So," he said, sauntering over to where they stood.

Sam's hand left Aston's only to wrap protectively around her waist.

Princeton noticed, and the snarl on his face changed again, into an angry sneer.

"You're with the convict now?" he asked Aston, raising his voice.

"Prince!" Her voice held a note of icy warning. "Don't start."

"Oh, I'm fucking starting," he shot back. "I'm definitely starting, A. This isn't you. I don't know what he did to you, but this isn't you. You're not a slut."

Her face snapped to the side as if she'd been slapped.

Sam reacted, stepping in front of her and getting into Princeton's personal space.

"Say something like that to her again," he growled. "And you're gonna have to be carried out of here."

Princeton had to look up to Sam at that distance, and he backed up a step.

"Whatever," he said, shrugging his shoulders. "I'm just saying, A. If you wanted a convict, you could have found one native to N.I. You didn't have to bring this one back from VA."

Aston's eyes narrowed, and she stepped out from behind Sam.

Reed appeared then, walking up from the deck outside. He stood silently off to the side, watching, in case he needed to step in. Blaze, Finn, and Tate soon joined him. They all looked on warily, their eyes moving from Sam to Princeton to Aston.

"How do you know about Virginia, Princeton? We haven't even had time to fill everyone in on what happened. We just got back yesterday."

Princeton shrugged again, but a look of concern crossed his features. "Rumor mill. Small town."

"You're lying," Reed said. "You've always been a bad liar, Prince."

Princeton turned around angrily to face Reed. "Shut the fuck up, Hopewell."

"Easy, Prince," Blaze warned. "You're on the wrong side of right here, man."

"Oh, really?" Princeton spat. "So you're all on *his* side, now? He's a newbie. A summer flea that's gonna be gone next month. You really want to throw away years of friendship for him?"

"Did you turn him in, Princeton?" Aston asked quietly. Her voice was laced with rage. "Did you?"

Princeton faced her, his face scarlet with his fury.

"You know what?" he said. "Yeah. Yeah, I did. Because I found out what he really was, a *murderer,* and I couldn't stand by while he stole you out from under me, Aston. He's fucking trailer trash under your feet. You don't end up with him."

Aston's eyes flashed their old, cool blue. She hadn't been this angry since she'd met Sam, but now she was on the warpath. And she was superb on the warpath.

"Princeton Alexander, you listen to me," she hissed. "Sam is mine, and I'm his. There's not a damn thing you can do to change that, you *asshole*. Even if Sam wasn't in the picture, I'd never go back to you."

Sam tightened his arm around her waist, almost as if to hold her back. But his heart thumped with the pride of being able to call her his. And his hard-on throbbed with the promise of what was to come, when her fiery temper cooled.

"And you know what else?" she went on. Princeton was staring at her, his jaw clenched.

"It didn't even matter," she said smugly. "Sam was innocent. So now he's here, and he's working at Hopewell Enterprises, and he's *staying*. He's enrolling at U of C this month. So you can chalk your tattling up to a wasted effort."

Blaze put his hands together and started to clap. Reed, grinning, joined him. It didn't take long for Finn and Tate to join in the applause, and soon the entire bar area was clapping for Aston's tirade. She grinned in satisfaction, breathing heavily and leaning into Sam's side. Princeton looked around him with disgust. "You've all lost your fucking minds. I'm out."

He walked past them all and exited the bar, slamming the wooden door behind him so hard the glass behind the bar rattled.

Aston turned and took a bow, and the applause grew thunderous.

She grinned at Sam. "Shall we?"

"We definitely shall," he answered.

He picked her up and tossed her over his shoulder, carrying her squealing to their table outside.

Their group sat around the table, and Sam explained what had happened in Virginia, and why he was taken away in handcuffs in the first place.

"Holy shit," Tamara said, her eyes wide. "So you actually were a wanted man."

The awe in her eyes sent a smile to Sam's face, and he answered her quietly.

"Yeah, I was."

Blaze let out a whistle. "That's heavy, dude. I'm glad everything is cleared up now. So you're starting a new life here in N.I. That's awesome. We're really glad to have you, man."

Sam nodded. "I'm glad to be here. And it's N.I. *and* Charleston. I go to the University of Charleston now, remember?"

Reed clapped Sam on the back. "I always knew you had it in you, Sam. Damn motherfucking right."

Sam shot Reed a grin. "So. I see that stage up there is empty tonight. No live band?"

"Nah," he answered, shrugging. "Kelly said that Friday Night Rhapsody had to cancel. Food poisoning or something. So she's just playing some tracks over the speakers tonight."

"Oh, that's a shame," Sam said, looking pointedly at Reed. "Considering we have a perfectly good guitarist and songwriter right here in our midst."

Tate, who was closest to Reed out of the bunch, began to smile slowly. He'd caught on to what Sam was doing, and he liked it.

"Yeah," he answered, elbowing Reed. "Just do it, man. Enough is enough."

Reed stared at them. "Y'all have lost your fucking minds. I'm not going up there."

Aston cocked her head to the side. "What—?"

Sam squeezed her thigh. "Just wait, Princess."

She clamped her mouth shut, darting suspicious glances between her brother and Sam.

Sam leaned close to Reed. "Come on, Reed. It's now or never. Show us what you got."

Reed looked doubtful, but that was his breaking point. Tate saw it and ran up to whisper across the bar to Kelly. She grinned and nodded. Tate looked back and gave them a thumbs-up.

Ten minutes later, Reed was climbing onto the stage with his black guitar, which he kept in his truck.

"We have something special for you tonight, folks," Kelly said into the mic as Reed pulled up a stool. "The sweet, smooth stylings of Reed Hopewell, our one and only."

She stepped away from the mic and rubbed Reed on the shoulder before leaving the stage.

Reed leaned forward on his stool and cleared his throat into the microphone. "Uh. Hey. It's strange for me, being up here, but yeah. I'm gonna play you something that you know real well first, and we'll go from there."

He began to strum, and the strains of Jason Mraz's "I Won't Give Up" drifted through the crowd. Everyone watched, transfixed, as Reed began to sing, leaving his heart on the stage with him.

Aston leaned into Sam, never taking her eyes from the stage where her brother sat pouring out his soul.

Reed had the entire bar in the palm of his hand, and when he finished the song the floor shook with the standing ovation he received. Everyone knew him, and they hooted and hollered their approval of his secret talent.

Reed smiled, his grin sparkling under the spotlight. And he leaned into the microphone again.

"Yeah? You liked that? Thanks. Now I'd like to play you something of my own."

And he did, and everyone went wild again. Reed Hopewell was a hit, and he continued to light up the place for the rest of the night.

Twenty-Four

Sam backed Aston up until her back was pressed against the wooden wall of Sunny's exterior.

"I've been sitting next to you…" he began, murmuring against her neck. He pressed his lips to her skin, gripping her hips tightly with both hands.

Aston strained to get ahold of herself. She was attempting to remain calm and in control of her body and her emotions.

"For nine hours in Reed's truck," he continued in the growly voice that made her immediately want to rake her nails down his back. "Then all night at this damn bar. I can't just sit next to you anymore."

"Oh?" The word escaped in a strangled gasp, not at all the picture of control she was trying to be. "What'd you have in mind, Waters?"

His lips traveled from her neck down to her exposed collarbone, where he began to suck. Then he dragged a small circle on her skin with his tongue, his teeth scraping lightly against her. She clutched at his soft T-shirt and dropped her head back against the wall. His hands slid up the front of her shirt, cupping her breasts and squeezing, and she uttered a breathy moan at the shock and pleasure.

"Sam," she said in a strained voice. "We're outside the bar. You want to go home? Because we rode here in Reed's truck, too."

She reached into the waistband of his jeans and gripped his hardness in a firm fist, relishing the groan she received in response.

He trembled beneath her exploring fingers. His mouth froze on her neck. He lifted his eyes to peer at her and then he closed them briefly. "*Shit,* Princess."

Suddenly, he lifted her, holding her under her thighs and pulling her flush against him. She squirmed, and white-hot need shot straight to his already throbbing, very swollen dick.

"I can't wait," he whispered into her ear. And it was her turn to shiver. He carried her into the bar and held out his hand to Reed, who was done with his performance and basking in the glow of it at the table with their friends.

"I need your keys," Sam demanded, holding out his hand.

Reed eyed them both; Sam gripping Aston tightly with one hand to hide his current state of horniness and Aston giggling, her head buried in his shoulder.

Reed sighed. "Keep it clean in my fucking truck."

Sam snatched the keys tossed by Reed out of the air and carried Aston back out into the night, climbing right up into the Silverado with her straddling his lap, and slamming the door.

"We aren't going to make it home," he warned her as he

gunned the rowdy engine. "I waited too long as it is to be with you, and I missed you like hell when I was in that jail cell."

She smiled at him. "It's really, really dark over there on that side of the parking lot."

He glanced that way, and shook his head.

"Uh-uh. I'm not doing this in the dark corner of a bar parking lot. Never with you."

He put the truck in drive and pulled out of the lot, riding a few torturous miles down the highway. Then he pulled over and drove off the road through a sea of tall grass growing out of the sandy soil. When he pulled to a stop, they were completely alone under a dark blue blanket of sky and stars and miles of quiet South Carolina calm.

"This is more private," he mused, glancing at her still in his lap.

His deep tawny eyes were wide and completely open to her; she could read every emotion written there, and in addition to the desire in his eyes he was looking at her with rugged, raw, rough-around-the edges love. She sighed happily, and he exited the truck with her heaped in his arms.

She placed her hands on his broad shoulders as she slid down his long body. He stood in front of her, his hands braced on either side of the vehicle and leaned down until their noses were nuzzling.

"I'm so sorry I waited this long to tell you how I felt about you," he whispered.

His eyes fluttered closed. "This summer with you, especially after what happened with my brother and Ever, has been more than I ever expected to earn in this life. And making love to you the other night was the single most amazing experience of my life. I want to be wrapped up in you like that again and again, Aston. Only you."

She stared at his lips as he spoke, wondering how long it would take until they claimed hers again. She reached up and framed his face with her hands. He opened his eyes, and they bore into hers.

"I would have waited for you as long as it took," she answered simply. "Because you're worth it. You saw what I needed before anyone else did. You saw right through the wall I put up for everyone. So for me, it's also only you."

His lips met hers, soft and gentle. He lifted her against him as he kissed her tenderly, carrying her around the truck and setting her down on the edge of the tailgate.

He stood between her thighs and leaned into her, his kiss becoming more urgent as he tangled one hand in her long hair. She pulled away from him and climbed into the bed of the Silverado, reaching into the metal box by the window and pulling out a thick afghan. She spread it out and sat down, crooking her finger to beckon Sam toward her.

Watching her bend over in those skintight jeans to spread out a blanket in the back of a truck bed...he nearly stopped breathing altogether. At her request, he climbed in and crawled to where she sat. Her fingers hitched up his shirt, and he raised his arms so she could pull it off him. His lips were immediately on hers again, and his hands explored all the glorious softness that her skin always offered. Making quick work of those skinny jeans and tight top, he grabbed hold of her under the knees and behind her back and deftly flipped their positions.

"This is new," she said, a wry smile tugging her lips.

He cupped her round little ass with his hands and squeezed. "I like to keep things interesting."

She leaned down to kiss him, but the cleavage brushing his face was far too tempting, and he caught hold of her front clasp, letting the skimpy fabric of her bra fall away from her breasts. He pulled her toward him and caught a taut nipple between his teeth.

She hissed, raking her nails down his bare chest as he sucked, leaving her tingling and aching in the very best way.

"I'm going to be honest with you," he said as she pushed her hips against his hard-on. His hips bucked up to meet her. He stared at his hands covering her breasts in amazement, then raised his eyes to hers.

"There's never been anything so sexy as the sight of you ready to rock my world in the back of this goddamn truck."

She threw back her head and laughed. "Don't get used to it, Waters. I'm a lady."

"You are," he agreed. "A lady about to ride me in the back of a truck."

His lips smothered her giggle as he pulled her head toward him and devoured her mouth with his once again. His hands ran down her bare sides, and she trembled under his gentle fingers. He reacted to her shiver, grinding his hips up against hers, and she closed her eyes in euphoria.

She reached down to pull off his jeans and boxer briefs; she worked with a haste that let him know she wanted to feel him without any more barriers between them.

"Sam," she whispered.

He gazed up at her, using his strong hands to still her hips above him.

"Yes, Princess?"

"Put it in."

He grinned at the sexiest statement he'd ever hear. "Seriously? My, you're bossy tonight."

She grabbed his length and squeezed. "Are you really gonna argue?" Her eyes glittered dangerously.

He moved, guiding himself to her entrance so that she could press down onto him. The quickness with which she moved surprised them both; they cried out at the sensation caused by the unexpected friction.

"You're incredible," he said. "So hot, so wet. So…mine."

"So yours," she agreed. "I'm all yours, Sam."

She ran her hands over the tattoo stretching across the defined abdominal muscles of his stomach.

"Rise," she whispered. "Have I told you that I love this tattoo?"

He smiled up at her. "No. Do you? Have I told you why I got it?"

She shook her head. He shifted the position of his hips and she moaned as she took friction in the sweetest of spots. His pupils dilated and he pulled her down until their bodies were pressed tightly together.

"I'll tell you later," he said. His voice was so rough and sexy it sent tremors through her.

She nodded, and then gasped as he rocked his hips against hers.

His eyes burned directly into hers while she moved against him and she didn't break the contact. Making love to him while staring into his eyes was an experience she wouldn't trade for anything in the entire world. It just reminded her that she belonged to this man. She'd never belonged to anyone, not really, and being in Sam's arms in this completely intimate way was right.

He used his hips and his hands to help her climb, creating delicious friction just where she needed it; and as she reached the brink of her pleasure she fell ecstatically over the edge with his name on her lips. He followed quickly behind her, unable to continue to hold out when she was coming apart all around him.

She might have lost any sense of reality, because the next thing she knew she was on her back, staring up at the stars, and he was kissing her mouth, her nose, her forehead, and then resting his forehead against hers while they unraveled from the high they were riding. When their breathing had calmed, he rolled over onto his elbow, and the absence of his body over hers affected her immediately.

"I just…I just want to listen to you say my name that way all night." He glanced at her, a small smile pulling his mouth upward.

"That can be arranged," she said with a smirk. "So tell me about the tattoo."

He snuggled her closer to his side, lying back on the blanket with one hand behind his head and the other pulling her against him. He stared up at the stars and contemplated.

"It says RISE," he began. "Because that's what I've always had to do. No matter what shit I had to go through on any given day—and there was plenty—I rose again the next day. I had to, if I was ever going to get to my goal of getting out of there and making a life for myself." He finished, still staring skyward.

She rubbed tiny circles on his chest with her finger. "And now you have. Made a life for yourself, I mean. Here…with me."

He glanced down at her and smiled. He kissed her temple. "Yeah, Princess. Here, with you."

"We have to get registered for classes."

He raised his head to look at her this time. "We?"

She turned on her full grin, dazzling him with her beauty. "Yep. I'm transferring. This fall, we start at Charleston together. So it's you and me from here on out, Waters. Is that okay with you?"

He was stunned into silence. Then he rolled over her once more so that he was floating above her. He grabbed her face in his hands and kissed her, a fierce meeting of their lips that went on and on until she was breathless.

"I take that as a yes?" she asked dizzily.

His grin widened and he chuckled. "Damn, I love you, Princess."

She stilled. Gooseflesh broke out all over her body and the stars swam even brighter in the dark expanse above them.

His arms tightened around her and he gazed worriedly into her eyes. "That's not pressure, Aston. I'm not expecting anything in return. I just…love you. I do. And I'm not afraid to say it. This summer has changed my entire life. Not just the fact that your dad has given me monumental hope for my future as a man, but because *you've* given me a reason to live freely. Free of obligation, free of oppression. You opened your heart to me when you didn't have to. And damn...I love you for it. I can't wait to start proving it to you."

She reached up and wrapped her arms around his neck and squeezed. "You owe me nothing, Sam. You don't have to prove anything. I already know your heart. I've never been so safe in my life as I am in your arms and wrapped up in your love. So I accept your love completely. And I love you back."

He smiled enormously, lowered his lips to hers, and proceeded to lose himself in her again, and again.

Epilogue

This is the most beautiful wedding I've ever been to." Tamara pushed a strand of her dark red hair off of her face. Summer hadn't quite begun, and her skin was pale in the muted glow of the moon overhead.

Soft strains of a slow song drifted over the long, driftwood farmhouse tables sitting in the sand. The twinkling stars overhead littered an inky landscape, and everything was perfect.

"Me, too," agreed Sam.

He glanced at the girl laughing in the seat beside him. Almost perfect.

"Baby," he whispered. "Do you want to dance?"

Aston looked over at him, pausing in her conversation with Kelly. A gorgeous grin broke out on her face that still stopped his heart cold. She sent Kelly an apologetic smile, who waved her off with a knowing look.

Aston took his outstretched hand, standing. Her long dress cascaded down over her heels, and the picture of statuesque beauty was complete.

"Heard you guys graduated yesterday," someone called out as they passed, on their way to the dance floor.

"We sure did," answered Aston.

An answering whistle caused a sense of wondrous elation to course through Sam.

He still couldn't believe he'd done it. After transferring his community college credits from Virginia and putting in overtime coursework and internship hours, he'd just completed his senior year at the University of Charleston, with the girl he loved by his side. Sam's business degree coupled with Aston's double degree in finance and business would hang in their brand-new offices at Hopewell Enterprises.

Two years ago, he was merely a ranch hand, a new and quite possibly temporary arrival in this town.

And look at him now. His life was perfect.

Almost perfect.

Two slender arms wrapped around his neck, commanding his immediate and complete attention. Aston swayed in front of him, and as he looked down at her, her smile was captivating.

"I think Ashley makes the most gorgeous bride in the world," she said. Her long, dark hair was pulled into an elegant knot at the nape of her neck, and all he wanted to do was release the pins holding it up and allow its full weight to tumble down around her shoulders.

"Mmm," he commented. Ashley was, indeed, a beautiful bride. And Finn would probably burst from happiness and pride right there on the dance floor. But Ashley couldn't hold Sam's attention. Not with Aston in the room.

"You're very…contemplative tonight." Aston stroked a finger over his lips. "Anything you want to talk about?"

He shook his head. "Just appreciating everything I have. Taking a minute to thank whoever's responsible for it all."

She nodded. "I know the feeling. I'm so ready for what's next, though, aren't you?"

He smiled. That was Aston. Ready to hurtle forward to the next challenge, the next adventure. He was always right there with her. Her partner, her equal.

A catcall erupted around them, and their eyes were drawn to the stage set up close to the rising tide.

"This next song belongs to the bride and groom," said Reed.

He began strumming something slow and sultry on his guitar. The songs he'd written for this occasion were phenomenal, and Sam had no doubt that Reed would achieve his dreams of musical stardom one day.

"God, he's amazing." Aston watched her brother, with pride and awe trading places on her face. "I feel like he's been doing this forever."

"He's something special. Only a matter of time before the whole world knows it," Sam agreed.

They watched him for a few moments longer, and then Aston sighed, leaning into Sam.

"I wish he had someone."

Sam nodded. She'd shared this worry with him more than once. She hated seeing Reed partying with different girls night after night. She knew what he was missing, although he still assured her that his happily ever after would never involve a serious relationship.

"One day," Sam soothed. He bent and kissed the spot on her neck that called to him like a siren. "Let's go tell Finn and Ash 'bye," he said, leaning down to speak into her ear. "I'm ready to get you home."

She shivered, and he smiled. Their ability to affect each other with a single breath would never fade.

Back home to the tack house, which they'd taken over as their own, now that they'd graduated and moved back to the island full-time.

Her grin curled at the corners of her lips. "Let's."

She pulled off her heels and ran with him across the sand. He fastened her helmet on her carefully as she pulled on her light leather jacket over her flowing bridesmaid's dress.

He climbed onto the Harley and waited until her arms were squeezing his middle before roaring off down the dark streets of N.I. He smiled under his helmet visor, knowing that he wasn't heading for the ranch, and knowing that Aston wouldn't be able to grill him on their destination while on the bike.

Five minutes later, they were walking along the Sunny's pier.

"What are you up to, Waters?" asked Aston, her voice full of suspicion. "I thought you were going to take me home and have your way with me."

Sam laughed. "Hold your horses, Princess. We'll get to that."

He stopped walking, pulling her to a halt with him. He smiled down at her, wrapping his arms around her waist and gripping her tightly. "I wanted to give you your graduation present first."

The ocean lapped gently against the wood on the pier, and he was reminded of another night, which ended right in this very spot. He was broken then, until the woman standing in front of him helped put him back together.

Eventually, Hunter and Ever had been forgiven. In time, Sam had been able to see that his childhood sweetheart and his brother belonged together in a way that he and Ever never had. He'd wished they'd arrived at that conclusion in a different way, but everything had worked out the way it was supposed to. Without Ever and Hunter's transgression, he may not have found his way into Aston's waiting arms.

Finding a way to put that water under the bridge had given him a relationship with his brother again.

Aston's eyebrows rose. He knew she'd never been able to resist a present. He chuckled.

"This pier? This is where my life started. At one point, I thought my life was ending here. And then my eyes were opened up to a world I never thought I could be a part of. My eyes were opened to you."

Her eyes softened at the corners, and she smiled up at him. "My life began that night, too. It just took you awhile to realize it."

He nodded. "God, Aston. My life is almost perfect now. Every crooked, twisted road I took…brought me here, to you."

She nodded, her eyes full of reflections from the stars. Then her brow furrowed. "Wait a minute. Almost perfect?"

He nodded, reaching into the interior pocket of his black leather jacket. "Here. I had this ordered for you."

She smiled as she pulled the shiny piece of platinum out of a long envelope. "A nameplate! For my new office at HE. Thank you, baby."

She stared down at it, the light of the moon serving to assist her in reading it. Sam could have counted backward from three. He watched her face read the name on the plate, her eyes narrowed, and then they flew back up to lock with his.

As the realization registered on her face, he clasped her hand and dropped to a knee.

"What do you think?" he asked softly. "Was I too presumptuous when I ordered an ASTON WATERS nameplate for your door?"

She shook her head fervently, biting her bottom lip. Tears pooled in her eyes as she tugged his hand. "Sam?"

"Marry me, Princess. Make my life perfect." He slid the carefully chosen diamond solitaire out of his pocket and slipped it onto her finger with a trembling hand.

She tugged his hand more urgently, and he rose to his feet. He scooped her up into his arms, and the feel of her lips pressed firmly against his was the only answer he needed. *Yes.*

Perfect.

Acknowledgments

God's unrelenting love for me is what led me to finally embracing what I always was…a writer. Thank you to my Lord and Savior.

Wanting Forever is my first traditionally published book, and also the first book in which I used the invaluable help of a critique partner. Thank you, Skillet, for all of your astute enlightenments when it came to this story. You loved Aston and Sam like I did, and have been so enthusiastic about this new career of mine. Friends like you don't come along every day, and I'm so grateful to be able to call you one of my besties.

Melody, you are always my first reader, but I gave you a break this time so you could actually enjoy a finished product. I hope you love it!

None of this would be possible had I not entered a pitch contest on Twitter and thus collided with my incredibly beautiful and hilarious pit bull of an agent, Stacey Donaghy. Thank you for being the feisty go-getter you are, and for believing in what I do! Support like yours is a pure blessing, and I look forward to many years together.

To my fabulous, super-smart editor, Leah Hultenschmidt, Nelson Island is coming into the light because you loved and believed in Sam and Aston! Thank you so much for your support and for making this transition into the publishing world completely painless and totally fun! I hope I do you proud!

All of my friends and family who have asked me questions and shown their unwavering love and support during this process is what has kept me going. I love all of the interest; it makes me feel as if what I'm doing is a real job! You're irreplaceable.

Thank you to my amazing little family who lives with my crazy every single day. Our two little wild things are my entire world, and my husband is the sun in our galaxy. Without you all, I wouldn't have a purpose, or a reason to want to make our lives even better with this amazing career. Thank you for being perfect for me.

And to the readers who wander onto the tiny little place that is Nelson Island, thank you for coming, and I hope you stay awhile. There are so many more stories to tell!

About the Author

Diana Gardin is a wife of one and a mom of two. Writing is her second full-time job after that, and she loves it! Diana writes contemporary romance in the Young Adult and New Adult categories. She's also a former elementary school teacher. She loves steak, sugar cookies, and Coke, and hates working out.

Learn more at:
DianaGardin.com
Twitter @DianalynnGardin
Facebook.com/authorDianaGardin

Get Ever and Hunter's side of the story in

EVER ALWAYS

A Nelson Island novella

Turn the page for a special preview

Hunter loved his brother with every breath in his body. Sam was his little brother, full of grand ideas and no clue how to make them happen in real life. This was no exception.

Not for the first time, Hunter thought his brother was a fucking idiot.

He'd left her. She'd just shot her father. The turmoil that was going to come from that for Ever was going to be life-changing. And Sam should be there to walk her through it.

But he'd left.

Hunter glanced over at Ever as they trudged through the woods, walking quickly toward the house where her father lay dead. Her gaze was aimed straight ahead, her chin held high. Her graceful, petite hands were balled into tightly clenched fists at her sides, as if she were preparing for war. And in a way, she was.

Hunter clenched his jaw. There was no way in hell he was going to let her fight this battle alone.

Two sheriff's cruisers were parked in front of the house when they arrived, blue lights flashing. Hunter was suddenly grateful for all things small town.

"That you, Ever?" asked Sheriff Lincoln.

"It's me," she called out.

"And me," said Hunter.

"Where the hell have the two of you been? Got the call about a gunshot fifteen minutes ago. Been bangin' on the door, nobody answered."

Hunter snorted. "So you got a gunshot report but just waited patiently outside?"

That was Duck Creek's finest, all right.

Sheriff Lincoln glared at Hunter. There was no love lost between the Waters family and the town's law enforcement. Hunter and Sam weren't bad growing up, but they did what they had to in order to survive. Their mother could barely place food on the table. When they were old enough to work, Hunter got a job at the lumberyard where he now made a good living, and Sam had worked at a garage in town in order to pay their mother's bills. But before that, they had to do what they could to bring money home.

"I wasn't talkin' to you, Waters. Where's that no-good brother of yours? He's never far behind."

"That's enough," Ever cut in, sick of the bullshit. Hunter could tell by her tone that she wasn't in the mood for any of it. She wanted to get this over as quickly as possible.

Hunter caught her gaze, silently asking her if she really wanted to do what she was about to do. If she did, he'd back her up. There wasn't a time in his life he could recall that he hadn't backed her.

She was his brother's girl; he knew that just as well as he knew the sky was blue. But at one point, she'd just been Ever Allen from across the field. The field that separated the good from the bad. And aside from Sam, she was his very best friend.

She nodded so slightly he was the only one who noticed, and he reached for her hand. She tightened her fingers around his palm and squeezed.

"You better come on inside," she said to the sheriff. Hunter heard a door shut, and turned. Brandon Charles, who graduated in the same class as Ever and Sam a few years back, climbed out of his deputy vehicle.

"Why?" asked Sheriff Lincoln. "What the hell happened? Where's your daddy?"

"Lying on the living room floor. Sam shot Daddy dead tonight when he tried to beat me with a baseball bat."

The five hours that followed were like every cop show Hunter had ever seen, only made into parody by small town methods and thinking.

Ever was stoic in her repeated version of the night's events. The biggest problem was Ever had never reported one of the beatings she had received from her father. Hunter could see Sam's line of thinking. No one would have just accepted her self-defense story as truth. And they definitely weren't buying it that Sam killed Graham Allen in order to protect his girlfriend. But they processed the scene, gathered the gun and the baseball bat into evidence, and carted Ever's father off in an ambulance to be examined by the coroner.

When Ever slammed the door on the last person to leave, who

just happened to be Brandon Charles, the deputy, she leaned back against it. She shut her eyes tight, and Hunter could see her body beginning to tremble all over.

"Aw, Ev," he said quietly, closing the gap between them. He scooped her up into his arms before she could fall to pieces in the living room and carried her past the bloodstain on the floor to her own bedroom. He hesitated in the doorway, realizing she'd never felt safe there.

"It's fine, Hunter," she said, her voice soft. "He can't hurt me here anymore."

He placed her gently on her bed, where she threw an arm over her eyes and curled her legs into her chest.

Sinking down beside her, Hunter reached out to smooth her dark red hair out of the way. He stared down at her.

From the moment he'd laid eyes on her, she was the most beautiful thing he'd ever seen. Back then, he hadn't registered it as beauty. She was spunky and fun, and she liked to run just as much as he and Sam did. What more could a seven-year-old boy ask for? She was perfect. Then when he was a little older, maybe around eleven, he'd noticed the way her jewel green eyes sparkled when she laughed, and the way the light dusting of freckles on her skin made her face so much more interesting than any other girl he knew. The sunlight would catch in her thick hair, and he'd lose whatever stupid-ass words he'd been about to utter. The summer he turned fifteen and Ever and Sam were thirteen and a half, he noticed the way her head tilted to the side when she was thinking hard about something, and that she was beginning to develop migraine headaches when she felt upset. He tried to comfort her when she felt that way, tried to figure out what was bothering her. Sam was the fixer; he would rather make her headaches go away than find out what caused them in the first place.

"Your head hurting?" he asked her.

She nodded, lying still and quiet on the bed.

"What can I get you?"

She removed the arm covering her eyes, and stared up at him. His chest clenched with something achy and sharp, and his hand involuntarily went to the spot to clutch it and make the strange pain go away.

"Can you get me your brother back here where he belongs?" she asked, her eyes just as hard as the feeling in his chest.

His head dropped. He never wanted to disappoint her, never wanted to let her down. He and Sam had always been alike that way.

But *fuck,* she asked for the one thing he couldn't give her.

His brother was an idiot.

"Go home, Hunter," said Ever.

"I'm not going anywhere. Not tonight."

She winced against the overhead light's glare. Hunter rose from the bed, went to the light switch by the door, and shut it off. He went into the bathroom, where he knew her prescription migraine medicine was kept, grabbed two pills, and brought her a glass of water to accompany them.

"Here," he whispered, placing the water on the nightstand and holding out the pills. He helped her to sit up, handing her the medicine. She sipped the water, her eyes glittering softly in the darkness.

"You can go on home. I'll be fine."

"There's no doubt in my mind that you will be fine one day, Ev. Today isn't that day. I'm staying. Go to sleep, and get rid of that headache. I'll make you breakfast in the morning."

She hesitated for a second, and then she nodded as she sank back into her pillows. "Thank you."

The fact that she felt she needed to thank him for taking care of her when Sam wasn't there to do it blew his mind to pieces.

"Sleep," he told her.

She awoke to the pounding on the front door that matched the pounding in her head. She sat straight up in her bed, the light streaming in her window confusing her. Was it a dream? When she went to answer that door, would she see her father sleeping off a drunken stupor on the couch?

She stood and realized that she was somehow now wearing her pajamas. One of Sam's big T-shirts and a pair of old boxer shorts. It was all she ever slept in.

She pulled a robe out of the closet and padded barefoot out into the living room.

Her father definitely wasn't on the couch. Instead, she saw rumpled blankets and a pillow occupying the space. There was no giant bloodstain on the floor.

Maybe it really had been a dream.

Except for the sharp scent of bleach that hung in the air and the fact that Hunter was standing next to the front door in nothing but a pair of low-slung sweatpants. Ever could hardly believe she'd never noticed how built his chest and arms were.

"It's Sheriff Lincoln. You ready?" he asked her with concern. "How's your head?"

"Feels like my daddy hit me with that baseball bat after all," she said.

Hunter's brow furrowed. And when she looked into his face it was like breathing air into her lungs for the first time since she'd squeezed that trigger. His hazel eyes were locked on hers, his dark blond hair a spiky mess from sleep.

He took in her stare with serious eyes, and then he frowned. "Do you want me to get rid of him?"

She contemplated. She really didn't want to deal with the sheriff, but she also didn't want to cause Hunter any problems. He'd gotten away from his mom, bought himself a little house in town, and worked hard at his job to make a life for himself. He didn't need the shit storm about to rain down all over her.

She shook her head. "No. Go put a shirt on, for God's sake, Hunt. What will they think?"

His frown deepened. "I don't give two fucks what they'll think. And neither do you."

A small smile tugged at her lips. He was right about that. She never cared what any of the people in Duck Creek thought. Except for Sam and Hunter, and Lacey, her boss at the bakery.

"You're right. I don't give a crap. Let's just get this over."

He shot her a small, proud smile and allowed the front door to swing open, aiming his smirk at the sheriff. "Morning, Link. What can we do for you?"

James Lincoln, also known as the former best friend of Graham Allen, nearly stumbled as he took in the sight of Hunter answering Ever's door shirtless. Ever could see that Hunter was going to enjoy the situation far too much.

"Come in, Sheriff," she called.

He gathered himself, striding past Hunter and aiming a stern stare at Ever. "Young lady, I knew your daddy for more years than you've been alive—"

"And yet," she interjected, "you turned a blind eye every time he raised a hand to his daughter. I know he loved my mother, Sheriff, and lost a big piece of himself when he lost her. But that's no excuse for the way he treated me. I knew it, and so did you. What the hell do you *want*?"

Lincoln stared at her with his mouth agape. Ever had never had the nerve to speak this way when her daddy was still alive. She'd even surprised herself, and Hunter, who stood stock-still by the door, was unable to tear his eyes away from her face. It was looking like there would be some changes in Duck Creek.

"I want to know where that son of a bitch boyfriend of yours is," answered the sheriff. "You know, the one who killed your own flesh and blood? Where is he? We know he left town on his bike last night. And I know that you two"—he shot his glare toward Hunter, still frozen by the door—"know exactly where he went."

"Actually, we don't," said Hunter evenly. It never took Hunter long to get himself together again after a shock. "We haven't heard from him. If we do, Sheriff, you'll be the first to know."

"Yeah." Lincoln's voice dripped with sarcasm. "I'm sure I will."

He turned back to Ever, his tone and demeanor softening. "Listen, Ever. I know you're going through a lot right now. You must be in shock, confused. Don't let the wrong type of people get you mixed up in something you can't get out of. You want to come stay with Missy and me?"

Only in a town as tiny as Duck Creek could someone piss you off and then invite you to stay the night within the same breath. Did she want to go stay at the sheriff's house, while his wife babied her, like they hadn't known for years that she was getting beat senseless in her own house? Was he serious?

"No, thanks," she said with cool certainty. "I'll stay right here in my own house, where I feel safe for the first time in years. You can see yourself out, Sheriff."

He stared at her for a solid minute, and she knew he was wondering where the timid little girl he'd once known had gone. But he'd never known the real Ever.

Had anyone?

Hunter closed the door behind Sheriff Lincoln. He leaned against it, studying her. She had the uncomfortable feeling he was sizing her up. But then she remembered that this was Hunter. She'd known him her entire life, right? He knew her. She knew him. She tucked a strand of hair behind her ear and slowly sucked air into her lungs. She spent a moment just remembering how to breathe again.

She suddenly couldn't pinpoint the exact moment in her life she'd forgotten.

Finally, he pushed off the door and cocked an eyebrow. "This might be a dumb question. Okay, it definitely is the dumbest-ass question I've ever asked anyone. But I gotta ask it, and you gotta answer. How are you this morning? Other than the headache, I mean. How are you…emotionally?"

She sighed. "I shot my father yesterday. I don't have a clue where my boyfriend is. I don't know what tomorrow holds for me, or the day after that. So I'm…kind of a wreck, Hunter. Does that answer it?"

His head tilted to the side as he considered her, and she had to admit he was achingly adorable. His jaw was lined with scruff, glinting softly in the sunlight streaming through the windows.

"I know what you need," he said suddenly.

"I need to sleep for a week."

"Nah," he answered, shaking his head. "That's not you, Ev. You aren't going to bury your head in the sand. You're going to grieve, sweet girl. Because he was your father and maybe at one point in your life, he was a good one. But he wasn't good anymore. Not to you, not to himself. And you did what you had to do."

He crossed the tiny room and cupped the back of her neck with both hands. "Do you hear me? You will grieve, and then you will heal. And I'm going to be here every step of the way to help you."

She met his steady gaze head-on. It had been years since she'd stared into his eyes this way. They used to have staring contests when they were little, she and Hunter. Hunter had always blinked first. She smiled.

His lips turned upward into a smirk as he read her mind. "Go."

They stared each other down, neither wanting to be the first to blink or look away. Finally, against his will, Hunter's eyes blinked closed just before he muttered a curse. Ever laughed out loud.

"I win," she said. "I still got it."

"Yeah, Ev," he whispered, letting go of her neck. "You do."